MW01133174

THE COMPLETE GIRL'S GUIDE TO GROWING UP

The 3-in-1 Puberty, Friendships & Emotions Handbook for Tween Girls 8–12

Abby Swift

TABLE OF CONTENTS

BOOK 3. A TWEEN GIRL'S GUIDE TO FEELINGS & EMOTIONS

A TWEEN GIRL'S GUIDE TO PUBERTY

Love and Celebrate Your Changing Body

The Complete Body and Mind Handbook for Young Girls

Abby Swift

INTRODUCTION

Welcome to puberty!

Puberty is an important time in your life. It is a sign that you are growing into a young woman, and your body is changing from a child to an adult. While puberty is something to look forward to, it can sometimes be a little overwhelming. Your body is about to undergo many changes — some may have already begun! During this time, you might feel uncertain about how to handle those changes and what to expect in the future. But don't worry! This book is here to help you understand what puberty is, why it happens, and how it affects your body.

Puberty is described as "the process of physical maturation where an adolescent reaches sexual maturity and becomes capable of reproduction" (Breehl & Caban, 2023). While it may sound complicated, puberty is pretty simple to understand. During puberty, your body prepares for the possibility of having a baby, which means you can become pregnant. For a woman to become pregnant and have a child, certain hormones and traits are required. As you enter puberty, your body begins to release the necessary hormones to make pregnancy possible.

Puberty marks your body's preparation for the possibility of having a baby, and one of the most significant changes it includes is having your first period. Many cultures celebrate a girl's first menstrual cycle as a symbol of her transition into womanhood. While puberty can sometimes feel a little scary, it is the world's most natural and common experience. Did you know that there are more women than men on Earth? That means that many young girls around the world are going through puberty, just like you, and can relate to the same emotions you may be experiencing. Always remember, you are not alone on this journey.

Boys also go through puberty. While their journey isn't exactly the same as yours, they also experience changes as their hormones cause them to grow and develop into men. Puberty is a time full of transformations and new experiences, and the more you understand it, the easier it will be to navigate the changes happening to your body. This knowledge can also help you support your friends who may be feeling uncertain about their changing bodies, just like you.

What Will I Learn in This Book?

As your mind and body undergo so many changes during puberty, it is natural to have questions. And that's where this book comes in — it will help answer those questions! Inside, you'll learn about the physical and emotional changes you experience during puberty, such as changes in your body shape, your breasts growing bigger, and hair growing in new places.

You'll also learn about your first period, including what it is, how to prepare for it, and what you should expect when it arrives. And let's not forget about the exciting milestone of choosing and buying your first bra! We'll help you navigate the process and find the prettiest and most comfortable bra.

Personal hygiene becomes more important as you enter puberty. We'll cover topics like getting enough sleep, taking care of your skin, using deodorant, and everything you need to know about looking after your changing body. Additionally, we'll look into friendships and the importance of building and managing them during puberty. This includes managing strong emotions, handling conflict better, and building lasting relationships.

But most importantly, this book will show you that you are unique. Out of 7.8 billion people in the world, there is only one of you. Your body and mind are capable of so many incredible things, and together, they shape the person you are. This book will help you better understand how to love and appreciate your body and boost your self-confidence. Your body is beautiful, strong, and capable of achieving many wonderful things.

Finally, as you enter puberty, you might start feeling differently about people, and that's completely normal. But it is crucial to understand how to navigate your emotions and relationships. Eventually, you may even develop romantic feelings for someone. Knowing what to expect and how to manage those feelings is essential when that happens.

Why Should I Read This Book?

As you can see, many things happen and change during puberty. It's normal for you to have questions about puberty and what to expect in the coming years. This book will provide you with answers to many of these questions.

In today's world, social media has many ideas about puberty and how it "should" be. Still, it's important to remember that every girl is unique. That means your puberty journey will be unique to you. You may experience puberty earlier or later than your friends, and this can sometimes make you worry that something is wrong — especially if you read conflicting advice online. But not everything you read online is true or applicable to your experience. The truth is puberty is a unique and personal journey. Everyone is different, and what you experience is normal and natural.

By reading this book, you will understand why your experience with puberty may differ from that of your friends. You'll learn how to navigate your changing emotions, friendships, and relationships as you enter puberty. This book will also equip you with the necessary skills to mature into an adult and help you manage all the changes you will go through.

The primary purpose of this book is to help girls in the same position as you understand their growing and changing bodies. By the end of this book, you'll understand how puberty works, how your body changes during this phase, and why it's essential to love and celebrate your body just the way it is. Are you ready to go on this journey of self-discovery, learning to love yourself and care for your growing body? Let's get started!

1

EMBRACING YOUR CHANGING BODY

"Womanhood is a whole different thing from girlhood.
Girlhood is a gift...womanhood is a choice."
— Tori Amos

Puberty is an exciting time in a girl's life, and knowing what is happening to your body will help you feel prepared for when it starts happening to you. If you notice significant changes occurring in your own body or the bodies of your friends, it is a sign that you (or they) have entered puberty.

During this time, you may also begin to feel different and more emotional compared to before. Some girls may experience these emotional changes earlier than others, while others may not experience as many emotional changes. But rest assured, it's all a normal part of puberty. So, what is puberty anyway, and why does it happen?

Understanding Puberty: What's Happening, Inside and Out?

Lots of changes occur when you enter puberty. These changes include sudden growth spurts, changing body shape, and growing hair in new places. But that doesn't fully explain what is happening to your body and why. To help you understand puberty and embrace your changing body, you must first learn what puberty is.

What Is Puberty, and When Does It Start?

Puberty is the period in your life where your body starts changing to reach sexual maturation. That means that your body becomes capable of having a baby. Your body changes from a child to an adult — even if you are still a child when it happens. These changes are caused by a hormone released by your brain when you reach a certain age ("Everything You Wanted To Know About Puberty," n.d.).

What Are Hormones?

Hormones are chemical messengers that your brain and other organs release to make things happen in your body (Mandal, 2022). Hormones are usually secreted by your brain and travel through your bloodstream to reach your organs and other body parts. In the case of puberty, hormones are secreted from your brain, pituitary glands, and ovaries. They relay messages to the rest of your body, such as your sex organs, signaling to them that it is time to change and mature.

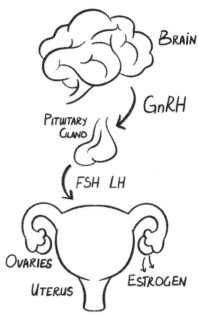

The hormone that your brain releases is called the gonadotropin-releasing hormone (GnRH). GnRH travels to your pituitary gland (also in your brain) and then through your bloodstream. When the pituitary gland receives the GnRH, it releases two other hormones: follicle-stimulating hormone (FSH) and luteinizing hormone (LH). These hormones are responsible for most of the changes in your body.

FSH, LH, and GnRH travel through your bloodstream to your ovaries. Your ovaries are in your lower abdomen and form a part of your sex organs. They contain all the eggs that can be used to make a baby when you get pregnant. Additionally, your ovaries also produce and release another hormone called estrogen. Estrogen works with the FSH and LH to help your body reach sexual maturity.

These hormones work together to help your body mature and cause various physical and emotional changes. Let's explore some of these changes, remembering that everyone is unique, so your physical and emotional changes might differ from your friends.

Physical Changes During Puberty

Since your body is changing from a child to an adult capable of getting pregnant, you can expect many physical changes. These changes won't happen all at once. Instead, they will occur gradually over time. Some physical changes may start earlier than others. Here are some of the physical changes you may experience during puberty:

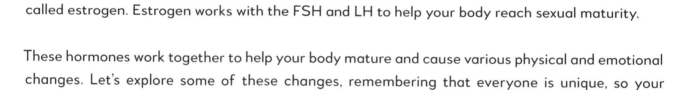

- Sudden growth spurts (suddenly getting taller).

- Changes in your body shape. You may get wider hips, a curvier figure, or bigger breasts.

- Skin changes. You might start getting more pimples or acne.

- Stronger body odor. Your body odor may smell stronger, and you might sweat more.

- Hair growth. You will notice hair growing in new places, and the hair you already have might become darker.

This book teaches you how to manage these physical changes and embrace your changing body. Remember that puberty is a normal part of growing up and is experienced by everyone on Earth, men and women alike. So, you are definitely not alone in this journey.

Emotional Changes During Puberty

According to Planned Parenthood ("Puberty," n.d.), the hormones that cause all of these physical changes in your body also trigger emotional changes. When you enter puberty, you may experience your emotions more intensely. This can include happiness, excitement, frustration, anger, and sadness. While not all of these emotions are always positive, they are entirely normal. It will take time for your body and mind to adjust to these hormones, which can result in challenging emotions.

Sometimes, you might not even understand why you feel how you feel. Don't worry — these feelings result from the hormones in your body. They will come and go, and as you get older, your body will adjust to the hormones, resulting in less frequent intense emotions. Later in this book, you will learn how to manage your emotions effectively.

When Does Puberty Typically Start?

Puberty usually begins between the ages of 8 and 14 in girls. However, it's important to note that some girls enter puberty a bit earlier or later than this. In addition, not all the physical changes will occur simultaneously. In fact, you may experience some changes, such as changes in your body shape and skin condition, before others. While your first period usually indicates that you have entered puberty, other signs may come beforehand.

As mentioned earlier, every girl is unique, and so is her body. You may start puberty earlier or later than some of your friends, and that's completely normal. If you notice your friends are going through puberty, you can support them by being an understanding friend. This will make the entire process much easier.

WHAT ABOUT BOYS? DO THEY ALSO EXPERIENCE PUBERTY?

While boys don't have periods like girls do, they do go through puberty. Boys typically go through puberty between the ages of 8 and 14, although it's common for boys to start puberty a bit later than girls. Similar to girls, there are many physical and emotional changes in boys during puberty. These changes include:

· Sudden growth spurts.

· Their voices get deeper.

· They develop stronger body odor.

· The possibility of acne.

· Hair growth on the face, genitals, and under the arms.

· Their sex organs (testicles and penis) grow bigger.

Boys, like girls, also experience stronger emotions due to hormonal changes during puberty. This can sometimes affect their behavior. Again, it's important to remember that puberty in boys is entirely normal, and the timing of these changes may vary by individual.

Growth Spurts and Body Shape: Celebrating Your Unique Figure

One of the changes you experience when entering puberty is growth spurts. A growth spurt is when you suddenly gain height or weight (Growth spurts & baby growth spurts, 2021). While you usually grow steadily for most of your life until you reach adulthood, you grow a lot faster in a short period when you are a baby, and when you enter puberty. In addition, during puberty, some parts of your body may grow even faster than others. In boys, you may notice that their arms and legs grow faster than the rest of their bodies.

But why do growth spurts happen when you enter puberty? Just like all the other changes in your body, growth spurts happen because of your hormones. The same hormones that cause your breasts and eggs to develop will cause other body parts to grow quickly.

You will also see changes in your body shape. For example, you may notice that your hips become wider, your legs and bottom become bigger, and your breasts grow. However, that isn't always the case. Some girls are naturally curvier than others, and everybody is unique and beautiful in their own way. Some girls may have larger breasts and hips, while others don't experience significant changes during puberty.

Just because you don't experience many physical changes during puberty doesn't mean something is wrong. Since your body is unique, it might not develop in the same way as those of other girls. Many girls have similar body shapes to their mothers. So, if your mother is curvier, your body shape might also be curvier. If your mother is slimmer, you might also have a slimmer figure.

The beauty of genetics, which includes the physical, intellectual, and emotional traits you get from your parents and grandparents, is that it makes you unique. You are a combination of your parents, but you are also your own person. That means that you develop at your own pace. Whether you experience growth spurts at 8, 14, 16, or never at all, it is entirely normal. There is no right or wrong way to enter and experience puberty.

Instead of comparing yourself to your friends and classmates, you should focus on celebrating your unique body shape and growth spurts. Remember that your body is strong, capable, and beautiful. It will enable you to do many great things, including having children, if and when you are ready.

Hair, There, and Everywhere: The Lowdown on Body Hair

Body hair is natural — everyone has it. Some people have more body hair than others, and some people's body hair might also be darker. But no matter who you are, you will develop more body hair as you enter puberty. The same hormones that cause your body to change and let you experience stronger emotions also increase your hair growth. You may notice more hair growing in these areas:

- On your legs.

- Under your arms.

- On your face (on your lip and brows).

- On your labia and pubic bone (pubic hair).

Additionally, the hair you already have on your body might become darker. This is an entirely normal part of puberty. Although you don't have to do anything about hair growth, you might choose to manage it somehow. There are many ways to handle your body hair, but whether you remove the hair is entirely up to you.

HOW TO HANDLE BODY HAIR

There are several methods for managing and reducing body hair. However, it's important to remember you don't have to remove any hair if you don't want to. If you keep your body hair, maintaining your personal hygiene is still essential. This includes keeping the area where the hair grows clean.

If you want to remove your body hair, exploring the various hair-removal options is helpful. Here are five methods you can consider.

SHAVING

Expense:
 $ $ $ $ $

Difficulty:

Hair regrowth time:
A few days

How it works:
Cuts it off near the skin

Which Body parts :
Legs, underarms, bikini area
(with caution)

Cautionary note:

There is a chance of nicking yourself with the blade, and the hair may grow back thicker and darker. Avoid using it on your face. Some people get rashes from shaving.

TRIMMING

Expense:
$ $ $ $ $

Difficulty:

Hair regrowth time:
A few days

How it works:
Cuts it off (not as close to the skin as shaving)

Which Body parts :
Legs, underarms, pubic hairs

Cautionary note:

Trimming is not suitable for very short hairs on the face and legs.

WAXING

Expense:
$ $ $ $ $

Difficulty:

Hair regrowth time:
A few weeks

How it works:
Plucks it from its root beneath the skin

Which Body parts :
Anywhere

Cautionary note:

Use caution when using wax at home to avoid skin damage or burns.

HAIR REMOVAL CREAM

Expense:
$ $ $ $ $

Difficulty:

Hair regrowth time:
A few days

How it works:
Dissolves the hair

Which Body parts :
Anywhere but your intimate areas

Cautionary note:

Some people may develop a reaction to the hair removal cream as it is a chemical.

LASER HAIR REMOVAL

Expense:
$ $ $ $ $

Difficulty:

Hair regrowth time:
Months or years; sometimes never

How it works:
Dissolves the hair from the root to the tip.

Which Body parts :
Anywhere

Cautionary note:

At-home laser hair removers are available, but therapists administer the most effective treatments during multiple sessions.

Other options for hair removal include threading and sugar waxing, each with their own pros and cons. If you want to remove some body hair, it is worth exploring your options and trying different hair removal methods to find the best option. Remember, what works for one person might not work for another, and what works on one part of your body might not work on every part.

Hair Removal Is Not Necessary!

While you may consider some of the hair-removal options above, it's important to know that you don't have to remove any hair you don't want to. Body hair is completely normal, and there is no reason to remove it if you don't wish to do so. However, even if you don't want to remove any hair, it's still important to keep it healthy.

Grooming your body hair involves keeping it clean and dry. Washing the area regularly with warm water and soap and applying deodorant to your underarms will help keep your body hair in good condition. Remember, removing body hair in some places while leaving it in others is perfectly acceptable. How you choose to manage your body hair is entirely up to you. Do whatever makes you feel comfortable and confident.

 **Key Takeaways**

- Puberty is the process of your body maturing from a child to an adult, triggered by hormones released by your brain.

- During puberty, you will experience numerous physical and emotional changes. These include shifts in body shape, breast growth, and changes in your skin. You may also feel your emotions more intensely.

- Boys also go through puberty, although the signs and changes they experience may differ. Hormones play a significant role in puberty for both boys and girls. Puberty typically begins between the ages of 8 and 14 for both girls and boys.

- Puberty brings about growth spurts, where your body shape may change, and your breasts will grow and develop. Remember, regardless of how your body changes, it is unique, beautiful, and deserving of celebration.

- When entering puberty, you will also notice hair growing in new places, including under your arms, on your legs, and in the genital area. This hair growth is normal. You can leave it as is or use one of many hair-removal methods. It's important to know that there is nothing wrong with body hair, and removing it is a personal preference.

Getting your first period is one of the significant signs of puberty. While your first period may feel new and unfamiliar, there is no need to worry — it's an entirely natural process. In the next chapter, we will discuss everything you should know about your first period and every period after that.

YOUR FIRST PERIOD—A RITE OF PASSAGE

One of the changes your body goes through during puberty is that you start getting your period. When you experience your first period, it can feel unfamiliar and might be a little intimidating, especially if you aren't prepared for it. However, just as going through puberty is a natural part of life, so is having your period. In this chapter, you will learn everything you need to know about your first period to help you prepare for it and celebrate this milestone when it occurs.

Understanding Periods

If you understand what is happening in your body, your first period won't feel nearly as confusing. As discussed in the previous chapter, your body changes from a child to a woman during puberty. One aspect of being a woman is the possibility of getting pregnant and having babies someday. Consequently, every month, your body prepares for the possibility of conception. It releases an egg from your ovaries that travels to your uterus, where it waits to be fertilized by a sperm cell.

If your egg is fertilized by a sperm cell (which can happen if you have sex), the egg attaches to your uterus, and a fetus starts to grow. This fertilized egg needs a lot of nutrients to grow and develop. These nutrients come from your blood. Every month, your uterus produces a thick lining of blood to support the growth of a possible fetus.

However, if your egg is not fertilized by a sperm cell, it does not attach to your uterine lining. In this case, the thick blood lining detaches from your uterus and exits your body through your vagina. This process is called a period — when the blood and tissue from your uterus come out of your body. Several hormones, such as estrogen, progesterone, and FSH, control your menstrual cycle. Your brain controls these hormone levels, which fluctuate throughout the month, ultimately resulting in your period if fertilization does not occur.

While your first period can be confusing, there is nothing to worry about. The blood discharged from your uterus through your vagina doesn't mean you are injured. Instead, it is part of the uterine lining in your womb that is no longer needed by your body. Even though it looks like a lot of blood, the blood cells in period blood are already dead and won't be missed.

While it might look like you are losing a lot of blood, most girls typically lose only two or three tablespoons of blood during their period ("Heavy Menstrual Bleeding," 2022). Some girls might lose a little more, and others a little less. This is known as having a heavy or a light period. Both variations are normal and depend on the size of your uterus and the thickness of the lining.

How Long Does a Period Last?

Your menstrual cycle is typically 28 days long. This cycle consists of four phases: the menstrual phase, the follicular phase, the ovulation phase, and the luteal phase ("Menstrual Cycle," 2022).

The menstrual phase marks the beginning of your menstrual cycle and starts on the first day of your period. Generally, periods last between four and seven days but can vary in duration. After your period ends, your body enters its *follicular phase*. During this phase, one of your ovaries develops an egg that it will eventually release for possible fertilization. This process takes approximately 14 days. Around the 14th day of your cycle, the mature egg is released from the ovary. This is known as the *ovulation phase*. The egg then travels through the fallopian tube to the uterus, awaiting possible fertilization. This is known as the *luteal phase*.

During the follicular, ovulation, and luteal phases, your uterus is hard at work producing a nutrient-rich, blood-filled lining to support a fertilized egg. If the egg is not fertilized, it will trigger your next period when it reaches the uterus.

While a typical menstrual cycle takes around 28 days, many factors influence the actual length of your cycle. Some people have longer menstrual cycles, while others have shorter ones. Both variations are entirely normal. When you start having your period, it may be less regular, and the cycles may vary in length. Sometimes, they may be longer than 28 days; other times, they may be shorter. This is normal as your body matures and adjusts to the hormones. As your body changes, your periods will become more regular.

Period Basics: What to Expect and How to Prepare

As you get older and your periods become more regular, you will better understand how and when to prepare for them. However, your periods will likely be less predictable when you enter puberty. One month, you might have a very light period or just a bit of spotting. Spotting is when you see a little bit of blood, but it's not enough to require a pad or tampon to absorb. It's just a few spots of blood. Spotting also sometimes occurs between periods and is normal when you first enter puberty and have your first periods.

The following month, you may have a heavy period that lasts longer. There's no need to worry. Your body will adjust, and your periods will become more predictable as you mature. However, being prepared and knowing which signs to look out for can help you manage your period better.

For many girls, periods usually start between ages 8 and 14. But again, because your body is so unique, your period may start slightly earlier or later than that. A few days before your period starts, you may notice some changes. Many girls experience mood changes, such as sadness or irritability, before and during their periods. This is due to the hormonal changes in the body. Some girls also notice more pimples or acne just before their periods start.

You may also experience cramps in your lower abdomen. For some women, these cramps are pretty light and hardly noticeable, while others have cramps that cause discomfort that disrupts their day. These cramps occur because the muscles in the uterus contract to expel the blood lining. In addition to menstrual cramps, you may also experience a sharp pain in your abdomen, which might feel like a pain in your fallopian tubes or ovaries. And you may also experience discomfort in your lower back.

Thankfully, there are many remedies for period pain. Heat pads, such as warm beanbags or hot water bottles, work wonderfully to reduce menstrual cramps and reduce back pain. Over-the-counter pain medication can also help to relieve these symptoms. In addition, light exercise, such as walking or running, can help reduce cramping and menstrual discomfort (McCallum, 2021).

When your period begins, you may notice that the color of the blood is brown or dark red. It may then change to bright red for a few days before switching back to brown before ending. This color variation is normal as the brown blood is older. Most women experience their heaviest flow during the first two days of their periods. However, this can change as your period becomes more regular. Some women may not experience these symptoms, and their period produces the same flow throughout.

Your period symptoms might differ from those around you, but that does not mean anything is wrong with any of you. Every girl's period journey is different and unique. Initially, when your period first starts, you may experience a mix of symptoms as your body adjusts to the hormonal changes. Over time, however, you will learn to better predict your period and be more prepared for it. Of course, you will also need the right products to manage your period.

Period Products: Finding What Works Best for You

When managing your period, you will need to choose from various period products available on the market. Each product has advantages and disadvantages, so determining which ones work best depends entirely on your needs and preferences. It may help to try a few products before deciding which one you prefer. Here are five period products you can consider.

Pads

Pads are one of the oldest period products available. They are made of cotton or absorbent material and are attached to your underwear. When the blood comes out of your vagina, it is absorbed by the pad, which prevents it from staining your underwear or clothes.

Pads are easy to use and are relatively inexpensive. However, they cannot be worn when swimming, as they won't stick to a wet bathing suit and will also absorb the water. There is also a risk of leakage if they shift out of place. Unfortunately, most disposable pads contribute to plastic pollution, although some environmentally friendly reusable pads are now available.

Tampons

Tampons also absorb blood. However, unlike a pad that sits in the underwear, a tampon is inserted into the vagina to absorb it before it exits the body. Using a tampon is relatively easy. It has a string that hangs outside of the body, and the tampon is removed by pulling on the string.

Tampons are smaller and more compact than pads and can be worn when swimming and doing other sports activities, but they are more expensive than pads and require some practice to use correctly. Environmentally friendly tampons with biodegradable packaging are available to reduce plastic pollution.

APPLICATOR TAMPONS

Applicator tampons work just like regular tampons, but come with a long dispenser made of plastic that makes inserting them into the vagina easier than a regular tampon.

They are more expensive than pads and regular tampons and contribute to plastic pollution if they have a plastic applicator. However, many applicator tampons are now made with cardboard applicators, which are kinder to the environment.

MENSTRUAL CUPS

Menstrual cups have gained popularity in recent years. They are small, round cups made from medical-grade silicone. The cup is folded and inserted into the vagina, where it collects the blood. The cup must be removed and emptied regularly before reinserting.

Menstrual cups can be used for up to five years, making them cost-effective and environmentally friendly. They can be worn during any activity and don't require frequent changes like tampons or pads. However, using a menstrual cup requires practice, as there are different shapes, sizes, and firmness levels to consider.

MENSTRUAL DISCS

Menstrual discs are similar to menstrual cups. However, whereas a menstrual cup is inserted into the vaginal canal, a menstrual disc is inserted deeper into the vagina, below the cervix. They offer similar advantages, including being more environmentally friendly than pads or tampons. However, using menstrual discs correctly without spilling blood may take some practice, and they don't last as long as menstrual cups.

Regardless of the period products you choose to use, there are some things to remember when it's that time of the month.

TIPS FOR USING PERIOD PRODUCTS

When you first start having your period, learning how to use each period product can be challenging. Since you have to replace the products often, you may wonder what you should do with the used products. Here are some essential tips:

- **Replace your period product every 6–8 hours to avoid leakage.** Pads, tampons, menstrual cups, and discs can only handle limited volumes of blood, so they must be changed regularly. If your pad or tampon is at capacity, it is time to swap it out.

- **Do not flush period products down the toilet.** Period products can block the drains. Wrap them in toilet paper or put them in a small bag and dispose of them in the trash.

- **Wash your hands before and after changing your period products.**

- **Keep a few extra products with you, just in case.** Having a few extra products is always recommended to use or share with a friend.

- **One size does not fit all!** There are different sizes for each period product, based on the size of your vagina and the heaviness of your flow. Choose the right size and absorbency level for your body and flow to ensure comfort and minimize period pain.

- **Don't be embarrassed to ask for help when you need it.** Learning to use period products can be daunting, but remember that you aren't alone. Every woman on Earth knows what a period is and how it feels, so don't hesitate to ask your parents or trusted adults if you have questions or need help.

Remember, every woman goes through this experience, and there is no need to be embarrassed or afraid to seek assistance when needed.

Period Positivity: Embracing Your Menstrual Cycle

"Society has placed a taboo surrounding periods and menstrual health, as if we should be ashamed of this natural and miraculous process that ultimately keeps the human species alive."
— Tracy Lockwood

While having your first period can be scary, it is also a special moment worth celebrating. It's a sign that you are growing into a woman, and one day you might have the incredible ability to bring new life into the world (if that's what you choose).

Getting your period is a significant step in your journey to becoming a woman. It means your body is preparing for the remarkable ability to create and nurture life. The hormones driving your period and puberty also play a crucial role in shaping you into a strong and extraordinary individual. It's essential to embrace and value these changes as symbols of the amazing person you're becoming.

For a long time, society made people feel that periods were not something to be discussed. Thankfully, times have changed, and many people are challenging that perspective. There's absolutely nothing to be ashamed of when it comes to your period. Whether you get it earlier or later than your friends, whether your flow is light or heavy, and whether you choose to use pads, tampons, menstrual cups, or discs, it's all a normal part of being a woman.

In many cultures around the world, a girl's first period is celebrated with elaborate ceremonies. It might be time to introduce this tradition to your own period celebration. Why not have a period party when you get your first period? You can eat cake, watch your favorite movie, and celebrate this milestone with friends and family. It's time for society to start celebrating the miracle of life and everything that comes with it, including periods.

Your menstrual cycle is a part of who you are and deserves to be celebrated. Even if you don't always feel like being grateful for your period, especially when you're experiencing emotions or pain, remember that without your body, hormones, and uterus, humans wouldn't exist.

Having a period party when you get your first period is an excellent way to embrace and celebrate this wonderful milestone in your life. It can make the experience more positive for you and your friends.

 **Key Takeaways**

· Your first period can be a scary experience, but understanding what happens in your body can help you embrace it. It usually happens between 8 and 14 years old, and occurs when an unfertilized egg reaches your uterus.

· Period blood is the blood from the lining in your uterus that is expelled when the egg isn't fertilized. The muscles in the uterus contract to expel this lining, causing menstrual cramps and bleeding.

· Exercise, painkillers, and heat pads work wonderfully for reducing period pain. It's normal for some girls to experience much heavier periods and cramping than others.

· There are lots of period products you can use, including tampons (regular and applicator), pads, menstrual cups, and menstrual discs.

· Having your first period is a big milestone and deserves to be celebrated. It signifies that you are becoming a woman.

Another part of entering puberty is the growth and development of your breasts, which means it is time to buy your first bra. This is an exciting part of growing up. In the next chapter, you will learn all about buying your first bra.

BEMBERTON
BOOKS

SOMETHING FOR YOU

Thanks for buying this book. To show our appreciation, here's a **FREE** printable copy of the "Life Skills for Tweens Workbook"

WITH OVER 80 FUN ACTIVITIES **JUST FOR TWEENS!**

Scan the code to download your FREE printable copy

FINDING THE PERFECT BRA —
A BEGINNER'S GUIDE

Owning and wearing a bra is an important step on the journey to womanhood. Unsurprisingly, many girls are excited about buying their first bra. However, as you will learn, not all bras are the same. It's important to know what to look for when buying a bra to ensure it is as comfortable and functional as possible. So, when is the right time to shop for your first bra?

When to Shop for Your First Bra

There is no right or wrong time to shop for your first bra. Some girls start wearing bras at eight, while others only need them at 14 or 15. Since everyone's body develops differently, it's natural for each person to require a bra at different times. If you feel self-conscious about your breasts, you might find a training bra a comfortable way to ease into wearing a bra.

While there is no set time to start wearing a bra, there are signs that indicate it might be time to go shopping for your first bra. Remember that a bra is meant to support your breasts. If your breasts or nipples start feeling uncomfortable or you feel self-conscious about them (though you have no reason to — your body is beautiful just the way it is), it might be time to go bra shopping. Here are some signs that it might be time.

1. Your Breast Buds Are Developing

Breast buds are the tissue around and under your nipple that grows during puberty ("The First Bra Guide," 2019). As your breast buds develop, your breasts will start to grow, and there will be more actual breast tissue. This is a sign that your breasts are developing, and getting a bra might make you feel more comfortable. As your breast tissue develops, your breasts may feel sore or swollen. In this case, a bra can offer support and help ease any discomfort.

If you have larger breasts, a bra can provide much-needed support and reduce the strain on your lower back.

2. Your Nipples Are Sensitive or Show Through Clothing

The hormones responsible for the changes in your body, including your breasts growing, can make the nipples feel sensitive or stand upright, causing them to show through clothing. Wearing a bra with soft padding can alleviate discomfort caused by hard or sensitive nipples.

Sometimes, the nipples may also darken. This is normal, but it might cause them to show through light-colored tops. A flesh-colored bra can help prevent nipples from showing through clothing and help you feel more confident wearing any outfit.

3. You Feel More Breast Movement During Exercise

If you notice your breasts more when you exercise and feel like they are bouncing up and down, it may be time to buy a sports bra. These bras are designed to offer more support when exercising and can stop your breasts from bouncing around.

They're also important as your breasts grow to prevent sagging as you get older. Whether your breasts are small or large, wearing a sports bra during exercise becomes essential.

4. You Feel Self-Conscious About Your Breasts

If you feel self-conscious about your breasts being more noticeable in certain clothes, wearing a bra can help you feel more confident. Of course, you have absolutely no reason to feel self-conscious about your breasts — they are unique and a part of your beautiful body. But if it bothers you, a bra can help you feel more secure and confident. Wearing a pretty bra can boost your confidence and help you appreciate and love your breasts.

5. Your Friends Are Wearing Bras

While you shouldn't compare yourself to anyone else, it can feel strange when your friends are all wearing bras, but you aren't. It's fine if you want to wear a bra to fit in with your friends.

Remember that everyone develops at their own pace. Just because you don't *need* a bra now doesn't mean you won't need one later. Shopping for pretty bras with your friends can be a fun experience, so if you want to, you can buy a bra.

6. Do You Need to Wear a Bra?

While you might want to wear a bra for support, comfort, or any of the above reasons, no rule says you must wear one. Some women prefer not to wear bras, which is completely fine. While a bra offers structure and support, you can choose not to wear one.

Whether you wear a bra or not — and, if so, which type of bra you wear — is entirely up to personal preference. Determining when to wear a bra, if you want to wear one, is only half the story. The other half is deciding which type of bra is right for you. There are many different types of bras, each with their own characteristics. Learning to differentiate between these bras can help you choose the most suitable bra when shopping. Let's explore the different types of bras available.

Navigating Different Types of Bras

In addition to training and sports bras, various other kinds of bras are available. Some bras provide support, while others are designed to make the breasts look more shapely. Understanding the different types of bras can help you decide which is most suitable for you.

There are several things to look for in a bra, but most importantly, it needs to offer enough support and be comfortable. If it stabs you, pinches you, or digs in, it won't be comfortable. Finding the perfect bra can be a bit of a challenge, but it's worth the effort. Here are some different types of bras you'll come across:

Training Bras

Training bras are a common choice for girls starting out. These bras are usually made from thin cotton, making them soft, comfortable, and lightweight. Some training bras have a clasp in the back, like a regular bra, while others have a stretchy band that you can pull over your head.

Training bras don't offer much support for growing breasts, but they are perfect for girls whose breasts have just started developing or who have sensitive breasts and nipples. Training bras help you get used to the feel of wearing a bra.

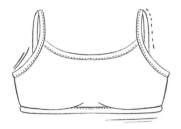

Bralettes

Bralettes are similar to training bras, but sometimes have soft padding, as well. They often have a clasp at the back, like a regular bra, and can be made from cotton, stretchy fabric, or lace. They also help cover the nipples to prevent them from showing through a shirt.

Like training bras, they don't offer much support, but they are extremely comfortable. While training bras are usually for girls just entering puberty, bralettes are available to anyone. Many women who don't need additional support from their bras prefer bralettes because they are lightweight and comfortable.

Soft-Padded Bras

Soft-padded bras have more structure than bralettes and training bras. These bras have a thicker, sometimes removable cup that fits over the breast. These cups help to give breasts a rounder appearance and prevent nipples from showing through clothing. They usually have a clasp in the back and can have thick or thin straps.

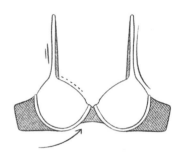

Because of their comfort and support, soft-padded bras are one of the most popular bras.

Push-Up Bras

Push-up bras look similar to soft-padded bras, but their cups have different inside designs. These cups often have a wave pattern on the bottom, with slightly thicker padding. Push-up bras are meant to push your breasts up and make them look bigger.

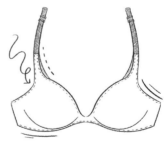

However, push-up bras don't offer more support than soft-padded bras. Women usually wear them because they like how they make their breasts look. When you first enter puberty, your breasts may not be big enough for a push-up bra, as there needs to be enough breast tissue to push up. But if you like the look of these bras, they can be something you look forward to buying when you are a bit older.

Underwire Bras

Underwire bras look like soft-padded bras, but they have a wire running along the bottom seam of the bra. This wire gives the bra more structure and support, especially for larger breasts. Some people prefer underwire bras, as they can provide more support. However, it's a personal preference, as others find the wire uncomfortable, especially when worn for long periods.

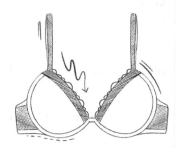

Some underwire bras also have padding or push-up padding. If you buy an underwire bra, it's crucial to ensure it fits properly. Otherwise, the wire may dig into your skin and be uncomfortable.

Sports Bras

Sports bras are just as popular as soft-padded bras and are worn by most women when exercising. Sports bras are designed to fit tightly and offer more support. They are specially designed to support breasts during vigorous exercise and protect them from bouncing up and down.

Regardless of how large your breasts are, it is recommended to wear a sports bra while exercising for maximum support. If you notice your breasts moving around a lot when you're active, a sports bra might be the best option as a first bra. That being said, it's important to know that sports bras are designed to be functional rather than to look nice.

Now that you know about the different types of bras available, it's important to understand how to find a bra that fits you correctly. If the bra doesn't fit properly, it can soon become uncomfortable and may not provide the necessary support.

Getting the Right Fit: Tips and Tricks

When buying your first bra, the priority is getting the fit right. There are many different styles of bras available, but it's all about getting the one that is perfect for you and your individual body.

Getting a bra that fits correctly will help you feel comfortable and give your growing breasts the best support. But how can you tell if a bra fits correctly? First, let's consider some signs that indicate a bra does not fit right.

How to Tell If a Bra Doesn't Fit Right

There are a couple of things to consider when trying on a bra. If the bra does not fit correctly, it will become uncomfortable throughout the day and may not offer the right support. These are common signs that a bra doesn't fit well:

- The straps dig into your skin or fall off your shoulders.

- The band around your body rides up in the front or back.

- The bra's wire or band digs into your ribs.

- The bra's band is too loose; you can easily pull it away from your body.

- Your breasts spill over the bra's cups.

- The bra cups gape away from your body.

If you notice any of these signs, it means the bra doesn't fit you properly. While you might not consider these big issues initially, they can become problematic when you wear the bra for a long time. Remember that you will be wearing a bra for most of the day, every day. So, if it doesn't fit properly in the store, it won't fit properly at home, either. Wearing a bra that is too small or too big is like wearing shoes that don't fit you properly: The longer you wear them, the more uncomfortable they become.

MEASURING YOUR BRA SIZE

The best way to ensure your bra fits you properly is to get measured for your correct bra size. Although you can try on bras in the store to see if they fit, having your measurements will help you determine which size bras to try. This is especially important when shopping for bras online since you can't exchange them easily. So, how do you measure your bra size?

Bra sizes work differently than other clothing sizes. A bra usually has two indicators of size: a number and a letter. The number represents the band size, while the letter is the cup size. For example, a 30A means the band size is 27 inches, and the cup measurement is one inch bigger than your band measurement. It may sound complicated, but it is pretty straightforward once you know how to measure your bra size. So, let's see how to determine your bra size.

Measuring Your Band Size

Measuring your bra band size is simple. Place a measuring tape around your ribs, right under your breasts. Ensure the measuring tape is level all around your body. Then, write down the number of inches your body measures around. It will be much easier if someone helps you to measure your band size, as they can ensure the measurement is accurate.

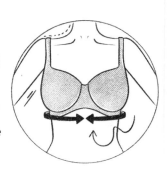

Measuring Your Cup Size

To measure your cup size, take the measuring tape and run it across your body, with the tape lying across the fullest part of your breast. It's best to do this while wearing a non-padded bra. Again, ensure the measuring tape is level to get an accurate measurement.

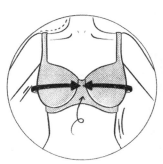

Determining Your Bra Size

Once you have these measurements, you can get your bra size. The band size comes first. Add 3 inches to your first measurement to determine your band size. For example, if your band measurement is 27 inches, you'll need a size 30 bra. If your result is an odd number, you will want to go up to the next size. For example, if your measurement is 28, 28+3=31, round up to a 32 band size. Take a look at the chart to help you determine your bra's band size based on your measurement.

To find your cup size, you need to subtract the measurement of your band size from the measurement of your breast size. For example, if your breast measurement is 33 inches and your band measurement is 30 inches, you would do the following: 33 – 30 = 3. This means that your bra cup size is a C. Here is another table to help you determine your cup size.

Measurements	Bra Sizes
27 in.	30
28 - 29 in.	32
30 - 31 in.	34
32 - 33 in.	36
34 - 35 in.	38
36 - 37 in.	40

You can use these numbers to determine your bra size. For example, if your band measurement is 29 inches and the difference between your breast and band measurement is 2 inches, your bra size is 32B. Knowing your bra size can make it easier to find bras that are suitable for you.

If you're unsure about measuring your bra size at home, you can also have it professionally measured at a clothing store. Many stores offer this service for free to help their customers find the perfect bra. If you feel more comfortable, you can ask a friend or family member like your mom, aunt, or sister, to measure their bra size with you. Once you know your bra size, you can focus on finding the right type of bra that suits your needs.

 **Key Takeaways**

- Buying your first bra is an exciting experience. There are so many bras to choose from; the best bra for you depends on your needs and the level of support you want.

- There is no right or wrong time to buy a bra. If your breasts start to grow, your nipples are visible through your clothes, your breasts are sensitive, or you notice them moving more when you exercise, it might be a good time to consider getting your first bra.

- There are various types of bras, including training, bralettes, soft-padded, push-up, underwire, and sports bras. Each has unique functions. Choosing the right bra is all about personal comfort and finding what works best for you.

- Measuring your bra size is essential to ensure a proper fit, which is crucial for comfort and support. Taking accurate measurements can help you find the perfect bra size for your body, making it easier to find the right bra.

As you enter puberty, along with choosing your first bra, it's time to adopt a fresh approach to your personal hygiene and skin care. In the next chapter, we will consider the importance of personal hygiene during this stage of your life and provide practical tips to help you develop effective routines.

PERSONAL HYGIENE —
TAKING CARE OF YOUR GROWING BODY

As you start puberty, you will notice many changes in your body. In the previous chapters, you learned that these changes are a result of the hormones released by your brain, which help your body mature. However, these same hormones also affect your body odor, the amount of sweat you produce, hair growth, and your skin. This chapter will explore how to manage these effects with good hygiene.

The Importance of Personal Hygiene

Before puberty, your daily routine was more straightforward. You didn't have to worry about body odor, sweating, hair removal, or your period. But all of that changes when you enter puberty. Developing a more detailed daily personal hygiene routine is essential to ensure you care for yourself properly.

Personal hygiene means caring for your body and keeping it clean — and it's crucial for everyone. The habits you put in place now will likely be with you for the rest of your life. Establishing an easy-to-follow and complete personal hygiene regimen now will save you a lot of time and make you feel more confident throughout the day.

A good personal hygiene regimen can boost your confidence by ensuring you are well cared for. It also helps improve your mental health and reduces stress, which is good for your well-being. For example, by showering daily and using deodorant, you can be sure that you smell nice, which boosts your self-confidence and reduces stress.

Maintaining good personal hygiene also ensures you are physically healthy. Showering, brushing your teeth, and washing your hands all help keep your body healthy and protect you against germs. This helps prevent you from getting sick, which most people want to avoid.

As you can see, personal hygiene is essential for many reasons — but what exactly does it entail, and how do you keep your body clean?

Skincare: Tackling Acne and Developing a Routine

One important aspect of personal hygiene is caring for your skin — especially your face. The hormonal changes during puberty often affect your skin, making it oilier, which can lead to pimples, acne, and breakouts. Even girls with non-oily skin experience breakouts, especially before and during their periods. Increased acne and pimples are normal during puberty but usually clear up as you get older.

That said, following a simple skincare routine can greatly help your skin. A daily skincare routine helps keep your skin clean, moisturized, and protected from the sun. It can also help prevent acne and breakouts and reduce the chances of acne scars.

A skincare routine doesn't have to be complicated. You don't need expensive products that celebrities and influencers often promote. You simply need a cleanser (or gentle face wash), moisturizer, and sunscreen to keep your skin clean and healthy. Using these products daily will significantly help your skin.

A morning and evening skincare routine also helps you focus on keeping your skin clean and healthy. It also gives you time to relax and focus on caring for yourself, which is crucial for your mental health. This is why it is a good idea to set aside time for your daily skincare routine each morning and evening.

If you wear makeup, you should remove it before starting your skincare routine. Use a makeup-removing wipe, micellar water, or a gentle makeup-removing oil to lift all the makeup from your skin.

Then, wash your face with warm water and a mild, oil-reducing cleanser or face wash. Gently pat your skin dry with a soft towel, then apply a light moisturizer to keep your skin soft and glowing. Finally, don't forget to apply sunscreen. Using sunscreen daily can prevent wrinkles and protect your skin from sun damage as you get older.

It's also important to clean your face at night to remove all the dirt and sweat from your day. Wash your face again with a mild cleanser and use a moisturizer. You don't need sunscreen at night.

The Importance of Dental Hygiene

Looking after your teeth is equally important. By the time you start puberty, you have likely lost most of your baby teeth, so the teeth you have now are the ones you will have for the rest of your life. If you don't care for your adult teeth and gums, you may get cavities, which is a painful and unpleasant experience requiring a trip to the dentist.

Practicing good dental hygiene is vital. Brush your teeth twice a day with a soft toothbrush and toothpaste to keep your teeth and mouth healthy. Regular flossing also helps prevent the development of cavities and ensures your mouth is clean and fresh. Clean teeth also help keep your breath fresh, boosting your self-confidence.

Avoid eating too many sugary foods or soft drinks, as the sugars in them harm your teeth. And, if you can, it's a great idea to go to the dentist once a year for a checkup to ensure your teeth are healthy. By following basic dental hygiene practices, you can maintain a healthy smile!

Showering, Deodorant, and More: Keeping Fresh and Clean

Another essential aspect of good personal hygiene is showering every day (or every other day, if you have sensitive skin). As mentioned earlier, the hormones during puberty cause you to sweat more, which leads to body odor.

Body odor occurs when sweat combines with the trillions of bacteria naturally present on your skin. When sweat comes into contact with the bacteria, it mixes with the fats and salts and can produce an odor. Not all body odors are the same — some may be unpleasant, while others don't smell at all.

Fortunately, there is an easy solution to combat body odor. Showering daily and using deodorant can help reduce sweating and prevent unpleasant odors. Additionally, washing your clothes regularly and wearing clean clothes can help reduce odors, since your clothes absorb sweat and can start to smell if not washed.

Of course, there might be days when you need to shower more than once. For example, a shower after sports practice or a visit to the gym can help you smell clean and fresh.

Applying deodorant after a shower and in the morning before getting dressed can also help control sweat and body odor throughout the day. There are various types of deodorant available, including:

- Deodorant sprays

- Deodorant sticks

- Roll-on deodorants

- Gel deodorants

- Antiperspirant deodorants (which block pores to reduce sweating)

- Natural deodorants made with ingredients like baking powder, coconut oil, and essential oils. These are environmentally friendly and don't contain aluminum, which may be harmful to your body. Natural deodorants may not prevent sweating entirely, but they prevent sweat from smelling.

You can use whichever deodorant you prefer to help you feel clean, fresh, and confident.

Hair Care: Keeping Your locks Clean and Healthy

Caring for your hair is as important as keeping your body clean during puberty. When you enter puberty, changes in your hormones can affect your hair. It may become oilier at certain times of the month, or your scalp might become dry and flaky. That's why using the right hair products for your hair type is crucial to keep it clean and healthy.

You don't have to wash your hair every day, unless it becomes very oily or dirty. How frequently you wash your hair depends on your hair type and how active you are. For instance, if you exercise regularly, your hair may become greasy. Pay attention to the condition of your hair to determine how often it needs washing.

Understanding the changes in your hair during puberty and using the proper hair-care routine can keep your hair looking and feeling its best.

Overall, good personal hygiene helps improve your health and confidence. When you are clean and well-maintained, you will feel more energetic, confident, and self-assured. You may also find that people around you treat you with more respect.

As you enter puberty, it becomes clear that personal hygiene is vital, and these habits will remain essential throughout your life. However, caring for your growing body extends beyond personal hygiene and cleanliness. So, what else can you do to practice self-care during puberty?

Exercise and Sleep: Prioritizing Your Well-Being

Getting enough sleep is crucial, especially during puberty. Your body needs enough rest to develop properly. Lack of sleep can affect your mood, attention span, and school performance (Jitesh et al., 2021). As a tween, you should aim for at least seven or eight hours of sleep per night.

Sleep is crucial for your health and well-being. While your body rests when you sleep, your brain is hard at work, releasing hormones and chemicals. These substances need time to work their magic. Furthermore, getting enough sleep will help you feel more energized during the day.

So, how can you get a good night's sleep? Here are some tips that can help you fall asleep faster and get a good night's rest:

· **Give yourself enough time to rest.** Aim for seven to eight hours of sleep.

· **Maintain a regular sleep schedule.** Try to go to bed and wake up at the same time each day.

· **Reduce caffeine intake in the daytime.** Highly caffeinated drinks, like coffee and energy drinks, take up to 12 hours to go through your body and can negatively affect your sleep.

· **Keep your room dark, quiet, and cool.** Cover any flashing lights (such as computer lights), as they can disrupt sleep.

· **Avoid using screens or tablets at least one hour before bedtime.**

· **Turn screens off and make your bedroom a "no charge zone!"** Avoid charging or keeping screens in your room, as they can distract and wake you up.

· **Exercise in the daytime.** Regular exercise can help you sleep better.

The Importance of Eating Well

Eating a healthy diet during puberty can also benefit your overall well-being. Did you know sugary foods and preservatives can affect your skin and health? Eating too many sugary and processed foods can lead to oilier skin and more breakouts. Additionally, the preservatives in junk food can disrupt your hormones, contributing to acne and mood swings.

Drinking water and staying hydrated is another crucial aspect of managing your personal hygiene. Water makes up 60 percent of your body, and not drinking enough can negatively affect your body and mental health. Drinking water and being properly hydrated can improve your skin, energize you, and help reduce period pain and discomfort. Teenage girls should drink at least six to eight glasses of water a day. If you exercise, you may need to drink more to replace the water lost through sweating.

Healthy foods like fresh fruits and vegetables are rich in antioxidants, vitamins, and minerals. These nutrients are essential for growth, development, regulating hormones, and improving mental health. Eating a nutritious diet also enhances your physical health, which is vital during your teenage years.

The Importance of Regular Exercise

Exercise is beneficial for your physical health and plays a significant role in your mental well-being. Exercise releases endorphins, sometimes called your body's "happy hormones." These endorphins increase your energy levels and improve your mood. Exercise also reduces cortisol, the stress hormone, which helps to reduce feelings of stress and anxiety.

To keep your heart and body healthy, doctors recommend doing at least 30 minutes of exercise a day.

What kinds of exercise can you do? There are many types of exercise you can enjoy. You can go for a walk (like walking to school or walking your dog), participate in a team sport at school, or go for a cardio class at the gym. The specific type of exercise isn't as important as keeping your body active and moving.

If you find exercising challenging, ask a friend to join you. A workout buddy can make exercise more enjoyable and feel less like work. Whatever you do, get out there and exercise. It is so important for everyone to exercise. Just remember the many benefits for your health, including improved mood, increased energy levels, and better sleep.

 **Key Takeaways**

- Caring for your growing body becomes even more important when you enter puberty. This includes practicing good personal hygiene to ensure you are healthy.

- Personal hygiene involves various aspects, such as showering regularly, keeping your hair, teeth, and nails clean, getting enough sleep, and regular exercise.

- Hormonal changes during puberty can lead to acne and breakouts. A daily skincare routine can help prevent breakouts, keep your skin clean and fresh, and boost self-confidence.

- Dental hygiene is crucial as your adult teeth replace your baby teeth. Brush your teeth twice a day, floss regularly, and visit the dentist for checkups.

- Maintaining personal cleanliness, such as showering, using deodorant, washing your hair, and keeping your nails short and clean, can increase your confidence and protect against germs. It's important to shower daily and use deodorant to combat sweat and odor.

- Getting sufficient sleep is crucial, especially during puberty. Your body needs sleep to grow and regulate your hormones.

- Regular exercise is important during puberty. It can improve self-confidence while also reducing period pain. Aim for at least 30 minutes of exercise each day.

- Eating a healthy diet and staying hydrated by drinking enough water both contribute to improved skin, balanced hormones, and a better mood.

By practicing good personal hygiene, prioritizing sleep, exercising regularly, and maintaining a healthy diet, you can be sure you are taking good care of your body during puberty. These healthy habits will set you up for success as a teen and later in life.

The next chapter will discuss everything you should know about cultivating friendships during puberty. By following the proper steps, you can develop strong friendships that last a lifetime.

CULTIVATING FRIENDSHIPS

As you grow up and get older, you may notice that your friendships start changing, too. When you were younger, it was easier to make friends. You likely had girlfriends and boyfriends, and all played together without a problem. As you get older and develop more of your own interests, your friendships might also start changing.

Managing your changing friendships is an important part of growing up. It's crucial that your friends positively impact your life. Good friends should build you up, encourage you, and support you.

Building lasting friendships can be challenging in today's world, but in this chapter, you will learn how to navigate these changes and cultivate new friendships.

The Changing Landscape of Tween Friendships

As you already know, you can expect many physical and emotional changes when you enter puberty. The emotional changes you experience when you enter puberty can affect how you feel about those around you and how they feel about you.

As you get older, your interests also change. You may become more interested in a specific sport, instrument, subject, or after-school activity. You will meet new people who share these interests, and you might become closer friends with them. At the same time, your older friends will develop their own interests, and you may grow apart.

Changing schools can also lead to losing contact with older friends and making new ones. It's a natural part of growing up to lose touch with older friends and make new ones who share your interests. But just because you don't have shared interests with someone doesn't mean you can't be friends with them.

Even if you and your best friend have different interests, you can continue to be friends while making time for your own pastimes. As you make new friends, your best friend will too, and it's essential to give each other room to grow. This can help bring you closer together as friends and help you make even more friends.

During puberty, it's common for relationships with your male friends to go through changes. Just as hormonal changes affect your body, they can also affect how you perceive people, including boys. This is true for boys, as well. Sometimes, boys you used to be friends with might start acting differently, and you might develop different feelings toward them.

These changes are a normal part of growing up and discovering new emotions. It can be challenging to navigate friendships, especially when everyone has entered puberty and is undergoing physical changes. However, understanding how to manage your relationships and respecting the differences between you and your friends can help build stronger friendships.

Eventually, things tend to settle down as everyone adjusts to the new hormonal changes. Therefore, it's essential to keep your friendships as strong as possible. Try not to burn bridges or end friendships with people you might want to reconnect with later. While you may experience ups and downs in your relationships, it's crucial to have a core group of friends who can support each other through the challenges of puberty.

Sometimes, your friends might be mean to you or reject your friendship. In such cases, it's okay to step away from those friendships. Remember, you are fantastic and deserve friends who love and respect you. If your current friends don't treat you well, it's time to look for new ones.

Conflict is an unavoidable part of life, and learning how to manage it is important. No matter how hard you try, you won't always be able to avoid conflict. In those situations, it is crucial to learn how to react to and manage conflict without losing control of your emotions. So, how should you navigate conflict as a teenager or adult?

Navigating Conflict: How to Handle Disagreements

Conflicts and disagreements are a normal part of life. During the tween and teen years, it's common to experience sensitivity to certain emotions. You may feel more self-conscious or insecure, leading to strong emotional reactions to situations. Additionally, you may feel misunderstood, which can lead to conflicts with parents, siblings, or friends.

This heightened sensitivity may be due to hormonal changes, but could also be due to greater pressure to perform well at school, in your sport, and at home. You are growing up and will naturally have more responsibilities, and these heightened feelings of responsibility might cause more conflicts.

While it's normal to feel upset sometimes, and your feelings are entirely valid, knowing how to navigate conflict is essential. If you let your emotions escalate, you may do or say things you later regret.

By staying in control of your emotions, you can calmly navigate conflicts and find ways to peacefully resolve them. Harshita Makvana (2023) from Mom Junction shares these 10 steps to navigate and resolve disputes as a teenager. Following these steps will help you navigate conflict and remain in control of your emotions:

· Step back and consider the other person's perspective. Try to see the situation through their eyes.

· Carefully listen to what the other person is saying, especially when they talk about how something makes them feel. Don't interrupt them when they share their feelings.

· Share your feelings. Be honest and keep calm to help them understand your perspective.

· Don't let your emotions overwhelm you. Take deep breaths when you feel like you are getting too emotional.

· Avoid digging up past conflicts. Resist the temptation to say, "You always do this," as that won't help resolve a dispute. Instead, focus on discussing the current conflict and finding a resolution.

· Try to find a solution that respects both of your opinions. Aim for a solution that serves both of you.

· Learn to compromise. The solution might not give you precisely what you want, but it's important that both you and the other person are satisfied.

- Learn to say sorry. It can be difficult to admit when you've made a mistake. However, learning to acknowledge and apologize for your mistakes can help immensely in a conflict situation. People always appreciate a sincere and honest apology.

- If you cannot find a solution, it might be necessary to bring in a mediator. A mediator is a person who isn't on anyone's side. They are neutral and are there to listen to both parties and help find a solution.

- Accept the other person's apology. Holding a grudge won't make you feel better, and resolving the conflict is more important than who is right.

Staying calm and listening to another person shows maturity. Remember the saying, "You have a choice between being right and being happy." Sometimes, it's more important to be the bigger person and accept an apology than to prove that you're right and they are wrong.

Compromising and navigating conflicts positively doesn't mean you're a pushover. It demonstrates maturity by prioritizing your friendships over the need to always be right.

That's not to say you shouldn't stand up for yourself. If someone crosses a line or hurts your feelings, you need to tell them. This shows them that their words or actions are unacceptable and helps define your boundaries. Standing up for yourself and addressing inappropriate behavior helps cultivate self-respect and the respect of others.

Building Strong and Supportive Friendships: Creating Lasting Bonds

The goal of conflict resolution is to keep your relationships with your friends and family healthy. But another important part of being a teenager is building new relationships and strengthening the ones you already have. As we have already discussed, as you grow up, your interests will change — and so will the things you need from your friends.

Since we all have different personalities, we look for different things in our friends. For example, if you're shy, an outgoing friend can help you feel more comfortable in new situations. If you love sports, having friends who share this interest can give you more to talk about and opportunities to support each other.

Unlike family, you can choose your friends. The good friends you surround yourself with in school are the ones who will inspire and motivate you to achieve your goals, study hard, and be successful. These friends will also love and support you and your changing body during puberty.

Choosing supportive friends at school who truly want the best for you can help make you happier and more successful. But to *have* a good friend, you must also *be* a good friend. So, how can you build strong and supportive friendships?

BUILDING POSITIVE FRIENDSHIPS

Navigating strong emotions can be tricky during puberty. Your hormones might cause you to overreact sometimes, and even though that's normal, it can put pressure on friendships. The key is building strong relationships based on trust and understanding, where you and your friends feel loved and supported. So, how can you achieve this? Here are some tips:

Top Tips for Building Positive Friendships

- Respect your friends and their differences. Their differences make them unique, and that's why they are your friends.

- Be honest with your friends. Tell them how you feel and let them help you. And if they hurt or upset you, tell them.

- Protect your friends. Stand up for them when they aren't around, and never gossip about them behind their backs.

- Always make time for your friends. Neglecting them can make them feel like you don't care, and that can drive you apart. So, make time for them, especially when they need you.

- When your friend tells you a secret—keep it! One of the easiest ways to ruin a friendship is to betray a friend's trust. So if your friend tells you something in confidence, keep it to yourself.

- Give your friend space to grow. Just as you will grow and develop new interests, so will your friends.

- Support and encourage your friends to help them reach their goals. You expect your friends to support you, so do the same for them.

Quality Over Quantity

If there's one thing you should remember about friendships as you grow up, it's that quality is always better than quantity. When you were younger, you probably had many friends. But as you get older, you realize that not everyone who is friendly with you is your friend.

Having one or two close friends who support and encourage you and who are always there for you is better than having thousands of friends on social media.

Your priorities change. Instead of having many friends to play with, you need friends you can trust to keep your secrets and stand up for you, even when you're not there. That's why choosing your friends carefully becomes more important as you get older.

Social Media: Friend or Foe?

Social media has become an important part of our lives, influencing friendships positively and negatively. We spend a lot of time on social media, liking posts, sharing with friends, and exploring new interests. But social media isn't always positive for friendships, and it's important to use it mindfully. Here are some pros and cons to consider.

Using Social Media To Build Friendships

It allows you to communicate with your friends when you're not together. Platforms like WhatsApp, Instagram, and Twitter all have chat options to check in with your friends and keep in touch.

You can meet new friends who share your interests. You can join groups or communities to connect with like-minded people.

PROS

You can share photos and videos with friends, letting them know you're thinking of them even when apart.

You can share photos, videos, and information about things you love, which can help you make even more friends.

Social media can create pressure to fit in or do things you're not comfortable with, this is called peer pressure. For example, if your friend keeps sending you pictures of piercings and urging you to get one, you might feel pressured to do it. Remember, it's okay to make decisions based on what feels right for you.

People can act differently online. Sometimes, people are braver behind a screen and may say mean things, pick fights, or hurt others' feelings. But remember just because it's a text, doesn't make the words any less hurtful.

CONS

Cyberbullying is a real problem. Posting mean comments online is a form of cyberbullying, and it can cause a lot of hurtful feelings. Always think before you post.

It's always there. Once something is posted on social media, it's always there. Meaning it's available for everyone to see for ever. So before you post something ask yourself: "Would I be happy if this is always there for everyone to see?"

 **Key Takeaways**

- Friendships change as you get older. As you develop new interests, you'll make new friends. Some old friendships may fade, while new ones will form.

- Learning how to navigate and resolve conflicts is crucial. Everyone faces conflicts in their lives, and it's important to learn how to handle them with care and respect.

- As you grow up, you'll realize that having a few true friends is more important than many superficial ones. To have loving and supportive friends, always be a loving and supportive friend in return.

- Social media can be both positive and negative for friendships. Learn to use it safely and responsibly. and always consider your friend's feelings before putting something out there.

We've already explored the effects of puberty on your emotional well-being in this book, but now it's time to learn how you can control and manage your feelings. In the next chapter, you will learn about embracing and managing your changing emotions during puberty.

EMBRACING YOUR EMOTIONS — NAVIGATING MOOD SWINGS

During puberty, along with the physical changes you experience, you'll also notice some emotional changes. Understanding and navigating these emotional shifts is vital for your health and well-being. While these new emotions and mood swings are perfectly normal, they can cause challenges in your relationships if not managed effectively.

Managing your emotions and recognizing your mood swings before they occur is an important part of growing up. In this chapter, we'll focus on discovering why you sometimes have mood swings, which emotions you may experience, and how you can manage your emotions using helpful coping strategies. But first, what causes all these emotions and mood swings? Let's take a look.

Understanding the Connection Between Hormones and Emotions

As mentioned before, your brain and body produce more hormones during puberty. These include an increase in estrogen, progesterone, FSH, and LH, which are responsible for your body's physical changes. Some of these hormones (specifically estrogen) can affect your body's serotonin levels (Tallman Smith, 2017).

Serotonin is a chemical messenger that sends signals from your brain to the rest of your body and plays a role in many functions, like digestion, sleep, and mood. During your menstrual cycle, your body produces varying levels of estrogen. And just before your period, those estrogen levels fluctuate dramatically. Many scientists believe that your estrogen levels are linked to your serotonin levels. Some say that an increase in estrogen leads to a decrease in serotonin, which could cause sudden mood changes (Tallman Smith, 2017).

As a result, these hormonal changes can affect how your brain works and how you feel. Because of this, it's common for girls to experience mood swings before and during their periods. It's important to know that these mood changes are normal. In fact, research shows that most women — approximately 90 percent — experience mood swings throughout their menstrual cycles (Holland, 2019).

What Are Mood Swings?

Just like the weather can change throughout the day, your moods can also change during your menstrual cycle. These sudden mood changes are called mood swings, and they happen because of the changing levels of hormones in your body.

From the outside, it might seem like your mood suddenly changed for no apparent reason. The good news is that most, if not all, women experience mood swings during their menstrual cycles. This means that most women will understand when you have these sudden mood swings.

Of course, it's important to remember that sudden mood swings do not excuse bad manners or behavior. Later in this chapter, we will look at coping strategies for managing mood swings.

Although hormone fluctuations play a significant role, they aren't the only reason you may experience mood swings.

Other Factors That Cause Mood Swings

Several other factors might also contribute to mood swings. These factors can be made worse by fluctuating hormones, making the mood swings more intense and frequent. Here are some additional factors that can contribute to mood swings:

· Stress

· Too little sleep

· Caffeine consumption

· Eating highly processed and sugary foods

Fortunately, you can help manage and reduce your mood swings by addressing the factors contributing to them. We'll discuss these factors in a later section. However, before we do that, it's important to identify and understand the range of emotions you may experience during your menstrual cycle and which emotions are intensified by hormonal fluctuations.

Identifying Emotions

Emotions are a natural part of life. As you grow up, you'll notice they become more complicated and difficult to understand. When you were younger, emotions were pretty straightforward and easy to understand. If someone took your toy, you might have felt angry. If you fell in the playground, you probably felt sad. And you likely felt happy when something good happened, like your mom buying you an ice cream. But, as you get older, your emotions and how you express them become more complex.

Everyone experiences emotions differently. Some people cry when they're angry, happy, or tired, while others laugh when they are cross or become quiet when they're sad. As your emotions become increasingly influenced by hormonal changes during puberty, it's important to recognize and understand what you are feeling. This can help you manage your feelings and understand why you feel the way you do.

So, what do the different emotions feel like during puberty? Let's explore some common emotions and how they often present, which can help you better understand and make sense of your feelings.

Anger and Irritation

Anger is an emotion many women feel when their serotonin levels drop. Serotonin contributes to feelings of joy and happiness, so low levels can lead to anger or irritation. If you find that you are suddenly irritated with your friends and family for no reason, or you get angry with them even if they haven't done anything wrong, it may be due to hormonal fluctuations in your body.

Anger often results from frustration or feeling like you are being treated unfairly, and irritation can arise from being distracted or bothered by something. However, when your anger and frustration result from hormonal changes, it's important to remember it's not necessarily someone else's fault. It's normal to feel angry or irritated, even when your hormones cause these emotions. But it's important to manage these emotions, especially when they're influenced by hormones, as the person you feel irritated or angry with may not understand what they did to deserve such a reaction.

Sadness

Sadness is another common emotion many women experience before or during their periods. When you feel sad, you may cry or feel a sense of heartache, even if no one has physically or emotionally hurt you. Sadness is a natural part of life, and although it's not enjoyable, it's important to acknowledge and try to understand your sadness.

Sadness affects people in different ways. Some people release their sadness by crying, while others bottle up their sadness and pretend nothing is wrong. Feeling sad due to hormonal changes can be frustrating, because sometimes you may not even know why you are feeling sad. It could be triggered by something as simple as seeing a dog on the street, or you might wake up feeling sad for no obvious reason. Remember, sadness is a completely normal emotion. Although you'll likely want to overcome your sadness, allowing yourself to experience and feel these different emotions is important.

Sensitivity

Many women feel more sensitive before and during their periods. Mood swings often cause sensitivity because you may not understand why you feel the way you do. For example, if you wake up feeling sad or angry, even when nothing has happened to make you feel that way, you may also feel more sensitive because you don't understand the reasons for your emotions. Sensitivity is a perfectly normal emotion, even if it can be frustrating.

When you go from feeling happy to sad to angry to tired in a short time, you may also feel more sensitive because you may not know what's causing these emotions and why they change so often. Additionally, suppose you struggle to make simple decisions, like what to do, eat, or watch. In that case, you might feel extra sensitive, especially when someone gets annoyed that you can't make up your mind.

Knowing what causes your moods and indecisiveness might help you feel less sensitive. When your sensitivity is caused by your hormones, even knowing what is causing it might not make you feel better. Still, it might help you understand why you feel the way you do.

FATIGUE

You can feel fatigued if you experience any of the emotions we have discussed already. Fatigue occurs when you are so tired that you cannot think clearly. Women often feel fatigued during their periods, as their bodies are doing a lot of extra work to expel the uterine lining. Taking frequent naps, feeling too tired to do anything, and feeling physically and mentally exhausted are all signs of fatigue.

Unfortunately, because your fatigue stems from hormonal changes, sleeping more won't necessarily make you feel better. Still, giving your body more time to rest might help with your mood swings.

SELF-CONSCIOUSNESS

When you are self-conscious, you feel that other people are staring at you or judging you for certain things, such as how you look, dress, speak, etc. Many girls feel self-conscious when they first start puberty, and many women feel self-conscious during their periods.

Being self-conscious can also make you feel scared to do things. For example, you might not want to go to school during your first period because you think your friends will make fun of you. But self-consciousness is often a feeling we only have about ourselves — it isn't necessarily how others feel about us.

Many people are also self-conscious about their bodies. For example, you might feel self-conscious when your hair is a bit messy, or when you feel like you look tired. Being self-conscious is a normal feeling, but it can increase just before your period.

Recognizing that your self-consciousness might be because of your fluctuating hormones can help you ignore these feelings and focus on embracing your beautiful body instead.

Recognizing and understanding your emotions is an important first step to managing them. While all emotions and feelings are normal, learning how to manage them is a crucial part of growing up.

If you cannot manage your emotions, they might start to control you, which can lead to unpleasant experiences. Fortunately, there are several proven ways to help manage emotions, enabling you to feel more like yourself both before and during your period.

Coping Strategies for Managing Mood Swings

Although the mood swings you experience before and during your period are completely normal, it doesn't mean you should just accept them. Mood swings can make you feel miserable and might lead you to be mean toward others when they don't deserve it. If you learn how to manage your mood swings, you can avoid hurting other people's feelings, improve your mood, and make your period a much more enjoyable experience. So, how can you manage your mood swings?

GET ENOUGH SLEEP

Getting enough sleep is important for any tween and teenager, but focusing on your sleep is even more important during your period. Because your hormones fluctuate more, your body needs more rest. Being tired can increase mood swings and negative emotions like sadness, irritability, and self-consciousness.

By getting seven to eight hours of sleep, you will feel more refreshed and energized, and more in control of your emotions. Sleep quality is important, so remember to follow the tips in Chapter 4 to help ensure you get plenty of rest during your period.

DRINK MORE WATER OR CAFFEINE-FREE TEA

Caffeinated and sugary drinks can potentially impact your mood swings. Caffeine has been associated with increased feelings of stress and anxiety, which can contribute to mood swings and affect sleeping patterns. Furthermore, research has shown that sugary drinks and foods can also cause increased anxiety and irritability (Sheehan, 2010).

Water and caffeine-free tea help you stay hydrated, which can improve your mood and overall health. All your body's cells, including those in your brain, need water to function. When fully hydrated, your brain works well and helps regulate your mood. Dehydration, on the other hand, can lead to tiredness, irritability, and a drop in concentration. Remember to drink water throughout the day to stay healthy.

Do Light to Moderate Exercise

Exercise is one of the best things you can do to stay physically and mentally fit. Research has shown that exercise can positively affect your mood by increasing dopamine and serotonin levels (Watson, 2019).

Even during your period, doing light to moderate exercise can help improve your mood. The combination of the mood-boosting chemicals and the fresh air from outdoor activity is known to improve your well-being and helps you sleep better.

Exercise also helps you think more clearly, which can help you manage your emotions a lot better. Going for a walk in the afternoon, participating in team sports, or taking a class at the gym can help improve your mood and help you manage your emotions and mood swings while on your period.

Eat Calcium-Rich Foods

Calcium is a mineral you get from eating certain foods, like milk, low-fat cheese, and leafy greens. Many studies have shown that eating calcium can help reduce fatigue and sadness during your period (Sheehan, 2010). Therefore, eating calcium-rich food can help you manage your mood swings.

It also helps you to feel better overall. Eating healthily and taking your vitamins also improves your body's immune system and energy levels, which helps to manage your hormone levels. If your hormone levels are regulated, so too are your mood swings.

Sit in the Sun

Did you know sun exposure can increase your serotonin levels? Studies have shown that sitting in the sun for just 15 minutes a day can increase your serotonin levels, which helps to improve your mood (Byzak, 2018). Sitting in the sun and getting fresh air can also help clear your mind, make you feel more positive, improve your mood, and reduce stress.

Just remember to wear sunscreen when going outside to soak up the sun's vitamin D.

Manage Your Stress

Stress management is also essential during your period. Increased stress can intensify mood swings, affect sleep, and make you feel more irritated and angrier overall. Therefore, before and during your period, it's important to focus on reducing stress.

There are many techniques for stress management, even when you are busy with exams or tests. Breathing exercises, light to moderate exercise, and a healthy diet can all reduce stress and help you manage your mood swings much better.

Speak to a Doctor or Medical Professional

Some women and tweens have a harder time managing their mood swings during their periods. Certain health conditions, such as polycystic ovary syndrome (PCOS) and thyroid conditions, can cause more significant hormonal fluctuations, leading to severe mood swings and other period complications. Women who struggle with these conditions are sometimes prescribed medication to help manage their hormone levels, which in turn helps manage their mood swings.

If you find that you struggle with severe mood swings despite following the tips above, it might benefit you to see a doctor to determine if something else is the cause of your fluctuating hormones. Fortunately, these conditions are rare and aren't common among young girls just starting their periods.

By implementing these strategies, you can effectively manage your mood swings and make your period a more enjoyable experience. Remember, it's normal to experience emotions, but learning how to navigate and manage them is an important part of growing up.

 **Key Takeaways**

· Mood swings during your menstrual cycle are caused by the fluctuation of hormones in your body. Just before your period starts, your estrogen levels spike, causing your serotonin (happy hormones) to dip, which can lead to mood swings.

· Many women feel sad, angry, irritated, sensitive, and self-conscious before and during their periods. These feelings are normal, but some strategies can help manage these mood swings.

· Strategies for managing mood swings include getting enough sleep, drinking more water, exercising, and sitting in the sun.

· Following these tips can also help you feel happier and more relaxed during your period.

One of the emotions you may feel during your period is self-consciousness. Many women struggle with this not only during their period but in general. In the next chapter, we'll look at ways to enhance self-confidence and love your body.

SELF-ESTEEM AND BODY IMAGE — LOVING YOURSELF INSIDE AND OUT

As you go through puberty, your body undergoes many remarkable changes that help make you wonderfully unique. It's natural to sometimes feel like you don't measure up, or have moments of self-doubt. However, it's important to remember that these thoughts don't reflect the truth.

In a world influenced by social media, prioritizing self-love and acceptance of your wonderfully unique body has never been more important. In this chapter, we will look at strategies to help you build your self-confidence and love your body.

Understanding Body Image and Self-Esteem

Before we dive into ways to manage your body image and self-esteem, it's vital that you first understand what these concepts are. Your body image and self-esteem are extremely important as you grow up, and developing a positive body image will help you immensely later in life. Your body image affects your self-esteem and confidence, so having a positive body image is crucial. But what exactly is body image?

WHAT IS BODY IMAGE?

Your body image refers to the thoughts you have about your body. Many factors affect how you feel about your body, and your thoughts may change as you get older. Most people have both positive and negative thoughts about their bodies. They like some parts, while disliking others.

Tweens and teenagers often become more aware of their body image. Since the body changes so quickly during puberty, it's normal for your perception of your body to change during this time.

Your body image is the way you *see* your own body. However, it's important to remember that how you feel about your body may not align with the reality of how your body looks, especially if you feel insecure about certain parts. For example, if you think your arms are too big, you might always see them as larger in the mirror than they actually are.

Your body image is also influenced by how you *think* about your body. How you think about your body often affects how you see it, too. If you think your body is beautiful, you will look at it and see it as beautiful.

How you see and think about your body significantly affects how you *feel* about it, also known as your affective body image. This is one of the most important parts of your body image, as it plays a crucial role in how you treat your body, and greatly contributes to your self-esteem.

Finally, all these aspects influence how you *treat* your body. A positive body image is important, as it leads you to treat your body kindly.

Your body image can affect your self-esteem, with a positive body image improving your self-esteem and a negative body image potentially damaging it. But what exactly is self-esteem?

What Is Self-Esteem?

Your self-esteem is your confidence in your abilities and skills. Essentially, it's how you feel about yourself. Your body image is a part of your self-esteem, and greatly affects it.

Having good self-esteem helps you value yourself more. This is important in your daily life, enabling you to recognize and appreciate your uniqueness. It can also help you speak up when you're not being treated fairly. Therefore, having good self-esteem is crucial for your mental health and well-being.

Lots of factors influence your body image and self-esteem. Understanding these factors and learning how to manage them can greatly improve your self-esteem and confidence.

What Factors Affect Your Body Image and Self-Esteem?

Your body image and self-esteem are affected by various factors, such as media, society, and the changes that come from puberty. When you enter puberty, your body goes through many remarkable changes. It's natural to compare yourself to others, even if you may not want to. If you feel that you are progressing at a different pace than your friends, it can sometimes lead to negative feelings and affect your self-esteem.

Society and the media also affect your body image and self-esteem significantly. Society has ideas about how people should look, dress, speak, and behave, and the media shapes ideas about body image and self-esteem.

These standards change frequently, but they can significantly affect your feelings. Unfortunately, social media has a big influence, exposing teens to society's standards, whether they want to pay attention to them or not.

Furthermore, the people you hang out with and peer pressure can also affect your body image and self-esteem. Understanding how to deal with peer pressure and the influences of social media — and not allowing them to affect you — is important. But how can you effectively deal with these pressures?

Dealing with Peer Pressure and Social Media Influences

People often like to voice their opinions, even when they're not asked for. When the people around you feel like they have a say in how your body should look, it can make you feel pressured to feel or look a certain way.

Social media often showcases and celebrates what they deem to be the "perfect body." This can lead to a negative body image if your body doesn't match these unrealistic standards.

Society's Ideas of the Female Body

Society's ideas of the ideal female body are ever-changing. For instance, in the early 1900s, the "perfect female body" was considered to have an hourglass figure and a tiny waist. In the 1960s, a thick body with no curves was considered the "ideal female body." And in the 1980s, having a more athletic body was more fashionable.

As you can see, society's idea of the perfect female body is constantly changing. So, what does that mean for your body? It means that your body is perfect just the way it is. Regardless of whether you feel your body is "ideal" according to today's standards or not, it is beautiful in its own right.

Beauty comes in many forms, including different body shapes, and each form deserves to be celebrated. The beauty of your body is its uniqueness, and that is something that deserves to be celebrated.

The problem arises when people believe everything they see on social media. If you constantly see photos and videos of strong, muscular women, you may think something is wrong with your body if it doesn't look that way. But nothing could be further from the truth. You are unique and wonderful, and what you see on social media often isn't reality.

Social Media and Peer Pressure

This problem often becomes more significant when you feel pressured by your friends and peers. For example, if everyone dresses a certain way, you may feel pressured to dress that way. And if you don't look the same as your friends in similar clothes, you might start to believe that there is something wrong with your body.

However, that couldn't be further from the truth. Every body shape is beautiful and deserves to be celebrated just as it is. During puberty, your growth spurts may occur at different times from your peers. Certain parts of your body may grow before others. Your hips may become curvier before your breasts start developing, or you may have a sudden growth spurt without developing curves for a while.

None of that matters. What matters is how you feel about your changing body. Remember that your body experiences numerous changes during puberty, and what you see on the outside reflects what's happening inside. Some people may go through "awkward" body changes during puberty, where they feel unbalanced. That is entirely normal and all part of growing up.

Things About the Female Body Social Media Doesn't Show You

Instead of convincing yourself that you should look and dress a certain way, it's important to focus on all the beautiful things about your body. The images you see on social media are often edited and airbrushed to make models appear flawless. Here are some things you don't see in those edited pictures.

Stretch Marks

Stretch marks are tiny lines that appear on the skin when it stretches rapidly. They often occur during growth spurts, when you grow so fast that your skin struggles to keep up. Initially, stretch marks may be red. They may also be itchy or sore. Over time, they fade to white or silver and become less noticeable.

Some women use skin oils and lotions to reduce the visibility of stretch marks. However, they are a completely normal part of being human. Most people have them, and they can appear on any part of your body, such as your legs, stomach, breasts, and arms.

Cellulite

Like stretch marks, cellulite is another normal part of the human body. Cellulite occurs when fat pockets gather beneath the skin, resulting in a dimpled or lumpy appearance. Cellulite is extremely common, with 80–90 percent of women having cellulite on some part of their bodies ("Cellulite," 2021).

Although there are some methods to help prevent or reduce the appearance of cellulite, it can be difficult to remove once it occurs. However, there is no need to remove cellulite or feel ashamed of it, as it is an entirely normal occurrence, and most, if not all, of your friends will also have cellulite.

Acne

Many social media influencers use filters to edit out skin imperfections and wear makeup to make it look like they have perfect skin. In reality, though, acne, dark undereye circles, pigmentation (dark spots on your skin), and freckles are normal.

Every influencer you see on social media has some skin imperfections, even though they may try to hide them. However, there is no need to hide them. It's normal to have skin blemishes, acne, or other skin concerns. That's real life, but what you see on social media is often not reality. Instead of hiding these imperfections, celebrate them as a sign that your body is maturing.

Body Fat

Body fat is entirely normal, despite what social media may have you believe. Hip dips, a lower belly pouch, thicker thighs, and back fat are entirely normal. Each person's body stores fat in different places.

Your body needs some fat to protect your organs, give you energy, and regulate your body temperature. Therefore, your body will naturally hold on to some fat. Body fat is nothing to be ashamed of. Even though many influencers may pose and edit their photos to make it look like they have "perfect" bodies, they also have body fat stored somewhere — everyone does!

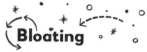

Bloating

Bloating occurs when your stomach feels swollen and inflated, and is usually due to factors like diet, hormonal changes, or stress. Many women experience bloating throughout their menstrual cycles. Although few people talk about it openly on social media, bloating is a normal part of being human. It can happen to anyone, regardless of their body shape or size.

Instead of believing everything you see on social media and idolizing models and influencers as having "the perfect body," consider all the amazing things your body is capable of and love yourself just the way you are.

Building Confidence: Tips for Boosting Your Self-Esteem

Since self-esteem and body image affect your confidence, mental health, and physical health, learning some techniques for building your self-esteem is important. By doing so, you can embrace your changing body and develop a positive body image. Here are 11 tips for boosting your self-esteem and cultivating a positive body image:

1. Surround Yourself with Positive Friends

One of the best ways to improve your self-esteem and body image is to surround yourself with positive and encouraging friends. Supportive friends can share similar struggles and help you feel better when you feel down about your body, providing support and encouragement. During challenging times, having a positive support system is crucial. Friends who love and care for you can help you overcome any challenge, reminding you that you are beautiful, powerful, and perfect just the way you are.

2. Don't Compare Yourself to Others

While it can be difficult to do so, it's important to focus on yourself and avoid comparing yourself to others. Your body is as unique as your personality and will change at its own pace. If you enter puberty earlier or later than your friends, it doesn't mean anything is wrong with you. Instead, it is simply your body going through things at its own pace.

Instead of comparing yourself to others, focus on appreciating the amazing aspects of your body. Doing so will help you embrace and enjoy your body's changes.

3. Focus on Improving Yourself

Rather than comparing yourself to others, focus on improving yourself. If you recognize areas where you want to improve, such as your fitness, concentrate on your own abilities and progress. Instead of wishing that you were as fit as your friends, think about how much fitter you are now than you were when you started training.

4. Prioritize Your Health

Taking good care of your body is essential for improving self-esteem and body image. Prioritize your healthy by getting enough sleep, eating healthily, drinking plenty of water, and exercising regularly. You will appreciate it more when you take good care of your body. You will also feel more confident that you are doing everything possible to ensure your body is healthy and well cared for.

5. Celebrate Your Accomplishments

Celebrate your accomplishments, no matter how small they may seem. Whether it's reaching a fitness goal, achieving a good grade at school, or having your first period, celebrate it. Celebrating your accomplishments releases serotonin, which improves your mood, body image, and self-esteem.

6. Be Kind to Yourself

It's easy to be hard on yourself. People often do it. They criticize themselves for every failure and flaw. But doing so only decreases their self-esteem. Instead of focusing on your shortcomings, focus on your strengths.

Of course, you should also work on improving areas that need attention, but you shouldn't focus only on them. Instead of looking at your shortcomings as failures, think of them as progress, and remember that nobody is perfect.

As Oprah Winfrey wisely said, "Think about yourself as a queen. A queen is not afraid to fail. Failure is another stepping stone to greatness." View your shortcomings as stepping stones to greatness and use them to empower you to reach new heights.

7. Do What Makes You Happy

Doing activities that make you happy is a great way to boost your self-esteem and confidence. Doing something you enjoy — even if you aren't good at it — can give you a sense of achievement and satisfaction. It also helps to reduce stress, anxiety, and depression. Additionally, it releases serotonin, which helps to improve your mood and overall well-being.

8. Be a Good Friend

Being a supportive and caring friend also enhances your self-esteem. By helping your peers when they need you and offering advice and support, you'll feel more self-confident.

Knowing you are a good friend who supports others and helps them will improve your self-esteem by making you feel more worthy. Showing appreciation for your friends, even if you have only one or two, is essential in fostering positive relationships.

9. Tell Yourself That You Are Beautiful

Start your day by reminding yourself of all the fantastic things you can do. Repeat positive affirmations to yourself, like "I am beautiful just as I am." These affirmations gradually build a positive self-image and improve self-esteem. The more you tell yourself these positive messages, the more you will believe in your own beauty. Eventually, these positive messages will help you disregard any criticism.

10. Avoid Negative Self-Talk

No matter how demotivated you feel, never speak negatively about yourself. Negative self-talk can affect your self-esteem and body image even when meant as a joke. Focus on building yourself up rather than tearing yourself down.

11. Remind Yourself of Things You Are Grateful For

It's natural to for people to get stuck on their shortcomings or the things they don't like about themselves. However, adopting a more positive outlook, such as focusing on what you are grateful for, can greatly improve your confidence.

Be thankful for your strong and healthy body and remind yourself of this fact whenever you feel negative, and you will begin to feel more positive. Remember, you have many reasons to be grateful. Focusing on them can help boost your confidence.

By implementing these tips, you can shift your focus toward self-acceptance, self-appreciation, and self-love. Embrace your unique body and recognize the incredible capabilities it possesses. Building a positive body image and self-esteem will contribute to your overall confidence, well-being, and happiness.

 **Key Takeaways**

- Your body image is how you think about, feel about, and see your body. It is often influenced by your peers, social media, and society. Developing a positive body image is crucial for improving your self-esteem and self-worth.

- Your self-esteem is how you feel about yourself and your abilities. Having a positive body image helps improve your self-esteem.

- Social media often paints an unrealistic picture of beauty. The images and videos are often edited to remove imperfections. It's important to celebrate and embrace natural parts of your body, including cellulite, stretch marks, and acne.

- To improve your body image and self-esteem, avoid comparing yourself to others. Instead, focus on your own journey.

- Remember that you are worthy, powerful, and beautiful. By following the tips and strategies in this chapter, you can cultivate a positive body image and self-esteem.

In the next chapter, we will explore how to build positive relationships and manage the romantic feelings you may develop toward others as you get older.

PREPARING FOR THE FUTURE — HEALTHY RELATIONSHIPS AND ROMANTIC FEELINGS

As you grow up, you may begin to develop romantic feelings for others. These feelings can make you happy and excited but may be a little confusing at first. Understanding the difference between romantic and platonic feelings, how to set boundaries in a relationship, and the importance of communication are all crucial for a safe and positive experience when you enter the world of romantic relationships.

In this chapter, we will provide guidance on starting a safe and happy relationship when you feel ready. But first, let's explore romantic feelings and how they differ from other emotions.

Understanding Romantic Feelings: Navigating Crushes and First Loves

During puberty, your emotional state matures along with your body. One of the new feelings you may experience is that you may find yourself romantically interested in someone. Initially, you might not fully understand why you feel the way you do around them. Later, you will realize that your feelings for them differ from how you feel about your other friends.

You may notice different sensations, like butterflies in your stomach, a reddening of your face, or blushing when they are nearby. You might think about them often, wondering how they are and how they feel about you. These feelings are all completely normal. They are a sign that you have a crush on that person.

Having a crush is a natural experience, but it's important to treat the person respectfully and consider their feelings, as well. For example, they may not share your romantic interest. If they communicate that to you, you should respect their decision.

There's a difference between liking someone as a friend and having romantic feelings for them, and it's important to understand these differences. When you like someone as a friend, it's called a platonic relationship. In this case, you enjoy spending time with them, talking to them, and seeing them, but you don't have any romantic feelings towards them or see yourself being in a romantic relationship with them.

Regardless of your feelings for someone, you should respect their feelings and wishes. If someone has stated that they're not interested in you romantically, it's crucial not to pursue them further. Remember that you are a wonderful, beautiful, and strong individual deserving of a healthy relationship with someone who shares your feelings.

Finding someone who feels the same way about you may take time, but it will be worth the wait. When you find someone who likes you as much as you like them, you will have an entirely new challenge — navigating your first relationship.

Having your first relationship is an exciting but sometimes daunting experience. Your first relationship is something you will remember for a long time. However, there's no rush. In fact, you may not develop romantic feelings for someone until you are older.

When you enter a relationship, there are important factors to consider to ensure it is a safe and healthy relationship. Here are some of the most important ones.

Boundaries, Respect, and Consent

Being in a relationship comes with important points to consider, which determine whether it is a healthy relationship or not. When you start dating someone, it can be challenging to understand what is acceptable in the relationship. Above all, it is crucial that you feel safe and respected.

A healthy relationship is one in which both people respect boundaries and treat one another with respect. But what exactly are boundaries?

Boundaries are like lines that define what is okay and not okay in a relationship. Just as countries have borders, you also have personal boundaries. These are imaginary lines that you and your partner should not cross without proper permission. For example, when you begin dating, you might only feel comfortable holding hands and not ready to kiss. This is a boundary you have set.

Your partner will also have some boundaries, and it's essential to respect each other's boundaries and never pressure one another to do something you aren't comfortable with. It's always better to ask for consent before trying something new, especially if you're unsure about their comfort level.

Consent is the same as asking for permission. For example, before holding your partner's hand, ask, "Is it okay if I hold your hand?" If they say yes, that's great. But if they say no, respect their boundary, just as you would want them to respect yours. Remember, no means no, and you must never try to pressure your partner into anything they aren't comfortable with. Both of you should feel safe enough in the relationship to say no.

Saying no to someone doesn't mean you like them any less. It simply means that you aren't ready to do something. Building trust and taking things at your own pace is essential in any relationship, regardless of age. If your partner truly cares about you, they will respect your boundaries.

Healthy vs. Unhealthy Relationships

When you first start dating someone, it can be hard to tell if you are in a healthy or unhealthy relationship. Healthy relationships are great! They can improve your self-esteem, make you feel more confident, and make you happy. Signs of a healthy relationship include:

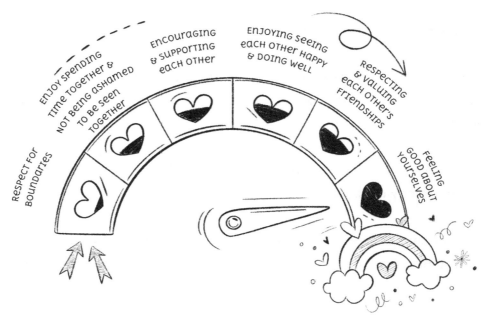

- Respect for each other's boundaries

- Enjoying spending time together and not being ashamed to be seen together

- Encouraging and supporting each other

- Enjoying seeing each other happy and doing well

- Respecting and valuing each other's friendships

- Feeling good about yourselves

In a healthy relationship, you have space to grow and mature at your own pace. This is especially important when you're still young and discovering who you are meant to be. If your partner doesn't give you room to grow and develop, it may indicate an unhealthy relationship. Signs of an unhealthy relationship include:

- Being mean to you in front of others or when you are alone

- Ignoring your boundaries or pressuring you into doing things you are uncomfortable with

- Putting you down, discouraging you, and pointing out your flaws and insecurities

- Lying to you

- Acting strangely or differently toward you in front of your friends

- Stopping you from spending time with your friends, isolating you, and talking negatively about your friends

- Not treating you with kindness and respect

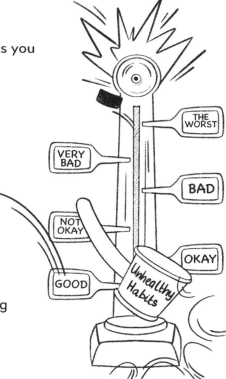

If you notice any of these signs, you are likely not in a healthy relationship. In that case, the best thing to do is to end the relationship before someone gets hurt. Remember, you deserve to be with someone who loves and supports you. Don't settle for an unhealthy relationship, no matter how much you like the person.

Red Flags in a Relationship

You might have heard people talk about "red flags" in relationships. Red flags usually signify danger in the real world, and it's very much the same in relationships. Red flags indicate that something isn't quite right or may be unhealthy. Red flags include not respecting your partner's boundaries, treating them unkindly, and not giving them space to grow and spend time with their friends and family.

Seeing red flags doesn't always mean the person is bad; it might just mean they're not the right person for you.

In general, any relationship or person who does not respect your boundaries or makes you feel like anything less than the beautiful and unique person you are is a sign of an unhealthy relationship. Consider these red flags and end the relationship as soon as possible.

Staying in a relationship with someone despite your friends and family raising red flags, or noticing red flags yourself, is dangerous and will only lead to more heartbreak. Therefore, it's best to end the relationship gently before anyone gets hurt.

When you decide to end a relationship, it's important to respect your partner. Don't blame them for the relationship ending. Instead, treat them kindly and explain why you don't think it is the right time for the relationship, then give them the privacy and time they need to process the end of the relationship.

It is never easy to end a relationship. Still, it is best to do so when you realize the relationship isn't healthy or brings you more sadness than joy.

The Importance of Communication in Relationships

Communication is crucial in any relationship. Discussing your feelings with your partner and allowing them to share theirs can help build respect and trust, and foster a healthy relationship.

It isn't always easy to talk about the more serious aspects of a relationship, such as your expectations, boundaries, and things that upset you. Still, if you don't focus on clear communication, you or your partner might not even realize when you've hurt or upset each other.

In many cases, you can keep your relationship healthy just by communicating with each other. Check in with your partner to see how they are doing. Support them if they are stressed and remind them of what a wonderful person they are. Listen when they tell you about the things they don't like about the relationship. Just doing these simple things can help you maintain a healthy relationship.

During conversations about your relationship, remember the following:

- Stay calm and listen to your partner.

- Treat them with kindness and respect, even if you disagree.

- Avoid interrupting them when they are speaking.

- Explain your feelings without blame.

- Don't leave important things unsaid.

- Don't get angry or defensive when you disagree.

- Don't pressure your partner into doing something they aren't comfortable with.

- Never disregard your partner's feelings; they are important.

By maintaining open communication in a relationship, you can deal with problems as soon as they arise and ensure you and your partner are happy. Communicating and listening to each other will make you feel loved and appreciated, helping foster a healthy relationship.

 **Key Takeaways**

- It's normal to develop romantic feelings for someone as you enter puberty. These feelings are different than platonic relationships.

- Respect, boundaries, and asking for consent (permission) are crucial in any relationship. Remember, no means no.

- Recognizing red flags is essential to identify an unhealthy relationship.

- Communication is vital in relationships in order to maintain respect, trust, and a healthy dynamic.

It's important to remember that not everyone feels ready for a romantic relationship at the same time, and that's perfectly normal. You should never feel pressured to be in a relationship if you don't want one or haven't found someone you're interested in romantically.

You are unique and beautiful just as you are, and the right person will come into your life when the time is right. Embrace your individuality and continue to grow and explore the world around you. Trust that love will find its way to you when the time is right.

CONCLUSION

Congratulations on completing this book!

You've learned a lot about puberty and navigating the changes in your body. Puberty is an exciting and unique journey that signifies your transition from a child to an adult. Remember, everyone goes through puberty at their own pace, so don't worry if you start earlier or later than others.

During puberty, hormones play a significant role in causing the physical and emotional changes you experience. Your body will go through growth spurts, your shape will change, and you'll notice hair growth in new places. You'll also start having your period, which is a normal part of becoming a woman.

Breast development is another change that occurs during puberty. If you feel the need, you might consider buying your first bra. There are different types of bras available, so finding the right size and style is essential for comfort and support.

Taking care of your body becomes more important during puberty. Establishing a personal care routine, including regular showers, using deodorant, and practicing good oral hygiene, will keep you clean and healthy. Remember the importance of exercise, staying hydrated, getting enough sleep, and maintaining a healthy diet.

Friendships may change as you grow older, and that's normal. Focus on being a good friend and surrounding yourself with friends who support and encourage you. It's better to have a few close friends than lots of acquaintances.

Mood swings are common due to hormonal changes, especially before and during your period. Understanding the causes of your emotions can help you manage them. Taking care of yourself by getting enough sleep, spending time in the sun, and managing stress can help stabilize your mood.

Body image and self-esteem can also be affected during puberty. Remember that your body is unique and beautiful, just the way it is. Avoid comparing yourself to others and focus on embracing your individuality.

Finally, as you enter puberty, you may develop romantic feelings for others. It's important to enjoy yourself, respect boundaries, ask for consent, and communicate openly in any relationship. Remember, you are in control of your own body and choices.

Embrace your journey, celebrate yourself, and use the knowledge you've gained to guide you. Remember, you are a beautiful girl, and you are growing into a strong and amazing woman.

As you continue your path through puberty, support and encourage your friends, too. Each of you is unique, and everyone's puberty journey happens at their own pace — but deep down, what's happening inside your bodies is the same. You're not alone in this journey, as billions of women have gone through what you're experiencing and stand beside you.

"Do not live someone else's life and someone else's idea of womanhood. Womanhood is you. Womanhood is everything that is inside of you."
— Viola Davis

You are unique, you are beautiful, and you are ready to conquer the world.

A TWEEN GIRL'S GUIDE TO FRIENDSHIPS

How to Make Friends
and Build Healthy Relationships

The Complete Friendship Handbook for Young Girls

Abby Swift

INTRODUCTION

Have you ever had a friend who just gets you and makes you feel amazing? Imagine if you could have more of those amazing friendships!

Being a tween and teenager can be full of challenges. During this time, you're dealing with a lot: puberty, physical changes, new emotions, and so much more. It's an exciting time, but it can be confusing and uncertain. You might find yourself questioning your friendships or wondering how to build the kind of friendships that support you through these transformative years. You're not alone in facing these challenges.

The truth is that navigating friendships during this stage of your life can be tricky. It's normal to feel a little overwhelmed by the changes in your relationships, the ups and downs in friendships, or the pressure to fit in with certain groups. You might have times when you feel alone or misunderstood, when you're not sure who your real friends are, or when you're dealing with conflicts, jealousy, and other friendship hurdles. Without the right tools, these challenges can affect how you feel about yourself, your happiness, and your well-being.

That's where this book comes in! It's your guide to help you understand and enjoy friendships during the tween and teen years.

In this book, you'll learn about:

· What real friendship looks like

· The different kinds of friends you can have

· How to make new friends and keep your old ones close

· How to spot the difference between healthy and unhealthy friendships

· Tips for managing conflicts and jealousy

· Strategies for dealing with friends growing apart, bullying, and peer pressure

· How to manage digital interactions with friends while staying safe

· Understanding how puberty can impact your friendships

By the end of this book, you'll have the tools and knowledge you need to be a fantastic friend and create strong, supportive friendships that make the ups and downs of growing up a little smoother and a lot more fun.

How to Use This Book

Each chapter covers a different topic. While the book is designed to be read from start to finish, you're welcome to jump around to the sections that interest you the most.

Every chapter includes a case study and an activity to help you put what you've learned into practice. By doing these activities and actively engaging with the content, you can gain hands-on experience and reinforce your understanding, ensuring you get the most out of this book.

Ready to begin this journey towards becoming a great friend and building strong, lasting friendships? Let's get started with the first chapter. Best of luck!

1

THE VALUE OF FRIENDSHIP

As you grow older, your friendships will change — and that's perfectly normal. You might find that your group of friends gets smaller, or your interests might change, and you'll make new friends. Having friends is special at any age, but it becomes even more important as you enter your teenage years. Friends can support you, make you feel like you belong, and help you through tough times.

Friendships are precious, and it's easy to take them for granted. But they're one of the best parts of life. In this chapter, we'll dive into what friendship means and look at the different kinds of friends you might have in your life. Let's start by answering a big question: What does it mean to have a friend, and why is it so important?

What Is Friendship?

A friend is someone you feel close to — someone who's there for you, no matter what. You share a special connection with your friends and can count on them when things get tough. You probably have things in common with your friends, like the same beliefs or values, which strengthen your friendships. We'll talk more about the different kinds of friendships in the next section. But at its core, friendship is about feeling connected to someone and really enjoying the time you spend together.

THE BUILDING BLOCKS OF A FRIENDSHIP

Most friendships are built on four key components. A good friendship will have most of these qualities, even though not every one may have them all. To truly understand friendship, it helps to consider how these four aspects play a role in your connection with people.

1. Shared Interests

Most friendships start through shared interests. Joining a new art class, school, sport, or hobby introduces you to new people interested in the same things you are. This common interest can be a starting point for making connections. Over time, as you discover more shared interests, these acquaintances may bloom into friendships.

Remember that shared interests aren't always what keep a friendship strong. You might discover new interests or outgrow the initial ones that brought you together. But once a strong bond is established, your friendship can flourish even when your shared interests change.

For example, imagine you became friends with someone because you both loved playing soccer. As time passes, you might become interested in different sports or hobbies. That doesn't mean your friendship has to end. True friendships can survive and grow despite changing interests.

2. Mutual Respect

Mutual respect is a must-have in any friendship. It means showing admiration and care for one another and, sometimes, acknowledging that your friend might be better than you at something. A friendship without mutual respect is like a garden without sunlight — it simply cannot grow.

Respect in a friendship means honoring each other's space, privacy, and needs. It also means understanding that your friend has other relationships that are just as important to them.

Have you ever had a friend who was always there for you, respected your privacy, and made you feel valued? How did it make you feel?

3. Trust

Trust is the foundation of any friendship. It means that when you make a promise to your friend, you keep it. Like keeping a secret your friend shared with you, trust involves respecting and protecting each other's privacy.

If trust is broken — for example, if a friend shares your secret — it can shake the foundation of your friendship. Trust is what makes you feel safe and respected. Without trust, there's no openness, and without openness, a friendship cannot truly thrive.

Can you think of a time when someone broke your trust? How did it make you feel? How did it affect your friendship?

4. Understanding

Understanding is the final piece that makes a good friendship. It's all about really "getting" your friend — how they feel, what they're going through — even if it's different from what you're experiencing. It's like putting yourself in your friend's shoes for a while and seeing the world from their point of view. It's not about always knowing the right thing to say, but it's about listening, offering a kind word, or just being a shoulder to lean on when they need it.

Being an understanding friend means being there for your friends when they need you, even if you can't fix the problem. Sometimes, knowing someone is there to listen can make all the difference.

Think about a time when a friend was there for you when you needed it most. How did it make you feel?

Now that we know the building blocks of friendship, how can we tell the difference between a good friend and a not-so-good one? Let's find out.

Good and Bad Friends

Every friend is different, and that's what makes friendships so exciting. But not all friendships are created equal. While some friendships can make you feel on top of the world, others can make you feel down in the dumps. Let's break down what makes a good friend and identify signs that a friendship may not be the best for you.

What does a good friendship look like?

· Good friends support you. They encourage you and cheer you on.

· They make you feel good so you can be yourself.

· They really listen to you. They want to be involved in your life and take an interest in what you're up to.

They recognize when they've made mistakes. They're quick to say "sorry" and are forgiving when you make a mistake, too.

These types of friends will always make you feel loved and supported. They encourage you to be the best "you" that you can be and inspire you to be a better friend to them and others.

Unfortunately, not all friendships are like this.

Here are some signs of a bad friendship:

- Bad friends gossip about their other friends.

- They only reach out when they want or need something.

- They are pushy — they only care about their opinions and needs.

- They don't accept different opinions.

- They are unreliable. They aren't there when you need them.

Staying in a bad friendship is unpleasant and can affect your health, making you feel drained, stressed, and even anxious. Instead, you need to surround yourself with people who will support and be there for you when things get tough, and you can find these friends in many different areas of your life.

Let's look at the different types of friends you can have.

Different Types of friends

Just as there are good and not-so-good friendships, there are also different kinds of friends. Having a mix of different types of friends is good, as they bring other things into your life. But remember, you also don't have to have friends in all these categories. Any kind of good friend is an excellent addition to your life! Let's look at three types of friends you might have at different stages in your life.

Best friends

Best friends are your closest confidants. You trust them with your secrets, dreams, and fears. They support you when times are tough and are there with you to celebrate your wins.

While the strong bonds of best friends are usually built over years of shared experiences, there are times when you might meet someone and instantly feel a deep connection with them. It's almost like you've been best friends for years.

School friends

School friends are the friends you hang out with at school. Some school friends may also be your best friends, but not always. They could be classmates, teammates, or people you meet at lunchtime. You may be closer to some than others, which is perfectly normal.

As you grow up and your interests change, you may find that you drift apart from some of your school friends. That's totally normal.

Casual friends

Casual friends are those you're friendly with but not super close to, like people you meet at a summer camp or on vacation. You enjoy spending time with them when you see them, but you don't often plan to spend time with them alone.

Sometimes, a friend of a friend becomes a casual friend. You get along and enjoy their company, but you wouldn't share your deepest secrets with them. Having casual friends is excellent, as these are often friends you can have a lot of fun with and are just nice to be around.

FRIENDS VS. ACQUAINTANCES

While you may have a small or large group of friends, chances are you'll have more acquaintances. Acquaintances are people you are friendly with but don't really hang out with. They could be people in school you've known for ages but haven't really hung out with outside school hours, or friends you used to be close with but have drifted apart from. Often, friends start as acquaintances until you get to know them better.

Acquaintances may not be as close to you as friends, but they are still good to chat with when you bump into each other. As you grow up, you'll see the value of having positive relationships with your acquaintances. You never know when you might be able to help each other out.

Now that you've learned what friendship is — the good and the bad — and the different kinds of friends you can have, let's see how this knowledge applies to real life. In the next section, we'll look at a case study of two friends and some questions for you to think about. Then, we'll explore a fun activity to help you understand the different kinds of friends in your life. Let's dive in!

The lifelong Friendship of Maya and Sophie

Maya and Sophie became best friends in middle school. They both shared a love of art, and spent hours after school doodling in the art room. But when they left middle school, their interests began to change. Maya started playing soccer, while Sophie became interested in drama. Despite these differences, they still hung out regularly and tried to support each other. Sophie always made time to watch Maya's soccer games, and Maya never missed seeing Sophie in her plays.

Their friendship was tested when Sophie moved away for a year due to her parent's work. Initially, this was tricky; with timezone differences to contend with, speaking every day wasn't always possible. Instead, they organized weekly video calls to catch up and share their news. The year flew by, and by the time Sophie returned, their relationship had become even stronger.

After leaving school, their friendship continued to blossom. Despite moving to different parts of the country, they chatted almost every day and met up as often as they could. Recognizing the importance of their friendship, they continued to support each other in every aspect of their lives.

Maya and Sophie's relationship shows the importance and lasting power of best friends. Their lifelong connection is a testament to the timeless nature of true friendship.

Answer the following questions about Maya and Sophie.

1. Maya and Sophie's friendship was initially forged over a love for art. Can you remember how you met your best friend?

_____

_____

_____

2. When Sophie moved away, how did she and Maya keep up their friendship? How can you keep up a friendship with someone who is far away?

_____

_____

_____

3. Why do you think Maya and Sophie's friendship strengthened when they were apart for a year?

_____

_____

_____

4. Maya and Sophie's lifelong friendship changed their lives for the better. Can you share how your friends have changed your life?

_____

_____

_____

Activity: Friendship Tree

Now that you understand friendships well, it's time to dive into your first activity. You're going to create your very own Friendship Tree. A Friendship Tree is a great way to visualize all the fantastic social connections in your life, with each branch representing a different part of your life and the friends you've made.

Here are the steps:

1. Draw a large tree trunk in the space provided. The main tree trunk represents you, so write your name on it.

2. Next, draw some branches coming out from the main trunk. Each branch represents a different aspect of your life. For example, include a branch for school, one for your hobbies, and another for any other activities. Write the name on the branch.

3. Now, it's time to draw the leaves! Each leaf represents a friend you've made in that part of your life (write their names on the leaves). For instance, any friends you've met at school will be a leaf on your school branch.

The Friendship Tree is a great way to see all of the wonderful friendships you have in your life. Look at your branches, and take a minute to think about all the friends you have and how they add to your life. How do they make you happy? How do they support you? How do they enrich your life? As you get older and explore more hobbies and new opportunities, keep adding new branches to your tree.

 **Key Takeaways**

Friendships are crucial, particularly during your teenage years. They offer support, provide assistance, and fill your life with fun and joy. Friendships come in many forms and from different areas of your life. Remember, not every friend will be your best friend, but each one holds unique value and contributes positively to your life's journey.

MAKING FRIENDS

Making new friends can be a rewarding experience that enriches our lives with diverse perspectives and shared experiences. However, it can also be challenging, especially for those who might feel shy, anxious, or concerned about fitting in. If you want to expand your circle of friends and form stronger bonds with people, you'll need to take proactive steps to overcome these hurdles. In this chapter, we'll provide practical tips to help you approach new people, start conversations, and create meaningful connections.

Whether you already have a large group of friends or not, learning how to approach others and strike up conversations is a valuable life skill that will serve you well beyond your teenage years. But how can you meet new people, start conversations, and make a great first impression?

Approaching New People

Starting a conversation with someone you don't know can be intimidating, regardless of how brave or outgoing you may be. Worrying about saying the wrong thing or not being well-received is natural. Developing the ability to confidently approach new people is a skill you'll use throughout your life. It can help you build stronger relationships, express yourself more effectively, and connect more easily with others.

In most situations, a friendly and genuine approach will be appreciated, and the conversation will flow naturally. The key is to approach others in a way that feels comfortable for you and them. So, how can you do that?

How to Approach New People

You may have noticed that some girls have this amazing ability to make friends with everyone. They confidently walk over to a group of people, and within minutes, everyone's laughing and chatting. If you are one of those girls, that's fantastic! It means you are a people person, and that's a skill that will help you a lot in life. However, if you struggle with approaching new people or striking up conversations, don't worry! In this section, we'll share tips to help you develop your social skills, even if it initially feels challenging.

When you meet and approach new people, there are a few key things to keep in mind that will help you come across as friendly and open. By following these tips, you'll be well on your way to making new friends and forming strong connections.

HOW TO APPROACH NEW PEOPLE

1 MAKE EYE CONTACT — Show you're listening!

2 SMILE — Be a friend magnet!

3 REMEMBER THEIR NAMES — It's like saying "hi" twice!

4 ASK OPEN ENDED QUESTIONS — Get the chat going!

5 FIND COMMON GROUND — What do you both 🖤?

6 SHOW REAL INTEREST — Listen and Laugh!

Make Eye Contact

Making eye contact is a powerful nonverbal cue that signals your interest in someone. It shows that you are engaged, attentive, and confident. In many cultures, eye contact is also seen as a sign of respect, as it demonstrates that you value and respect the other person.

Remember that you don't have to maintain constant eye contact throughout the conversation. It's okay to look away occasionally, as staring can make the other person feel uncomfortable. Aim for a balance that feels natural and comfortable for both of you.

Smile

A smile goes a long way. If making eye contact makes you uncomfortable, a simple smile is a great way to break the ice. Smiling at someone instantly puts them at ease and makes them more open to conversation. It also makes you seem welcoming and approachable, which can be helpful when you're trying to make new friends.

Remember Their Name

One common mistake when meeting new people is to forget the other person's name. You introduce yourself, they tell you their name, but it doesn't stick, and ten seconds later, you've forgotten it. Everyone does it. But learning people's names when you first meet them is an important skill to develop. When you're able to remember someone's name, it shows them you value them. It's a simple gesture, but it makes a lasting impression.

A simple way to remember a name is to repeat it in your head and use it in your first conversation. For example, if you meet someone called Clare, you might say: "Nice to meet you, Clare!" Then: "What hobbies are you interested in, Clare?" Using the name in the conversation a few times helps reinforce it in your memory.

Another tip is to associate their name with something memorable about them. For example, if you meet someone named Elen who's into soccer, you might mentally associate "Elen" with "soccer." You could even create a nickname like "Soccer-Elen" in your head. This association will help you remember their name the next time you see them.

Ask Open-Ended Questions

Open-ended questions encourage people to share more about themselves and their thoughts. They also show that you're genuinely interested in getting to know them. Unlike simple yes-or-no questions, these questions encourage the person to share more, helping you to get to know them better. Instead of asking someone if they like music, ask them what type of music they enjoy or what they like doing after school.

Here are some more examples of open-ended questions:

· "What do you usually do during summer break?"

· "I noticed you have a Thor badge on your backpack. Have you seen the latest *Avengers* movie? What do you think about it?"

· "What did you think about this morning's history lesson?"

Find Common Ground

Finding common ground with someone is an excellent way to establish a connection. When you share interests or experiences, it gives you something to bond over and talk about.

When you approach a new person, try to look for visual clues. Are they wearing a particular brand of clothes? Do they have unique badges on their backpacks? Do they carry a sports bag? These clues can tell you a lot about a person, making it easier to strike up a conversation and connect over shared interests.

For example, if you notice someone wearing a band t-shirt, you could ask about their favorite songs or concerts by that band.

Remember, the goal is to find topics that both of you enjoy discussing, so be open to exploring various subjects and interests.

Show Real Interest in Them

One of the most important things you can do when talking to someone is show genuine interest in what they say. It's easy to get excited and start talking about yourself, but listening and asking questions about their experiences can make a big difference.

How can you show real interest? It's simple! Listen when they speak, and try not to interrupt. Respond to their words with gestures like nodding, smiling, or showing other emotions. And ask questions to keep the conversation flowing.

Think about a time someone really listened to you. They probably nodded, seemed engaged, and asked you questions, right?

Imagine if that same person had cut you off, only talked about themselves, or seemed distracted.

Remember, making friends is not just about sharing your stories and interests. It's also about getting to know others and showing interest in their lives.

THE IMPORTANCE OF BODY LANGUAGE WHEN MEETING NEW PEOPLE

Meeting someone new is more than just saying the right things and listening to them talk. Your body language plays a big part, too. Body language is how you use your body to express your feelings and thoughts without words. It includes how you hold yourself, your facial expressions, how you move your hands, and how you sit or stand.

If you slouch, sigh, roll your eyes, or generally appear disinterested when someone is talking, they will pick up on those signals. This might make them uncomfortable and question if you're genuinely interested in getting to know them.

So, how can you make your body language more inviting? Try keeping your arms at your sides instead of crossing them, standing or sitting with a straight back, and looking up at the person. These gestures convey confidence. When you add a warm smile, make eye contact, and nod in agreement, you signal that you are genuinely interested in what they're saying.

Managing Shyness and Fear of Rejection

Even with all the tips you've learned about approaching new people, it's natural to still feel shy. Being shy isn't a bad thing. Some people, called extroverts, love being around others. They enjoy being the center of attention and feel energized in social situations. Introverts, on the other hand, often prefer quieter environments with fewer people. They might find big crowds a bit much and sometimes feel unsure in new environments.

Whether you're an extrovert or an introvert, both are totally normal. And everyone feels shy sometimes in certain situations.

MANAGING SHYNESS

Shyness might simply mean feeling uneasy in new situations or around people you don't know. You might feel nervous or anxious around others, particularly when you're the center of attention or being asked questions. While it's normal to feel shy sometimes, it's important to learn how to handle this feeling so you can make new friends and feel more at ease around others.

Remember, it's totally okay to be shy, and you're definitely not the only one who feels this way. However, learning how to manage your shyness is a valuable skill, as you'll often encounter new and unfamiliar situations in life.

Here are a few tips to help manage shyness when meeting new people:

- **Prepare in advance**: If you know you'll be in a situation where you'll meet new people, like joining a club or a new sports team, you could prepare a few questions and answers beforehand. For example, to start a conversation and break the ice, you might say, "Hi, I'm [Your Name], what's yours?" or "I noticed your [book, shirt, etc.], I'm a big fan of that, too!"

- **Practice in the mirror**: Now that you have some questions and answers lined up, instead of imagining how you'll respond, practice in the mirror. Talking to yourself might initially seem strange, but it can help you feel more confident and ready.

- **Find common interests**: It's easier to connect with someone when you have something in common, so try to find those shared interests. Visual cues like the clothes they wear or the bags they carry might give you hints about what they like.

- **It's okay to be shy**: Even the most confident people are shy in certain situations, so feeling shy is perfectly normal. Just try not to let it hold you back from doing what you want.

MANAGING FEAR OF REJECTION

Sometimes, the thought of talking to new people can be scary because we worry they might not want to be our friends. It's okay to feel this way; most of us do! But remember, just because someone doesn't click with you doesn't mean there's something wrong with you. In fact, they're missing out on getting to know a fantastic person: you!

Life is full of ups and downs, and everyone faces rejection now and then. But guess what? Rejection doesn't define your worth. Think about it: maybe you tried out for the school's hockey team and didn't get in this time. Instead of letting it get you down, use it as fuel to practice harder! When you achieve your goal later on, whether rocking the hockey field or finding a best friend, the joy will be even sweeter.

Keep putting yourself out there, and you'll find the friends and opportunities that are right for you.

The Story of Lucy and Liam

Lucy was a quieter girl at school, who found it tough to meet new people and make friends. Instead of playing outside at break, she preferred to read comics in the classroom. Then, one summer, Liam, a new student, joined the school. Much like Lucy, Liam was shy and enjoyed spending his breaks reading comic books.

When their teacher assigned them a project to create a comic book, Lucy saw this as the perfect opportunity to get to know Liam. Even though Lucy felt nervous about approaching Liam, she knew they shared an interest in comic books already, so that was a fantastic starting point.

After a few weeks of working together on the project, Liam opened up and came out of his shell. Lucy seemed to forget her initial anxiety. The project was a huge success, and fast forward to the end of the school year, and Lucy and Liam had become the best of friends.

The experience had taught Lucy that overcoming her shyness and putting herself out there to make new friends was worth it. It just took a bit of courage and, of course, a lot of comic books!

Answer the following questions about Lucy and Liam.

1. Can you think of a time when you started a conversation with someone new. What did you talk about? How did you feel?

   _____

   _____

   _____

2. What did Lucy and Liam have in common that made it easier to initiate a conversation?

   _____

   _____

   _____

3. How did Lucy overcome her shyness when she decided to speak with Liam? Can you think of a time when you overcame similar feelings?

   _____

   _____

   _____

4. How do you think Lucy's experience changed her confidence? How have your experiences with making friends boosted your confidence?

   _____

   _____

   _____

Activity: Role-Play Scenarios

In this role-play activity, you will imagine meeting three new friends at school. Each person has unique hobbies and interests. Your job is to engage with these people by asking about their hobbies and seeing if you can find a shared interest. Use the strategies you have learned in this chapter and consider how you will approach these people to make new friends.

You can also involve your family by asking one of them to role-play as the new friend while you practice what you have learned to communicate with them. Ready? Good luck!

Role-play 1: Gemma

Gemma's a new student at your school from Germany. She seems friendly, and you've noticed that she has a patch of Olaf from Frozen on her bag, so you guess she likes Disney. She's also in your art class, so she might like painting.

How could you start a conversation with Gemma?

_____

_____

_____

Role-play 2: Miguel

Miguel is another new student in your class, and he's just moved here from New Mexico. He's struggled to get to know the other kids since joining partway through the year. He's a bit shy, but you've noticed he brings a soccer ball to school and rides a skateboard, so those might be some of his hobbies.

What could you say to Miguel to start a conversation and make him feel more at home?

_____

_____

_____

Role-play 3: Abi

Abi was in your primary school class and just transferred to your school
this year. You never really talked before and aren't sure if she remembers
you. You know she likes swimming and the outdoors, since she talked about
it back in primary school. Talking to Abi might be awkward since you don't
know if she remembers you.

What could you say to Abi to break the ice and make her feel welcome?

_____

_____

🔑 Key Takeaways

Making new friends can be daunting. Being shy and worrying about what other people think can
make it tough to approach new people and make friends. But remember the tips we've shared: Look
people in the eye, ask questions that keep the conversation going, listen when someone's talking, and
use friendly body language. Doing these things can help you seem confident, open, and interested
in the other person. It will also make it much easier for you to make new friends.

NAVIGATING DIFFERENT PERSONALITIES

Today you are you. That's truer than true.
There's no one alive who is youer than you!
— Dr. Seuss

Just imagine how boring life would be if we were all the same. If we all thought the same, talked the same, walked the same, and did everything in the same way, the world would lack color, diversity, and fun. Lucky for us, we're all unique, each with our own special personalities — a mix of characteristics and traits that shape how we think, feel, and behave.

Think about your circle of friends. Some might be bubbly, confident, and always up for an adventure, while others might be more reserved and shy. The key is that there's no "right" or "better" personality type. Everyone is different, and embracing this uniqueness and individuality makes life more exciting and fun.

Why Personalities Matter

Understanding and navigating different personalities is a vital part of growing up. Wherever you go, you'll meet people who are different from you. They might look, talk, think, and react differently in certain situations. Even though differences can sometimes cause tension, it's crucial to cooperate with people and even be friends with those different from you.

This chapter will discuss how to understand and navigate different personalities. Before diving into the benefits and challenges of different personalities and viewing a case study, let's first look at the different personality types.

Understanding Personality Types

Your personality is like a puzzle, and each trait is a unique piece that fits together to form the complete picture of who you are. Each part of your personality contributes to making you special.

While it's true that some people are really similar, like siblings, parents, and even friends, no two people are exactly alike — not even twins. Many factors set two people apart from each other, and our personalities are just one of those factors.

As you get older, you'll notice that your friends have different personalities, too. Even though everyone is unique, most people share certain personality traits. Recognizing these personality traits (in others and yourself) is an important part of learning to interact with different personalities.

Researchers and scientists have spent much time figuring out exactly how many personality traits there are. There are many personality theories, and one well-known theory is The Big 5 model, presented by Kendra Cherry in Very Well Mind (2023). According to this model, there are five primary personality traits: agreeableness, openness, extroversion, neuroticism, and conscientiousness.

Let's look at these traits to help you understand yourself and your friends better.

- **Agreeableness**: Agreeable people are friendly, value teamwork, and enjoy helping others. They're great at making friends, but may struggle with low self-esteem and avoid conflict. Have you ever found it hard to say "no?"

- **Openness**: Open people are creative and like trying new things. They adapt well to change and see life as an adventure. But they can sometimes be seen as self-centered or unreliable. Do you like to explore new things?

- **Extroversion**: Extroverted people enjoy being around others and feel energized in social settings. They're often charismatic, but may come across as self-centered. Do you love chatting and sharing stories?

- **Neuroticism**: Neuroticism means being emotional — feeling both joy and sadness intensely. It's not necessarily negative, but these people may overthink and worry a lot. Do you often find yourself worrying about things?

- **Conscientiousness**: Conscientious individuals are responsible and considerate. They're great at planning, but may struggle to relax and let go of control. Are you the one in your group who always remembers everything?

Remember that no one fits perfectly into just one of these categories. Most of us exhibit all of these personality types to varying degrees. At the end of this chapter, you'll take the Big 5 Personality Test to see how you score for each trait.

So, what are the benefits and challenges of different personalities? Let's find out in the next section.

Benefits and Challenges of Different Personalities

No one is perfect, and neither are personality types. But by understanding the benefits and challenges of each personality type, you'll gain valuable insight into your friends. You'll find it easier to navigate the ups and downs of different personalities and build stronger, more meaningful relationships.

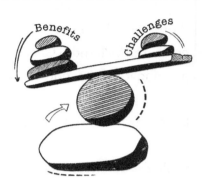

COMPLEMENTARY PERSONALITIES

Every personality type has its unique strengths that can complement others. Imagine your friend group as a team, where each member brings something special. An extroverted friend might help an introverted friend come out of their shell. A conscientious friend could ensure everyone stays on track and is never late. An open friend might have fascinating stories to share, while an agreeable friend can help the group make new friends. A friend with high neuroticism will always be open about their feelings, offering a sense of emotional honesty.

CHALLENGES AND CONFLICTS

Of course, blending different personalities can sometimes lead to disagreements. A conscientious person might get frustrated with the carefree attitude of an open friend, and an agreeable friend may find a neurotic friend overwhelming. When conflicts arise, it's crucial to respect each other's differences and work together to find a solution.

ACCEPTANCE AND CHANGE

Sometimes, you might not agree with your friends, and that's okay. Accept your friends for who they are, even if their personality traits can be challenging. Remember that people's personalities can change over time, and it's important to support and embrace those changes within your friend group.

Now that you understand the different personality types, their benefits and challenges, and their value in a group of friends, it's time to put your knowledge to the test. Complete the case study of Alex, Sandy, and Anika, and take a simplified version of the Big 5 Personality Test to see which personality traits you score high or low in. Good luck!

Case Study : Alex, Sandy, and Anika

Alex, Sandy, and Anika have been friends since kindergarten. Alex is a thoughtful introvert. She likes reading, being in nature, and spending time with her best friends, Sandy and Anika. Sandy is the complete opposite of Alex. She is loud and outgoing. She loves being around people, going to the shopping mall, and talking to strangers to pet their dogs at the park. Anika is an adventurer at heart. She loves trying new things, often meeting new people along the way.

Despite their differences, the girls have kept their friendship strong and complemented each other well. Alex always thinks of everything—what to bring, when to leave to be on time for the movies, and what potential problems they might encounter. Sandy, on the other hand, is impulsive and often persuades Alex to accompany her to parties. This helps Alex make more friends and come out of her shell more. And everyone can count on Anika to come up with something new (and sometimes crazy) for the girls to do.

Even though their personalities are different, the girls have learned to work together to complement each other's needs in the friendship, and they are always understanding and respectful towards each other.

Answer the following questions about Alex, Sandy, and Anika.

1. **Can you spot the different personality types in Alex, Sandy, and Anika? How would you describe each one's personality?**

   _____

   _____

2. **How do Alex, Sandy, and Anika's personalities contribute to and strengthen their friendships?**

   _____

   _____

3. **Can you think of a time when personality differences caused a misunderstanding in your friendship group? How was it resolved?**

   _____

   _____

4. **Alex, Sandy, and Anika all have different personalities. Can you identify the personality traits in some of your friends?**

   _____

   _____

Activity: Personality Quiz

Here's a test based on the Big 5 personality traits. Please note that this is a simplified version and not a scientifically validated test. It is just for informational and entertainment purposes only.

Instructions: For each statement, indicate the extent to which you agree or disagree by selecting the option that best describes you.

	Strongly Agree	Agree	Neutral	Disagree	Strongly Disagree
1) I am talkative and outgoing	😊	🙂	😐	🙁	☹️
2) I tend to be organized and efficient.	😊	🙂	😐	🙁	☹️
3) I am open to new experiences and enjoy exploring different ideas.	😊	🙂	😐	🙁	☹️
4) I am generally calm and emotionally stable.	😊	🙂	😐	🙁	☹️
5) I am dependable and can be relied upon.	😊	🙂	😐	🙁	☹️
6) I am curious and enjoy learning new things.	😊	🙂	😐	🙁	☹️
7) I tend to be reserved and quiet.	😊	🙂	😐	🙁	☹️
8) I am compassionate and care about others' well-being.	😊	🙂	😐	🙁	☹️
9) I am organized and pay attention to details.	😊	🙂	😐	🙁	☹️
10) I experience a range of emotions and can be easily affected by them.	😊	🙂	😐	🙁	☹️

SCORING

Assign the following values to each response:

Answer		Points
Strongly Agree	😊	5
Agree	🙂	4
Neutral	😐	3
Disagree	🙁	2
Strongly Disagree	☹️	1

To interpret your results, add up your score for each trait:

Trait	Add Points for Questions	Score
Extroversion	1 & 7	
Conscientiousness	2 & 9	
Openness	3 & 6	
Neuroticism	4 & 10	
Agreeableness	5 & 8	

Now, let's work out your results! The higher your score for a particular trait, the more you exhibit that personality type's characteristics. And if you have a lower score? It simply means those traits aren't as prominent in your personality.

But remember, this is just a bit of fun, and there's no "good" or "bad" in this quiz. It's all about celebrating who you are! Scoring high or low on any trait doesn't mean you're better or worse than anyone else. Instead, it shines a light on the colorful mix of traits that make you uniquely YOU. Embrace your results and enjoy learning more about your awesome self!

 **Key Takeaways**

Having friends with a mix of personalities can be incredibly rewarding, as your friends will complement each other and ensure balance in a group. However, different personality traits can sometimes lead to friction or conflicts. There are no "good" or "bad" traits; it's simply about understanding and accepting the different personalities.

HEALTHY VS. UNHEALTHY FRIENDSHIPS

Now that you're familiar with the various types of friends and how personalities can complement each other and sometimes clash, let's explore the difference between healthy and unhealthy friendships. Remember, there's a fine line between occasionally disagreeing with a friend and being in an unhealthy friendship.

Friendships are rooted in love and support. In a healthy friendship, there's a balance of give and take. You offer your friends attention, friendship, and support; they do the same for you. If your friends don't respect or support you, it might be time to reevaluate the health of the friendship.

In this chapter, we'll examine the features of a healthy friendship and the red flags that indicate an unhealthy one. After learning about these distinctions, you'll apply your knowledge to a case study on handling an unhealthy friendship and take a friendship checkup activity to assess your current friendships.

Before we get into all of that, let's start at the beginning. What makes a friendship healthy? How can you identify a positive relationship?

Characteristics of Healthy Friendships

Good friends are people you can trust, who support you when you need a helping hand, and whom you enjoy spending time with. We've touched on some aspects of what makes good friends in Chapter 1. They lift you up, make you feel good about yourself, listen to you, aren't afraid to admit when they've messed up, and never hold grudges.

Healthy friendships aren't always smooth sailing. Sometimes, you'll have differences of opinion. When both of you feel strongly about something, it may result in an argument. What matters is how you handle these differences and treat each other afterward.

What makes a good friendship? Here are seven characteristics of healthy friendships:

1. **Mutual Respect:** Respect is at the heart of any healthy friendship. It means honoring each other's personal space, treating your friends in the same way you would want to be treated, and listening to their opinions and views, even if they differ from yours. Mutual respect is the foundation for any healthy friendship.

2. **Trust:** Trust is essential in a strong friendship. Knowing your friends will be there for you when you need them is vital for building a healthy and long-lasting friendship. Trust also extends to secrets. If you share something private, your friend should keep it confidential.

3. **Open Communication:** Open communication is key to understanding each other's boundaries and enhancing trust. It means that you feel comfortable expressing yourself freely and openly. It also means you can talk about any topic, even if it may be tricky, and voice disagreements without fear of them escalating into an argument. If you can't express yourself openly in a friendship, it's not a healthy relationship.

4. **Balancing Give and Take:** Every relationship involves an aspect of give and take. You give your friends time and energy; they give some in return. You share your secrets with them, and they do the same. You prioritize seeing them, and they return the favor. That's just how a friendship works. But the give-and-take aspect of the friendship must be balanced. If it's one-sided, where one person gives more than the other, the friendship is unlikely to last.

5. **Celebrating Each Other's Successes:** In a healthy relationship, you celebrate each other's successes. If your friend makes the sports team, you should be happy for them, even if you didn't make the cut. While it's natural to feel disappointed if your friends achieve something you haven't, it's important to put those feelings aside and celebrate their successes. And remember, they should also do the same for you.

6. **Taking Interest in Each Other's Lives:** For a friendship to be strong, it's important to be actively involved in each other's lives. This means taking an interest in their hobbies, showing your support, and checking in on them regularly. If your friends aren't interested in your life, how will they know when you face challenges?

7. **Being There for Each Other:** True friends are there for you when you need them. Whether you need a good chat, a fun distraction, or just want to hang out, having friends there for you shows their reliability and trustworthiness. It doesn't mean you have to drop everything to support them. For example, it doesn't make you a bad friend if you're swamped with exams and can't visit them. The key is to support them when they need you and know they will do the same for you.

While these are all signs of a strong friendship, there are also some warning signs, or "red flags," to look out for. These signs might indicate that a friendship is unhealthy.

Red Flags in Unhealthy Friendships

Unfortunately, not all friendships are healthy. Even when you and your friends are good people, sometimes a friendship just isn't meant to be. Sticking around in an unhealthy friendship can be harmful, so it's important to recognize when to let go of a friendship that's no longer good for you.

But how can you spot when a friendship is turning sour? Here are some warning signs to look out for.

1. **Constant Negativity:** If a friend always sees the downside of a situation, that negativity may also affect you. Everyone has off days and tough times, but looking for positives in life is important.

   If your friends are always negative, you may lose sight of all the great things around you. This could end up bringing you down. Try to surround yourself with people who brighten your day, not darken it.

2. **Lack of Respect:** Respect is key in any friendship. Without respect, there's no trust. If your friend doesn't respect you, they might not consider your feelings or needs. This could lead to drama and heartache.

   Suppose you notice that your friends don't respect you, or they don't show you the respect you deserve. In that case, you should take it as a warning sign and consider whether these are friendships worth sticking with.

3. **Control Issues:** If a friend tries to control your choices — like what you wear, where you go, or what you say — it's a significant red flag.

   It's okay for a friend to offer advice; some friends naturally like to plan things more than others. Still, your friends should always respect your individuality and opinions. If a friend tries to control you and doesn't let you be you, they might not truly appreciate you.

4. **Imbalance of Give and Take:** A healthy friendship is built on a balance of give and take. If there's an imbalance, it's usually a warning sign that something isn't right. If your friend doesn't

offer you support in the same way you support them, or only reaches out when they need something, that's a sign of imbalance.

If you can't rely on your friends when you need them, or if you're always making sacrifices and they're not doing the same for you, it's a red flag in the friendship.

5. **Jealousy:** Jealousy can be damaging in friendships. If your friends are jealous of your success or something you have accomplished, it shows they aren't truly happy for you.

Jealousy can be destructive in friendships, so if you notice this trait, you may need to reconsider the health of the relationship.

6. **Constant Criticism:** If you always feel you are being criticized or judged by your friends, it can be hard to be yourself around them. For example, if your friends are critical of how you dress, your hobbies, what you eat, or how you talk, you might feel like they don't appreciate you.

Of course, everyone is entitled to their own opinions, but constant criticism is hurtful and unpleasant. If this happens, it might be a sign you're in an unhealthy friendship.

 Recognizing and acknowledging red flags in a friendship can be challenging and emotional, but it's important for your well-being. It's normal to feel sad or conflicted about letting go of a friendship, even if it's unhealthy. Ending a friendship or distancing yourself from an unhealthy friend is never easy, but remember that you deserve to be surrounded by people who uplift and respect you.

Now that you know how to distinguish between healthy and unhealthy friendships, it's time to put that knowledge to use. Below, you'll find a case study with questions to help you identify the features of an unhealthy friendship. You can also complete a friendship checkup to assess the state of your friendships and identify any warning signs you should address. Let's get started!

Isabella, Ava, and Zoe

Isabella, Ava, and Zoe were inseparable at the start of the school year. They shared a lot of fun times together, but after a while, Isabella started feeling left out. Ava and Zoe sometimes whispered and excluded her from their conversations, making her feel uncomfortable and anxious. Eventually, she spoke to her older sister about it, who helped her recognize the unhealthy elements in her friendship with Ava and Zoe. Isabella then made the brave decision to distance herself from Ava and Zoe. She started spending more time with other friends who included her in everything and treated her with kindness and respect. This tough decision led her towards healthier friendships where she felt happy and valued.

Answer the following questions about Isabella, Ava, and Zoe.

1. Can you identify the signs of an unhealthy friendship in the story of Isabella, Ava, and Zoe?

_____

_____

_____

2. How did Isabella handle the situation when she realized her friends weren't treating her well?

_____

_____

_____

3. What would you do if you were in Isabella's position?

_____

_____

_____

4. What do you look for in new friends? What are the most important qualities?

_____

_____

_____

Activity: Friendship Check-Up

You probably have some awesome friends you enjoy spending time with who support you and make you feel great. But you may also have other friends you're not quite sure about. Perhaps you can't pinpoint what it is, but something doesn't feel right. That's where this exercise comes in. In this activity, you'll answer a few simple questions about your friends to determine whether your friendships are on the right track.

Carefully consider each question before deciding whether you agree or not. Once you've completed the table, write a short summary of how you feel about this friendship. Is it good for you, or not so much? What are you going to do about it? Remember, it can be tough to let go of friendships, but sometimes it's the best thing for you.

Friendship Audit With [   ]

	AGREE	NEUTRAL	DISAGREE
I feel like I can be myself around my friend.	☺	😐	☹
My friend accepts me for who I am.	☺	😐	☹
I can count on my friend when I need them.	☺	😐	☹
My friend doesn't criticize me or make me feel self-conscious.	☺	😐	☹
I can trust my friend with all my secrets.	☺	😐	☹
My friend makes me feel special/valuable.	☺	😐	☹
I can express my opinions around my friend.	☺	😐	☹
I feel like I take just as much as I give in the friendship.	☺	😐	☹
My friend treats me with kindness and respect.	☺	😐	☹
My friend is never jealous of my success.	☺	😐	☹

If most of your answers (5 or more out of 10) are "neutral" or "disagree," there might be some issues in your friendship, and it might be time to reassess.

Review:

Key Takeaways

A healthy friendship is one where you feel loved, valued, and supported and can be yourself no matter what. Keep an eye out for warning signs, like jealousy, control issues, or lack of respect. These might indicate that you are in an unhealthy relationship.

OVERCOMING FRIENDSHIP CHALLENGES

Whether in a healthy friendship or facing some challenges, hitting a few bumps along the way is normal. Disagreements are a natural part of being friends, especially when you and your friends have different personalities. But don't worry — challenges like these are completely normal in any friendship. What's most important is knowing how to navigate and resolve any problems so that you can keep enjoying each other's company and have fun together.

In this chapter, we'll explore conflict and uncover why it might arise between you and your friends. We'll unlock the secrets of making up after disagreements and discover ways to handle tricky feelings like jealousy. At the end of the chapter, you can use the skills you've learned in a case study and role-play exercise. Ready to dive in?

Understanding Conflict

Conflict sounds like a scary word, but everyone deals with it — at school, at home, and even on sports teams. It's when you and someone else can't agree, leading to an argument. Some people confuse conflict with fighting. While they have similar traits, they are not quite the same. Conflict is a disagreement or dispute, while fighting involves hostile behavior, often accompanied by anger or aggression.

While disagreements aren't nice, they're not always bad. Sometimes, it's good to clear the air. In fact, working through an argument can make friendships stronger. Let's look at some common causes of friction in a friendship:

1. **Misunderstanding** — Little mix-ups can happen between friends. Maybe you misunderstood a joke, or perhaps you both got confused about plans for hanging out. These misunderstandings can lead to frustration but can often be resolved by talking it out.

2. **Jealousy** — Sometimes, if a friend has something you wish you had or they achieved something you wanted to, it might make you feel jealous. This is a natural feeling, but it can sometimes lead to negative feelings in a friendship if not handled with care.

CONFLICT

Causes

1. Misunderstanding
2. Jealousy
3. Diverging Interests
4. Different Values / Beliefs
5. Peer Pressure
6. Feeling Left Out

Resolution

1. Active Listening
2. "I" Statements
3. Fair Communication
4. Finding A Compromise
5. Apologizing When Necessary

3. **Diverging Interests** — As you grow up, your interests will naturally change, and you may enjoy doing different things. For example, you and your friend might have loved playing games together, but what if one of you now wants to hang out at the mall instead? This can lead to feelings of being left out.

4. **Different Values or Beliefs** — As you get older, you may develop different opinions or values from your friends. These differences can sometimes lead to disagreements.

5. **Peer Pressure** — Sometimes, friends might pressure you to do things you don't want to do. This pressure can cause stress, leading to disagreements or hurt feelings between friends.

6. **Feeling Left Out** — Feeling left out is a big deal in friendships. If a friend feels ignored or less important than others in a group, it can lead to sadness and tension in the friendship.

Remember that friendships go through ups and downs, and conflicts are a natural part of that journey. The key to maintaining strong friendships is not avoiding them but learning how to handle them with care, empathy, and open communication. That way, you can keep your friendships strong, even as you grow and change!

Let's look at how to manage and resolve disagreements.

Conflict Resolution Techniques

While conflict is normal in any friendship, it is important that you know how to resolve it effectively, without hurting your friends or them hurting you. Resolving disputes is an important life skill. The sooner you learn it, the better. Here are five conflict resolution techniques to try when you argue with a friend.

1. Active Listening

Active listening means allowing the other person to talk and paying attention to what they are saying. Sometimes, we get so caught up with how we will respond to their words that we don't really hear what our friends are trying to tell us. This can make the argument even worse. When you're in an argument, focus on your friend's words and feelings before responding.

2. Using "I" Statements

It's easy to play the "blame game" when involved in a conflict, but blaming a friend won't resolve the hard feelings, and can worsen things. Instead of blaming them for everything, focus on using "I" statements. For example, instead of saying, "You don't pay attention to me anymore," say, "I feel like we don't spend enough time together, which hurts my feelings." "I" statements help you communicate your feelings without blaming others.

3. Fair Communication

If you're in a disagreement with a friend, stick to what you're really arguing about. Avoid digging up past issues, as it will only draw the conflict out and prevent the issue from being resolved. For instance, if you feel left out, concentrate on discussing that. Don't bring up other issues, like jealousy, as the argument will only escalate, and you'll unlikely resolve the problem.

4. Finding a Compromise

The goal of conflict resolution is to find a compromise. A compromise is when you both agree on something fair. It usually involves a bit of give and take. If you actively listen to your friend and focus on the issue, you should be able to find a middle ground for any problem. For example, if you feel your friend is leaving you out, perhaps you could agree to hang out together on Friday afternoons, leaving Saturdays for her to spend time with her other friends. You may not always get everything you want when finding a middle ground, but the important thing is you both feel heard, cared for, and satisfied with the result.

5. Apologizing When Necessary

Saying sorry can be tough, especially if you feel it's not your fault. But knowing when to apologize and making the effort to do so is crucial for keeping your friendships healthy. If you know you made a mistake, it's important to apologize. It can help clear the air and get things back on track.

Conflict can happen for lots of different reasons. Knowing how to talk it out and make up with a friend can keep your friendships happy and strong.

So, how do you deal with jealousy in a friendship?

Dealing With Jealousy

Jealousy can be a tricky emotion, but it's one that everyone experiences from time to time. It's that feeling you get when your friend has something you want, or maybe they're getting more attention than you.

Feeling jealous of someone with more friends or better things than you is natural, but acting on those feelings won't change anything. Instead, it might hurt your friendship and make your friend feel bad, leading to problems. Here are some reasons you might feel jealous:

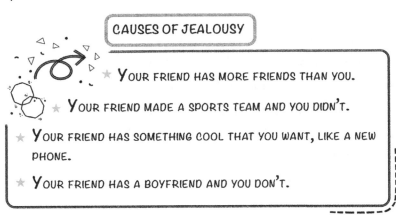

CAUSES OF JEALOUSY

★ Your friend has more friends than you.

★ Your friend made a sports team and you didn't.

★ Your friend has something cool that you want, like a new phone.

★ Your friend has a boyfriend and you don't.

Remember, it's normal to feel jealous sometimes, but acting mean or unkind because of it isn't fair to your friend. They haven't done anything wrong.

If you feel jealous of your friend, it's important that you focus on discovering the root of the jealousy. Here are some ways to deal with jealousy, so it doesn't cause problems in your friendships:

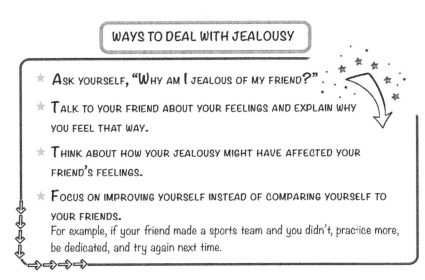

WAYS TO DEAL WITH JEALOUSY

★ Ask yourself, "Why am I jealous of my friend?"

★ Talk to your friend about your feelings and explain why you feel that way.

★ Think about how your jealousy might have affected your friend's feelings.

★ Focus on improving yourself instead of comparing yourself to your friends.
For example, if your friend made a sports team and you didn't, practice more, be dedicated, and try again next time.

Another common cause of conflict in a friendship is diverging interests. This happens when you and your friend start to like different things. It's not about someone being mean or doing anything wrong; it's just a natural part of growing up. But if it's not handled carefully, it can strain a friendship.

How do you manage this?

Diverging Interests

As you get older, your interests might change, and that's totally normal. You might find that you and your friends no longer like the same things. While this can cause tension in your friendships, it doesn't mean you can't still be friends. Here's how to manage diverging interests and keep your friendships strong:

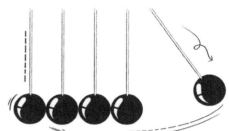

- **Accept That Change is Normal**: It's okay if you and your friends start liking different things. Everyone has unique interests.

- **Give Space and Support**: Allow your friends to pursue their interests, and ask for the same space in return. Support each other's individual passions.

- **Find Common Ground**: Look for activities or interests you still enjoy together, like shopping or watching movies.

- **Respect Individual Interests**: Understand that having different interests is okay, and focus on what you still have in common.

- **Make New Friends**: If your friend has a new interest you're not into, it's an opportunity for both of you to make new friends who share these new interests. This doesn't mean you're replacing each other; you're just expanding your friendship circles.

Remember, it's normal for friends to develop different interests as they grow up. What's most important is how you handle it. With understanding and communication, your friendship can still be strong and fun, even if you like different things.

Now that you have learned what conflict is, what causes conflict, and how to navigate conflict in your friendship, it's time to put that knowledge to the test. Below is a case study with some questions about how to handle conflict. You will also find a role-play activity where you can practice the conflict resolution techniques learned in this chapter. Good luck!

Case Study: Olivia and Sophie

Since kindergarten, Sophie and Olivia have been best friends, sharing everything from secrets to hobbies. But when Sophie started taking dance classes, she soon made a new friend, Mandy. Since Mandy was also in their school, Sophie started spending more time with Mandy and less with Olivia.

Olivia started feeling that Sophie was ignoring her for her new friend, leading to her feeling left out. However, after taking some time apart, they decided to talk about the issue openly. Olivia expressed her feelings of being left out, and Sophie apologized, explaining that she didn't intend to hurt Olivia.

After explaining how they both felt, the girls agreed to be more considerate of each other's feelings in the future. Olivia tried to understand Sophie's new interests, even attending a dance class or two. This not only strengthened her bond with Sophie, but allowed her to become friends with Mandy, as well.

Answer the following questions about Olivia and Sophie.

1. How did Olivia and Sophie sort things out?

_____

_____

_____

_____

_____

2. What strategies did Olivia and Sophie use to communicate their feelings effectively? (Hint: Consider how they expressed their emotions and listened to each other.)

_____

_____

_____

_____

_____

3. How can you apply these conflict resolution techniques in your own friendships?

_____

_____

_____

_____

_____

Activity: Conflict Resolution Role-Play

In this activity, you will explore three scenarios involving conflicts between friends. Your task is to apply the conflict resolution techniques you've learned in this chapter to address the issues in each situation. Write down the strategies and steps you would take, or role-play the scenarios with a friend or family member to practice in real time. Reflect on what you have done and learned after each scenario.

Scenario 1: Amy and Stephanie

Amy and Stephanie have to work together on a school project. They aren't really friends, and soon run into trouble with the project. While Amy wants to work together to complete the project, Stephanie isn't interested in working on the project. She assumes Amy will do all the work.

How should Amy broach the topic with Stephanie so they can work together on this project?

· Consider Amy's feelings and how she can communicate them to Stephanie.

· Think about how Stephanie might respond and how Amy can encourage teamwork.

_____

_____

_____

Scenario 2: Elsa and Liza

Elsa and Liza have been best friends for years, but after both girls tried out for the school soccer team, Liza was chosen for the team, while Elsa was not. This made Elsa feel jealous of Liza. As a result, she started acting differently toward Liza, hurting her feelings.

How can Liza and Elsa work together to resolve this conflict and remain friends?

· Reflect on the emotions involved and how open communication can alleviate the issue.

· Consider ways they can support each other, even though their circumstances have changed.

_____

_____

_____

Scenario 3: Merida and Odette

Merida and Odette have always been best friends. They had the same interests and dreamed of becoming professional dancers. However, when they went to high school, Merida started taking acting classes while Odette continued dancing. They started drifting apart, and Odette felt Merida was neglecting her to pursue new hobbies.

What can Merida and Odette do to preserve their friendship while giving each other space to grow?

· Think about the importance of understanding and respecting each other's evolving interests.

· Consider strategies to reconnect and find shared activities or interests.

_____

_____

_____

 **Key Takeaways**

As friendships evolve and interests change, conflicts may naturally arise. Navigating these challenges is crucial for maintaining strong, resilient friendships. Actively listening to your friends, using "I" statements, emphasizing fair communication, finding a compromise, and apologizing when necessary are just some of the ways to resolve disputes with your friends and keep your friendships strong.

LOSING FRIENDS AND MOVING ON

Losing a friend is not something anyone wants to experience. It can be painful, especially if you lose your best friend. But as tough as it is, losing friends is just something that happens as you get older. When you're younger, you might have lots of friends, but as you grow up and your interests change, you may naturally drift apart from some friends. It's not fun, but it's a normal part of life. The good news is that even if you lose some old friends, you'll make plenty of new ones as you grow older!

There are many reasons why friends might drift apart, and it's totally normal to feel a bit sad or confused about it. But there are ways to help you feel better and understand what's happening. It may not be the most fun thing to think about, but learning how to handle these feelings can turn something negative into a positive experience.

In this chapter, we'll explore why friends sometimes grow apart, and how to cope with the feelings that come with it. We'll give you some helpful strategies for dealing with these changes, so you can bounce back and feel great. Later, you'll get to use your knowledge in a case study about two friends who drifted apart, and try an activity that lets you explore your own thoughts about friendships.

Let's dive in and discover why these changes happen as we grow up, and how to handle them.

Reasons for Losing Friends

Have you ever heard the saying, "Life happens?" It's an old saying, but it's still true. Sometimes, no matter how hard we try or how much we care, we drift apart from a friend. It's a normal part of growing up, even though it's tough.

You may wonder why people lose friends in the first place. While there are many reasons for losing friends and breaking up friendships, here are five of the most common ones:

1. Changing Schools

Sometimes, friends drift apart when they go to different schools. When you leave elementary school, you might go to the same middle or high school as some of your friends, but other friends might go somewhere else. Whether that school is near or far, you could drift apart from the friends who aren't at your school.

Even if you try hard to stay close, it's tough to keep a friendship going when you're not in the same place daily. You're at school a lot, so you won't see friends from other schools as often. If you don't do the same after-school activities, you might not see them much at all.

It's sad to drift apart from friends just because you attend different schools, but it's natural. Once you get used to your new school, you'll make new friends, and your old friends might drift further away. That doesn't mean you can't stay friends if you're at different schools, but it might take more effort.

If you stop being friends because you or your friend changed schools, it's usually not anybody's fault. It's just a friendship that has run its course. You can always look back on the good times you had together and remember them with a smile.

2. Moving Away

Moving to a new place can be hard on friendships, just like changing schools. If you move to a different town, or even a different state or country, it can make it difficult to maintain friendships. You won't see your friends as often, and talking to them might be tricky if there's a time difference.

But don't worry, moving away doesn't mean you have to stop being friends. It's okay if you drift apart a little — it doesn't mean you did anything wrong or that your friendship was bad. Losing touch with friends sometimes is a normal part of growing up, and it can happen to anyone.

If you want to stay close to your friends after moving, you'll just have to try a bit harder to stay in touch.

3. Disagreements

Sometimes friendships end because of disagreements. While we discussed conflict resolution earlier in the book, some problems simply can't be fixed. When that happens, it might mean saying goodbye to a friendship. Ending a friendship over a disagreement is sad, and you might feel different emotions.

You should always try to work things out, but sometimes, it's just not possible. Maybe you both feel strongly about something, or neither wants to give in. That could mean the end of your friendship.

Even if an argument ends a friendship, it doesn't mean you have to be mad at your friend forever. Holding on to anger might make you forget all the fun times you had together, and leave you feeling upset. It's really important to understand how you feel about a friendship ending, no matter why it happened, so you can feel better and make new friends.

4. Diverging Interests

Another common reason friendships sometimes end is when you and your friend start to like different things. We have discussed this several times before, but diverging interests can cause friends to drift apart. As you grow up, you might find new hobbies or interests. Maybe you stop taking dance lessons or are no longer interested in swimming or collecting stickers.

If those shared activities were a big part of your friendship, growing apart can be tough. But it's okay if your interests change; that's just part of getting older.

If a friendship ends because you both like different things now, it doesn't mean you did anything wrong. Sometimes, friendships just naturally come to an end. You'll discover new hobbies and make new friends who enjoy the same things. Your old friend will do the same.

And remember, even if you don't share the same hobbies anymore, you can still be nice to each other. You'll always have the fun memories you shared when you liked the same things.

5. Unhealthy Friendships

You might remember learning about healthy and unhealthy friendships earlier in this book. Recognizing an unhealthy friendship is really important, and sometimes the best thing you can do for yourself and your friend is to end the friendship.

If you feel like you're not being treated with respect, support, or kindness, it might be time to look for friends who will treat you right. Trust is crucial, too. If you can't trust each other, it might be best to move on.

Ending an unhealthy friendship is a big decision and can be really sad, but it doesn't mean you did something wrong. In fact, it shows that you're wise enough to know when a situation isn't good for you and brave enough to do what's best for you and your friend.

It's normal to feel a mix of emotions when a friendship ends, no matter the reason. You might feel sad, confused, or even relieved, and that's okay. Healthily handling those feelings is a big part of growing up, and it helps you learn how to be a good friend in the future. Remember, you're learning and growing, and caring for yourself is important.

Dealing With the Loss of a Friend

Losing a friend can be tough, and it's normal to feel different emotions. You might feel sad one minute, angry the next, or even lost. It's okay to feel that way. Your feelings are normal, and you don't need to be embarrassed or ashamed.

However, it is important to process the feelings of losing a friend. If you don't process and overcome these feelings, they can have lasting impacts and may affect how you treat friends in the future.

Why It's Okay to Feel Sad When You Lose a Friend

It's natural to feel many different emotions when you lose a friend. You might feel angry or wish you could just forget about them. It's also totally okay to feel sad about it.

Even if you had a fight or didn't always get along, you were still friends. That friendship was special, and it's normal to miss it. You might feel a little lost or unsure about what to do next, and that's all right. Your feelings are real. It's important to recognize them and it's also essential to figure out healthy ways to handle those feelings.

Remembering the fun times and why you became friends in the first place can help. Think about the laughs, the shared secrets, and the great times you had together. Focusing on those happy memories can make the sadness a bit easier to handle.

Let's look at some other ways to process losing a friend.

COPING STRATEGIES AFTER LOSING A FRIEND

Losing a friend can be really hard, but there are healthy ways to handle all the feelings you might have. Here are some strategies that can help you process your feelings, focus on the good times, and feel better:

1. Giving Yourself Time

Healing takes time, and feeling sad or confused is okay. Give yourself time to process your feelings, and remember that those feelings will ease as you move forward.

2. Seeking Support

Seeking support from your friends and family can help you process the feelings of losing a friend. Talking to them can make you feel loved and cherished. No matter what, they're there for you, ready to listen and remind you that you're not alone.

3. Channeling Negative Emotions into Positive Actions

Turn your negative feelings into something positive, like exercising, journaling, or painting. Doing so can help release negative emotions and create something beautiful in the process. It's like giving those sad or angry feelings a new, happier home.

4. Seeking Healthy Outlets

You might want to write about your feelings instead of talking about them. That's okay! Journaling, meditating, or chatting with other friends can help. Even if you don't show your writing to anyone, getting those feelings out can help you understand them and make you feel much better.

5. Staying Positive

Instead of focusing on the negative aspects of a relationship, focus on the good memories and what you've learned from the experience. This can help you cherish the good times you spent together and keep a positive outlook for the future.

6. Seeking Professional Help

If those feelings just won't go away, or you're having a really tough time, it's okay to ask for help from a counselor or therapist. These experts know all about feelings and can help you find new ways to cope.

7. Joining Clubs or Groups

Finding a club or group that shares your interests can help you make new friends and keep busy. It can be a fun way to move on and find joy in activities you love.

Remember, it's okay to feel sad and emotional when losing a friend, and various coping strategies can serve as tools to help navigate those feelings. Experimenting with these tools lets you find what works best for you. With time and effort, the difficult emotions will begin to ease. Remember, you have the strength to get through this.

Ava and Lucy

Ava and Lucy were like two peas in a pod since kindergarten. They laughed together, shared secrets, and even had matching friendship bracelets. Growing up, they created loads of fun and unforgettable memories.

But then, something big happened. When they turned 12, Lucy's family decided to move to another city. Both girls promised to write letters, call each other, and remain best friends forever, but as time went on, things began to change.

They started to make new friends in their own cities, and their interests started to go in different directions. They tried hard to keep in touch, but the distance made things tricky. Ava missed Lucy a lot and felt really sad at first.

But then, Ava realized that it was normal to feel this way. She thought about all the good times she and Lucy had shared and smiled. She started to make new friends and found joy in new hobbies. Even though she missed Lucy, she knew their memories would always be a special part of her life.

This story shows that it's normal for friendships to change and that feeling sad about it is okay. It also teaches us to learn from these experiences, make new friends, and keep happy memories in our hearts.

Answer the following questions about Lucy and Ava.

1. Why did Ava and Lucy's friendship drift apart?

_____

_____

_____

2. How did Ava cope with losing her close friendship with Lucy?

_____

_____

_____

3. Can you think of strategies Ava used that might help you if you lose a friend?

_____

_____

_____

Activity: Letter to a Friend

Sometimes, writing down our feelings can help when we're sad or confused. In this exercise, you'll have the chance to write a letter to a friend you may have lost touch with or grown apart from. Don't worry, you won't actually send the letter, so you can be completely honest about your feelings.

You might find that writing this letter brings up strong emotions, and that's totally normal. If anything becomes too much, please don't hesitate to talk to an adult you trust. They can help you understand what you're feeling.

Take your time, and write whatever feels right for you. Here are some questions that might help guide your thoughts:

· What do you miss most about your friend?

· Are there things you wish you could have done differently?

· What happy memories do you still hold close?

· How have you grown or changed since your friendship changed?

· Is there anything you'd want to tell them if they were right in front of you now?

Remember, this letter is just for you. It's a safe space to explore your feelings, and there's no right or wrong way to do it. Take as long as you need, and be kind to yourself. You're doing great!

Here's a little prompt to help you get started:

Dear _ _ _ _ _ _ _ _ _ _ _ _ _ _ _ _ _

I've been thinking a lot about our friendship and all the fun times we used to have. Lately, things have changed, and I miss how close we used to be. I wanted to write you this letter to tell you...

_ _

_ _

_ _

_ _

_ _

_ _

_ _

_ _

_ _

_ _

_ _

_ _

 **Key Takeaways**

Losing a friend is never easy, but it is a normal part of growing up. Moving, changing schools, diverging interests, and arguments may cause a friendship to end. It's okay to feel sad when a friendship ends. However, developing the right coping techniques to deal with these emotions is important. Seeking support, remembering the past, channeling negative thoughts into positive actions, and seeking professional help are ways to process losing a friend or friendship.

BULLYING AND PEER PRESSURE

As great as they are, friendships can sometimes be challenged by bullying and peer pressure. These aren't minor issues — they are serious problems that deserve attention, even when they involve close friends. Bullying can stir up negative feelings, shaking your self-confidence. Meanwhile, peer pressure can push you to act in ways you're uncomfortable with, even doing things against your principles and beliefs.

Learning to recognize bullying and peer pressure is crucial. As you enter your teenage years, the nature of bullying will change, and peer pressure often becomes more complex. Since they can harm your happiness and well-being, knowing how to spot them and what to do when they creep into your friendships is vital.

In this chapter, we will uncover the signs of bullying and peer pressure and learn some effective strategies to tackle them. You'll also read a case study and several scenarios that show how peer pressure and bullying can appear in friendships, giving you a chance to apply what you've learned. But before we jump into the exercises, let's take a moment to understand bullying.

Bullying

Being bullied or bullying others is never acceptable. There's a massive gap between light-hearted teasing and joking among friends and bullying. Just because someone is your friend doesn't give them the right to bully you or for you to bully them.

Let's delve into what bullying truly means and how it's different from simple, friendly teasing.

Understanding Bullying

The Anti-Bullying Alliance defines bullying as "the repetitive, intentional hurting of one person or group by another person or group, where the relationship involves an imbalance of power" (n.d.). Put simply, bullying is when someone repeatedly hurts or upsets another person on purpose, taking advantage of a situation where they have more power or control. This behavior is always unacceptable.

When you're younger, you might have disagreements with your friends over small things, like which toy to play with, where to sit, or which snack to eat. However, when these disagreements escalate to name-calling or making fun of others, it becomes a type of bullying.

No one should have to endure bullying. Sadly, bullies can be found in most schools. But, identifying bullying is not always easy with all the different types. It becomes even more challenging when those involved are friends.

So, what exactly are the different forms of bullying?

Different Kinds of Bullying

Bullying takes many shapes and forms.

- **Physical Bullying**

  You might first think of bullying as pushing, hitting, or physically hurting someone else. This is known as physical bullying. It's just as serious as other types of bullying and is usually easier to spot.

- **Verbal Bullying**

  There's also verbal bullying. This happens when someone calls another person names, teases them, or spreads rumors about them. Verbal bullying often happens in the open, where many people can see or hear it. This can sometimes lead to an escalation in the bullying, where more people join in as the name-calling and rumors spread.

- **Cyberbullying**

  A type of bullying that's become more common with teenagers is cyberbullying. This is like verbal bullying, but it happens online or over social media. Because social media posts can be seen by so many people, this kind of bullying can spread fast and far. Posting embarrassing pictures of someone without their consent is also considered cyberbullying.

Each of these types of bullying is harmful and mean. If someone intentionally hurts another person without feeling sorry, they are a bully. Being a bully isn't a good thing, and you should look out for it in school and at home. But where does the boundary lie between friendly teasing and bullying?

The Difference Between Friendly Teasing and Bullying

Teasing can be a light-hearted way for friends to interact with each other. For example, if you have a fun nickname for your friend and they're okay with it, it's usually seen as friendly banter. Similarly, if your friends gently tease you about harmless subjects, like a crush you have, this isn't usually considered bullying.

These are examples of friendly teasing. So, what's the difference between friendly teasing and bullying? It comes down to why the teasing is happening and how it makes the other person feel. Friendly teasing comes from a place of love, laughter, and fun, whereas bullying results in tears and hurt feelings.

So, it usually isn't bullying if you don't feel hurt by your friends' jokes or actions. But situations and emotions change. If the same fun nickname you give your friend is used negatively or starts to make them feel bad, it's shifted into bullying territory.

Take a moment to consider how your words and actions might make the other person feel. This awareness can help you determine if your teasing is fun or might be causing unintentional harm.

Remember, no one deserves to be bullied, and it's never okay to bully others. It's okay to joke with friends, but not if it hurts their feelings. If you're unsure, it's always best to check in with your friends and ensure they're okay with the joke or teasing.

Peer Pressure

As you grow up and enter your teen years, you might face peer pressure. Wanting to fit in and being scared of being left out can make you more likely to feel peer pressure. Sometimes, peer pressure can lead to bad or unsafe situations. That's why it's important for you, as a tween, to understand peer pressure and how to deal with it.

1. STANDING UP FOR YOURSELF

Bullies usually don't like it when someone stands up to them. If you let them know that what they're doing isn't okay, they might stop. This might be tough, especially if it's your friends who are the bullies, but you have the right to tell them they're wrong.

2. GETTING HELP

If standing up to the bullies doesn't work, it's really important to talk to an adult you trust, such as a parent, teacher, or coach. They can offer help and advice on how to deal with the situation.

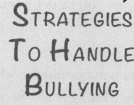

STRATEGIES TO HANDLE BULLYING

Bullying is never okay, and it's important to know how to handle it if you or a friend is being bullied. Here are four strategies that might help:

3. STAYING POSITIVE

Bullying can really hurt your self-esteem, but remember, you're not the one with the problem—the bully is. Try to keep your confidence high, and don't let their mean words affect how you feel about yourself.

4. HELPING OTHERS

If you see someone else being bullied, you can make a big difference by standing up for them. Knowing someone cares can be a huge help to a person who's being bullied. Even if you're not the one being bullied, you can help put a stop to it.

Understanding Peer Pressure

Peer pressure happens when your friends or group influence your choices or actions. It's like when your friends nudge or sway you to behave a certain way. Peer pressure can be positive. For example, your friends might encourage you to try harder on your homework or to put more effort into activities you enjoy.

But peer pressure isn't always good. It can sometimes be negative. This kind of peer pressure might push you to do things you don't really want to do, or that go against what you believe is right. For example, your friends might try convincing you to get a piercing, even when you don't want one. They might even encourage you to act in mean ways towards other people, which could turn you into a bully.

Peer pressure usually happens gradually, where you adjust your behavior bit by bit to feel more accepted by your friends. This typically happens when you become a teenager because fitting in with your friends can feel important.

Fear that your friends will reject you if you don't follow their lead is a big reason why peer pressure happens. When peer pressure is about good things, like studying more or helping others, it's not a problem. But, peer pressure can become a problem when it pushes you to do things that aren't good for you or make you uncomfortable. So, what should you do when you start to notice peer pressure?

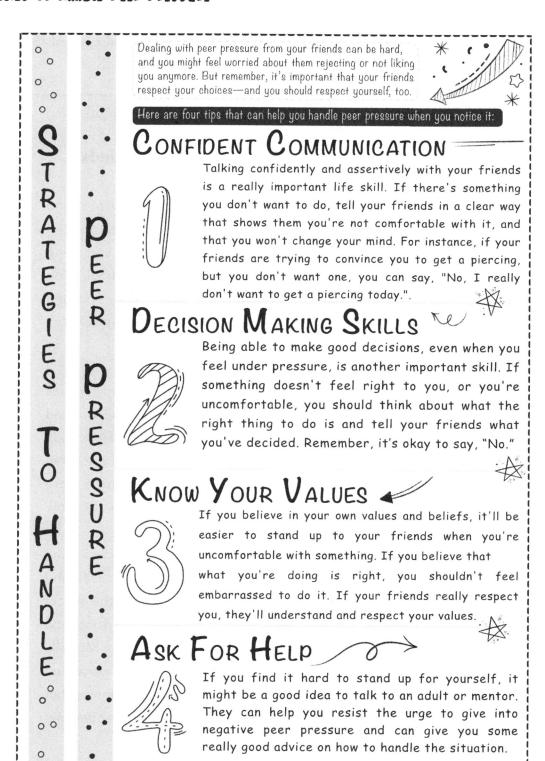

STRATEGIES TO HANDLE

Peer Pressure

Dealing with peer pressure from your friends can be hard, and you might feel worried about them rejecting or not liking you anymore. But remember, it's important that your friends respect your choices—and you should respect yourself, too.

Here are four tips that can help you handle peer pressure when you notice it:

CONFIDENT COMMUNICATION

1

Talking confidently and assertively with your friends is a really important life skill. If there's something you don't want to do, tell your friends in a clear way that shows them you're not comfortable with it, and that you won't change your mind. For instance, if your friends are trying to convince you to get a piercing, but you don't want one, you can say, "No, I really don't want to get a piercing today.".

DECISION MAKING SKILLS

2

Being able to make good decisions, even when you feel under pressure, is another important skill. If something doesn't feel right to you, or you're uncomfortable, you should think about what the right thing to do is and tell your friends what you've decided. Remember, it's okay to say, "No."

KNOW YOUR VALUES

3

If you believe in your own values and beliefs, it'll be easier to stand up to your friends when you're uncomfortable with something. If you believe that what you're doing is right, you shouldn't feel embarrassed to do it. If your friends really respect you, they'll understand and respect your values.

ASK FOR HELP

4

If you find it hard to stand up for yourself, it might be a good idea to talk to an adult or mentor. They can help you resist the urge to give into negative peer pressure and can give you some really good advice on how to handle the situation.

Now that you know how to spot and handle bullying and peer pressure, it's time to put that knowledge into action. You'll go through a case study and work through several scenarios with examples of peer pressure and bullying. This way, you can practice the strategies you've just learned. Good luck!

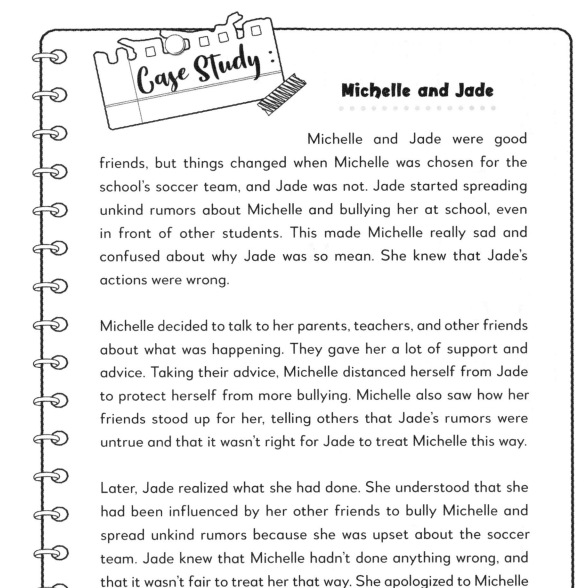

Case Study:

Michelle and Jade

Michelle and Jade were good friends, but things changed when Michelle was chosen for the school's soccer team, and Jade was not. Jade started spreading unkind rumors about Michelle and bullying her at school, even in front of other students. This made Michelle really sad and confused about why Jade was so mean. She knew that Jade's actions were wrong.

Michelle decided to talk to her parents, teachers, and other friends about what was happening. They gave her a lot of support and advice. Taking their advice, Michelle distanced herself from Jade to protect herself from more bullying. Michelle also saw how her friends stood up for her, telling others that Jade's rumors were untrue and that it wasn't right for Jade to treat Michelle this way.

Later, Jade realized what she had done. She understood that she had been influenced by her other friends to bully Michelle and spread unkind rumors because she was upset about the soccer team. Jade knew that Michelle hadn't done anything wrong, and that it wasn't fair to treat her that way. She apologized to Michelle and their friends, and told everyone that the rumors she had spread weren't true. Michelle accepted Jade's apology, understanding that Jade had been influenced by her other friends, and they became friends again.

Answer the following questions about Jade and Michelle.

1. How did Michelle handle the situation when Jade started bullying her?

_____

_____

_____

2. What role did Michelle's other friends play?

_____

_____

_____

3. Can you think of a time when you've faced peer pressure or bullying? What did you do to handle the situation?

_____

_____

_____

Activity: What Would You Do?

You'll find instances of bullying or peer pressure instances in the three scenarios below. After reading the scenario carefully, consider how to use the skills you've learned in this chapter to handle these real-life situations. Write down your actions and what you would say to help resolve the situation and support those involved.

Scenario 1: Becca's Photo

Becca is a classmate of yours. She's not part of the popular group and often gets teased or bullied by some of the popular boys and girls. One day, you find out that one of the popular girls has found a really embarrassing photo of Becca from when she was younger. This girl wants to share the photo with everyone in class, including all of Becca's friends, and even the boy she likes.

What actions could you take in this situation to help Becca?

_____

_____

_____

_____

_____

Scenario 2: The Popularity Contest

There's a popular online game that almost everyone at school is playing. Your friends have all joined and are pressuring you to do the same, even though you're not really interested. They say that everyone who's cool is playing, and you'll be left out if you don't. They're even ranking each other based on their game scores and discussing it at lunch.

What would you do in this situation? How would you handle the peer pressure?

_____

_____

_____

_____

_____

Scenario 3: Magdi's Lunch

Magdi is a student from India attending your school for a semester. Although she's friendly and intelligent, Magdi doesn't have many friends at school yet. One day, as you and your friends pass by Magdi's lunch table, one of your friends, Kate, starts making fun of Magdi for bringing packed lunch from home instead of buying something from the cafeteria. To make things worse, Kate teases Magdi for bringing a lentil curry to school and says it smells funny.

What would you say to Kate in this situation? Would you stand up for Magdi?

_____

_____

_____

_____

 **Key Takeaways**

As you grow older and become a teenager, you'll likely encounter more instances of peer pressure and bullying. It's important to know how to identify bullying and distinguish it from harmless teasing. In dealing with bullying, standing up for yourself, getting help, staying positive, and understanding the powerful role of helping others can make a big difference.

Peer pressure isn't always a bad thing. Sometimes, it can motivate us to do better. However, negative peer pressure can lead us to behave in ways that aren't true to ourselves or that we're uncomfortable with. Just like with bullying, being assertive, seeking support, holding strong to your values, and making wise decisions can help you navigate the challenges of negative peer pressure.

NAVIGATING FRIENDSHIPS IN AN ONLINE WORLD

The digital world is a big part of our lives and plays an important role in friendships. While you may not make new friends online, your friendships will likely evolve through social media, messaging apps, and other online platforms as you get older. On the one hand, this instant connection is a great way to stay connected, but it can also create some challenges.

This chapter is all about navigating friendships in an online world. We'll uncover the delicate balance of digital communication, ensuring that an emoji isn't misconstrued or a missed chat doesn't lead to feelings of exclusion. By the end, you'll know how to create your own digital safety checklist, ensuring you can safely navigate digital friendships.

Life Before Technology

Before technology, friends kept in touch via letters, waiting weeks or even months to receive a response. Then came the telephone, which offered an instant way to communicate and share news. Fast forward to today, and technology has revolutionized how we communicate with each other. Emails, instant messaging, social media, and video calls allow us to communicate in ways that even 20 years ago seemed impossible.

Let's look at some of the benefits of this instant communication.

EXPLORING AND FINDING SHARED INTERESTS ONLINE

 ONLINE FRIENDS ARE JUST A CLICK AWAY

 EXPLORING THE WORLD WITH ONLINE FRIENDS

 STAYING IN TOUCH THROUGH ONLINE FRIENDSHIP

 PRACTICING COMMUNICATION SKILLS

 LEARNING TO NAVIGATE THE DIGITAL WORLD

ADVANTAGES

ONLINE FRIENDSHIPS

DISADVANTAGES

 POTENTIAL FOR MISUNDERSTANDINGS

 WHO'S BEHIND THE SCREEN

 KEEP YOUR SECRETS SECRET

 WATCH OUT FOR BULLIES

 NO YUCKY STUFF

 YOU'VE GOT A LIFE OUTSIDE THE SCREEN

BENEFITS OF ONLINE & DIGITAL INTERACTIONS

Online interactions play an essential role in enhancing and building friendships. Here's why:

1. **Instant Connection:** When life gets hectic, physically spending time with friends can be challenging. Digital platforms provide a solution; you send a message and get a response instantly. This can help maintain a friendship and sense of closeness.

2. **Staying in Touch:** Have you ever had a friend who moved away or switched schools? Beforehand, you might have lost touch with them. But today, you can keep in contact wherever they are.

3. **Sharing Experiences:** Online tools make it easier to share experiences. Whether seeing your friends on holiday, watching a movie together on Zoom, or playing games online. It allows you to share and build a deeper connection.

4. **Practicing Communication Skills**: Chatting online can offer an excellent platform to practice and improve communication skills. For some, sharing feelings and thoughts in writing is easier than talking.

5. **Learning to Navigate the Digital World**: Using online tools responsibly teaches you how to be a good digital citizen. You learn about online etiquette, respectful communication, and the necessity of online safety.

CHALLENGES OF ONLINE & DIGITAL INTERACTIONS

Maintaining friendships online brings fabulous benefits. However, there are challenges too, and here's what you should keep an eye on:

1. **Potential for Misunderstandings**: Without the benefit of tone or body language, it's easier to get the wrong idea about what someone means in an online chat. It's always good to ask for clarification if you're unsure.

2. **Digital Boldness:** Sometimes, people behave differently when hiding behind a screen. They become bolder and more aggressive, forgetting that their words and actions can negatively affect others.

3. **Who's Behind the Screen**: Sometimes, strangers pretend to be someone they're not when they are online. They might say they're your age when they're really not.

4. **Privacy Concerns**: Don't give out any personal info to people you don't know. Stuff like where you live, your full name, or where you go to school should stay private.

5. **Comparing Yourself to Others**: It's easy to feel like everyone else's life is perfect when scrolling through social media, especially when comparing yourself to influencers. But remember, no one's life is perfect; everyone has challenges.

6. **FOMO (Fear of Missing Out):** Seeing friends share their experiences and activities can lead to feelings of missing out. Particularly if you're not part of the fun.

7. **Digital Distractions:** If you're not careful, the constant ding of messages and notifications can distract you from enjoying real-life experiences and conversations.

8. **Online Bullying:** Sadly, some people use the Internet to be mean to others. If anyone makes you uncomfortable or hurts your feelings, let a trusted adult know immediately.

9. **Inappropriate Stuff**: Let an adult know if an online friend shows you something that feels wrong or icky, like violent images or inappropriate content. You should never be made to feel uncomfortable.

10. **Life Beyond the Screen**: While the digital world is fascinating, nothing can replace face-to-face conversations and real-life experiences. It's essential to find a balance. Remember, there's nothing like stepping away from the screen, breathing in fresh air, and enjoying the world around you!

Remember, the Internet can be a fun place to keep in touch friends and learn new things, but always be careful and let an adult know if something doesn't feel right. Your safety is super important!

Online Friends: The Same Rules Apply
Like friendships in the playground or classroom, online friendships are based on the same principles: respect, trust, empathy, and understanding. The setting

might differ — you're communicating through screens rather than face-to-face — but the core values that make a friendship strong remain the same.

The same rules of friendship apply, whether you're chatting online or hanging out together after school. Here's a quick recap of those rules:

1. **Respect**: Always treat others how you want to be treated. Be considerate and kind in your online interactions.

2. **Trust**: Good friends trust each other. When you are online, this means being honest with your friends, keeping promises, and not sharing private conversations or personal information with others.

3. **Empathy**: Understand and respect the feelings of your friends. If they're upset or having a tough day, show them you care and offer your support.

4. **Understanding**: Everyone is unique. Celebrate these differences and try to understand others' viewpoints, even if they don't align with yours.

While these rules of friendship apply universally, the online environment does have certain nuances. As you navigate digital interactions, here are some digital-specific netiquette to keep in mind:

1. **Always Be Polite**: Just because you're online doesn't mean you can forget your manners. Treat your friends the same way you would want to be treated.

2. **Understand That People Are Different**: We all come from different backgrounds and cultures, and sometimes have different opinions. It's okay to disagree with someone, but always do it respectfully.

3. **Be Clear in Your Communications**: Since there's no body language online, ensure your words are clear and not likely to be misunderstood.

4. Take a Breather: If someone says something that upsets you, taking a break from the conversation is okay. Take a few deep breaths, think about what you want to say, and return when you're ready.

Now that we've covered online friendship netiquette, let's focus on another crucial aspect — online safety.

Online Safety

Digital interactions with friends can be fun and rewarding! However, just like in the offline world, there are a few things to keep in mind to ensure that everything stays friendly and safe. Think of the Internet like a big city: There are many amazing places to visit and people to meet, but just as you wouldn't share all your secrets with every person you meet in a city, the same goes for online.

- **What to Share and Keep to Yourself**
  When chatting on social media or in open groups, talking about your favorite movies, music, or games is fine. However, be cautious about sharing personal details. Your full name, address, school name, or other identifying information should be kept private. It might be tempting to share more, but remember that not everyone is who they claim to be, and sadly, not everyone has good intentions. Keep your real identity safe and avoid oversharing.

- **Set Your Privacy Settings**
  Privacy settings can help keep your personal data safe. When you're online, adjust your settings to protect information like your location and contact details. Remember, privacy settings ensure only people you trust and know can see your information.

- **Trust Your Gut**
  If something feels off or makes you uncomfortable, trust your instincts. For example, suppose someone is pressuring you to share personal information or send inappropriate messages. In that case, it's okay to end the conversation or block them.

- **Screenshotting and Recording**

  It's essential to respect privacy. Always ask your friends before taking a screenshot or recording a chat. If someone takes one without your permission, it's okay to tell them it's not right and to let a trusted adult know.

- **Handling Bullying or Harassment**

  Unfortunately, cyberbullying is a real issue. Recognize the signs of bullying, such as repeated aggressive messages, spreading rumors, or making threats. Also, remember that it's not your fault if it happens. Report any bullying or harassment to the platform and let a trusted adult know. Remember, no one has the right to make you feel bad or unsafe.

- **Strangers Online**

  Be cautious of friend requests or messages from strangers. While making new friends can be fun, online friendships should be people you already know. Not everyone is who they say they are. However, nice people may seem online; if you don't know them, they are still strangers. Speak to a trusted adult if you're unsure or uneasy about anyone or anything.

- **External Links and Downloads**

  Be careful when clicking on unfamiliar links or downloading files from unknown sources. They could contain viruses or other harmful materials.

- **Create Strong Passwords**

  Protecting your online accounts starts with strong passwords. Use a mix of letters, numbers, and symbols, and avoid using easily guessable information, like your name or birthday. Remember, your password is the first line of defense against someone getting access to your accounts.

Now that you've learned about digital interactions and staying safe online, it's time to put your knowledge to the test. The following case study is about Emma, a young girl who felt down after seeing her friends' seemingly perfect lives on social media. After reading her story, there are some questions for you to answer. Once you've done that, it's time to create a digital safety checklist to help you stay safe online.

Emma

Emma really enjoyed seeing her friends' adventures and hobbies, on social media, especially during holiday breaks from school. But, when she was at home during the holidays, she started to feel sad. It seemed like everyone was leading fun, exciting and happy lives, while she was just at home.

She felt left out and unhappy, wondering why her life wasn't as fun and exciting. She felt worse whenever she saw someone else's happy photos or read about their amazing adventures.

Emma's mom noticed she was upset and talked to her about it. She explained that people often only share their best moments online, creating a "highlight reel." This isn't a complete picture of their lives; everyone has regular days and faces challenges; they just don't usually post those.

After talking with her mom, Emma felt much better. She learned to focus more on enjoying her own experiences rather than comparing her life to the seemingly "perfect" ones she saw online. She understood that everyone has ups and downs, even if they don't share them.

Answer the following questions about Emma's story.

1. Why did Emma feel sad during her holidays?

_____

_____

_____

2. What did Emma's mom explain to her about people's online posts?

_____

_____

_____

3. Why is it important to enjoy your experiences instead of comparing yourself to others' online posts?

_____

_____

_____

Activity: Digital Safety Checklist

Understanding online safety is essential, but putting it into practice is where the real learning begins! In this activity, you will use the knowledge you learned in this chapter to create your digital safety checklist.

Once you've filled this out, take a moment to discuss it with a trusted adult. They might offer some additional insights. Remember, this checklist is to help protect you against online troubles. Keep it handy and stay safe!

MY DIGITAL SAFETY CHECKLIST

Once you've filled this out, take a moment to discuss it with a trusted adult. They might offer some additional insights. Remember, this checklist is to help protect you against online troubles. Keep it handy and stay safe!

WHAT'S A DIGITAL SAFETY CHECKLIST?
It's a personalized guide that helps you make smart choices online. It'll be your go-to handbook, reminding you of safe practices while you are browsing the web, playing games, or chatting with

☐ 1. PERSONAL DATA PROTECTION
List down the personal details you believe should never be shared online:

_____
_____
_____

☐ 2. PASSWORD SECURITY
Describe how you'll ensure your passwords are difficult to guess, & how often to change them:

_____
_____
_____

☐ 3. CLICKING CAUTIOUSLY
When faced with an unfamiliar link, what steps will you take before clicking?

_____
_____
_____

☐ 4. COMMUNICATION PROTOCOL
Write down your golden rules about online conversations, including who you will talk to and what things should never be discussed.

_____
_____
_____

☐ 5. BALANCING ONLINE AND OFFLINE LIFE
How will you ensure a healthy balance between online and offline time? What activities can you do that don't involve screens?

_____
_____
_____

☐ 6. SCAM AWARENESS
Write down a few warning signs that might indicate a scam:

_____
_____
_____

 ## Key Takeaways

The digital world plays an important role in maintaining our connections and friendships. Social media and messaging apps allow us to keep in touch with friends, regardless of distance. However, interacting online requires extra caution and responsibility. It's vital not to share personal information publicly and to remember the same rules of friendship of trust and respect apply. Be polite, stay safe, and remember not to believe everything you see online.

FRIENDSHIPS AND CHANGES IN PUBERTY

Puberty is a significant milestone in a young girl's life, marking the transition from childhood to adulthood. It's a time of physical, emotional, and social changes, which can impact your friendships. As you navigate this new stage of your life, it's essential to understand what's happening to your body and emotions, and how these changes can affect your relationships with others.

In this chapter, we will explore the impact of puberty on friendships. You will learn how to navigate the changes and challenges that puberty may bring to your friendships. Ready? Let's get started.

Understanding Puberty

Puberty is a period of rapid growth and development, signaling the shift from childhood to young adulthood. Your body will undergo many changes, such as growing taller, starting your period, and changing shape. But puberty isn't just about physical transformation. Your emotions and feelings will also evolve during this time.

The changes you undergo during puberty can happen all at once, or slowly over time. Remember that everyone's journey through puberty is unique. You might not experience things the same way your friends do, and that's okay. These changes might make you think and feel differently about many things, and that's a normal part of growing up.

As you progress through puberty, you may notice your interests starting to change. Perhaps you used to love playing with dolls, but now you're more drawn to painting or drumming. Maybe you still enjoy music, but your taste has shifted from pop to rock. All these changes are a natural part of growing up.

CHANGING EMOTIONS

Your emotions might start changing, too. You may feel differently about relationships, goals, and even your sense of self. As you navigate these new emotions, it's essential to remember that it's okay to feel a wide range of emotions. It's part of growing up, and exploring these emotions helps shape your experiences and understanding of the world around you.

SHIFTING FRIENDSHIPS

These changes may also affect your friendships. You might find yourself drifting away from some old friends as your interests diverge or your perspectives change. That's okay. As some friendships fade, you may find new friends who share your evolving hobbies or views. In Chapter 6, we discussed how friendships can end, and that's a normal part of life. If you find yourself drifting away from some friends, remember that it's okay to let go. You can still be friendly, even if you're not as close as you once were. Managing your emotions during this time is crucial, as strong feelings can sometimes lead to disagreements.

Since puberty plays such a big role in shaping friendships, let's take a closer look at how it may impact friendships in both positive and sometimes negative ways, and what you can do to help yourself at this time.

The Impact of Puberty on Friendships

CHANGING AT DIFFERENT PACES

During puberty, your friendships will likely evolve along with the many changes you're experiencing. It's essential to remember that not everyone goes through puberty at the same pace. You and your friends may be at different stages of your puberty journeys, leading to varied interests, experiences, and emotions. It's completely natural for these differences to emerge as you grow up.

NAVIGATING CRUSHES AND FRIENDSHIPS

The hormonal changes during puberty often bring in new romantic feelings or crushes. These emotions can sometimes introduce tension, especially if two friends are attracted to the same person. In addition, dedicating more time and attention to a new crush could make your friends feel left out. While these feelings are a regular part of puberty, it's essential to balance them to maintain your existing friendships.

The Role of Self-Image in Friendships

When you enter puberty, all the physical changes you experience may make you more self-aware, or even self-conscious. This might make you sensitive to comments from your friends, or you may find that you compare yourself with your friends more often, thinking that they are prettier or smarter than you. Although it's natural to feel this way, it's crucial to remember that everyone is unique and beautiful in their own way. These feelings and insecurities can strain your relationships, so it's important to communicate with your friends and seek support if needed.

The Effects of Puberty on Friendships

Beyond the influence of self-consciousness and romantic interests, puberty can also shape your friendships in other ways. It's worth remembering that every girl's journey through puberty is different. As a result, the effects of puberty on your friendships will be unique to your situation. These changes can strengthen or weaken your friendships.

Some Friendships Will Grow Stronger

Shared experiences during puberty, such as navigating the same challenges and emotions, can bring you closer together with some friends. These mutual experiences form a solid foundation, often making your friendships even stronger than before.

Some Friendships Will Fade

On the other hand, puberty may also lead to some friendships fading away. If you find that you and a friend don't share the same interests anymore, or if you argue a lot, it might be time to reevaluate the friendship. It's essential to recognize that some friendships might not survive the changes experienced during puberty, and that's okay.

New Friendships Will Bloom

As your interests and views change during puberty, you'll probably meet new people who share these interests and ideas. This is a great chance to make new friends. Many of these new friends will help shape who you become as a teenager and young adult, and some of them might even be your friends for the rest of your life.

Managing Changes in Friendships During Puberty

Puberty can bring about changes in your friendships. You might not always see these changes as they happen, but one day, you may realize that a friendship has changed, for better or worse. It's important to remember that your friends are also experiencing puberty and will be dealing with their own emotions and feelings during this time.

Even though everyone's experience of puberty is unique, we all go through it, and many of the changes and feelings are common. Keeping this in mind can help you relate better to your friends as you all navigate the challenges of puberty. Here are four strategies to help you manage changes in your friendships during puberty:

1. Open Communication

Talk openly with your friends about your feelings and thoughts. It can be hard to share your emotions, but it's key to building trust and understanding in your friendships. By opening up, you make it easier for your friends to share their feelings with you, too. Remember, they may be experiencing similar emotions and will appreciate having someone to talk to.

2. Understanding

Try to be more understanding when your friends' behavior, interests, or opinions change. They're going through puberty, too, and may have mood swings, lowered self-esteem, or conflicting emotions that affect their actions. Keep in mind that you may also have times when you struggle with similar feelings. Being understanding and giving each other the space to grow is vital for maintaining healthy friendships during puberty.

3. Patience

Being patient with your friends is crucial, especially when you have differing opinions. It's natural to feel confused or uncertain during puberty, as the physical and emotional changes can be overwhelming. You may also become more sensitive to criticism. Being patient makes it easier for your friends to feel understood and supported. In return, they'll likely extend the same patience to you.

4. Empathy

Empathy is the ability to understand and share someone else's feelings, even if they're not your own. Show empathy When your friends feel emotional, confused, or frustrated. While you may not share their feelings, you can understand what it's like to experience strong emotions for no apparent reason. Demonstrating empathy helps your friends feel supported and valued, even if your interests change or your friendship wanes.

Understanding how puberty affects friendships is essential for navigating this period of change. The following case study and questions will help you see the impact of puberty on friendships in real life. You can also complete the activity, where you'll write about your thoughts and emotions to process and embrace the changes you're experiencing during puberty. Best of luck!

Kayla and Madison

Kayla and Madison have been best friends since kindergarten. They've always been close, sharing everything from secrets to favorite games. But when they started middle school, things began to change. Madison started growing taller, getting pimples, and even needing a bra. On the other hand, Kayla didn't notice any big changes in her body.

Madison's other friends, who were also going through these changes, started forming their own group. They often talked about their new experiences, making Kayla feel left out and a little lost. She wasn't part of these new conversations and felt like she didn't belong anymore.

The distance between Kayla and Madison kept growing, and both of them felt sad about it. Finally, Kayla decided to talk to Madison about feeling left out.

During their chat, Madison reassured Kayla that their friendship meant the world to her, and it didn't matter who was taller or had more pimples. They promised to support each other through all the weird and wonderful changes that come with growing up.

Answer the following questions about Kayla and Madison's friendship.

1. How did Kayla and Madison handle the changes in their friendship when they started going through puberty at different times?

   _____

   _____

   _____

2. Why is it important to be understanding when your friends go through changes, even if you're not experiencing them yet?

   _____

   _____

   _____

3. What are some ways you can show support for a friend who feels left out because they're experiencing puberty at a different pace?

   _____

   _____

   _____

Activity: Journaling About Changes

As we have already explored, puberty is a time of changes, and sometimes it can feel overwhelming, especially with everything that's going on. Keeping a journal where you can write about your feelings can be a helpful way to express these emotions and make sense of them.

You don't always have to share your thoughts and feelings with others if you're not ready, or if you'd rather keep them private. Writing them down can give you the chance to explore your emotions without having to share them, and that's perfectly okay. In fact, it can help you process and better understand what you're going through, giving you a mature perspective on your feelings and experiences.

Writing might not be everyone's preferred way to process things, but it's definitely worth giving it a try. Journaling can give you a sense of control and a space to reflect on your thoughts and feelings. What will your journal entry be today?

Here are some simple prompts to help you get started:

1. Changes I've noticed in my interests lately...

2. How my friendships have evolved during puberty...

3. Emotions that were strong for me today...

4. My thoughts on the physical changes I'm going through...

5. Goals I want to set for myself...

6. Challenges I faced today and how I felt about them...

7. The best moment of my day was...

8. Three things I'm thankful for today...

9. What I hope for in the coming weeks...

DAILY JOURNAL
Date:

M T W T F S S

Key Takeaways

Puberty has a big impact on your friendships. Sometimes, the changes you go through during puberty, both physical and emotional, can either strengthen your friendships or cause them to fade away. As your interests change, you might also find yourself making new friends who share your new interests. Remember, everyone's experience of puberty is unique. By showing empathy, understanding, communicating openly, and being patient with your friends, you'll be able to support and care for them as they navigate their own puberty journeys.

10

FOSTERING KINDNESS AND RESPECT IN FRIENDSHIPS

Kindness and respect are essential for healthy relationships, whether with family, friends, or romantic partners.

In this chapter, we'll explore how to cultivate these qualities in your friendships. We'll define kindness and respect, explain their importance in lasting friendships, and offer practical tips on how to practice them.

We'll also take a closer look at a real-life example of a friendship where kindness and respect are front and center. This case study will help you understand how these qualities play out in day-to-day life and make friendships stronger.

Understanding Kindness and Respect

Kindness involves showing genuine care and helping others, regardless of their background or what they can offer in return. In friendships, kindness means being there for your friends, celebrating their achievements, and listening with empathy. Treating friends as equals who are deserving of love and respect is key.

Respect is about valuing others for who they are, even if you don't always agree with their opinions or values. Respecting friends means honoring their feelings and choices, creating a trust-based foundation in your friendship. This trust helps you handle disagreements constructively.

Being kind and respectful contributes to strong friendships and sets the standard for how you want to be treated. "Treat others as you want to be treated" remains a timeless guideline. Kindness and respect also benefit society, fostering community, understanding, and acceptance.

The Importance of Kindness and Respect in Friendships

As you go through puberty, face peer pressure, and experience shifts in interests, it's crucial to treat your friends with kindness and respect.

Let's explore why these qualities are essential in teenage friendships and beyond.

- **Resolving Conflict**: In your teenage years, conflicts can arise more often due to the pressure to fit in and the formation of strong opinions. Treating your friends with kindness and respect makes you more likely to approach disagreements with empathy, valuing friendship over minor disputes.

- **Improving Communication**: Respect involves listening, while kindness requires speaking with patience. Practicing these qualities in your friendships creates a comfortable environment for open conversations, fostering trust and facilitating honest communication.

- **Strengthening Bonds**: Kindness and respect create a trusting atmosphere where your friends feel comfortable sharing their lives with you. When you show respect and kindness, your friends are more likely to confide in you and seek your support in difficult times, which deepens your friendship.

THE IMPORTANCE OF MUTUAL RESPECT

Nurturing strong friendships requires mutual kindness and respect. Showing your friends respect and kindness is crucial, but you deserve the same in return.

Mutual respect means valuing each other's thoughts and feelings, even when you disagree. Differences can introduce new perspectives and enrich a friendship, provided both friends treat each other's opinions with respect and understanding. By fostering mutual respect and kindness, you create a safe space for open sharing and deeper connections.

Promoting Kindness and Respect

Being kind and respectful to your friends sounds pretty straightforward, but it can sometimes be challenging to know exactly how to put it into action. Here are four ways you can show kindness and respect in your friendships.

1. Expressing Gratitude

Show your friends that you value and appreciate them by expressing gratitude. Say thank you for their support, be there for them when they need a helping hand, and treat them in a way that reflects your appreciation for their friendship.

2. Offering Help

Being there for your friends when they need help, no matter how small the task, is a clear sign of kindness. If your friend is moving to a new place, offer to help pack their belongings or transport boxes. Being supportive and caring during their times of need strengthens your friendship and showcases your genuine concern.

3. Open Communication

Open and honest communication is vital in any friendship. Whether you're giving a compliment or addressing an issue, clear communication promotes mutual respect, kindness, and trust. Just as your friends should feel comfortable discussing things with you, you should also feel comfortable addressing your concerns. Friendship doesn't mean you'll always agree, but you should be able to communicate your disagreements with respect and care.

4. Respecting Personal Boundaries

Recognizing and respecting your friends' boundaries is key to showing kindness and respect. If your friend has asked for space or expressed discomfort with a particular topic, honor their wishes without pressuring them. Similarly, a respectful friend will respect your boundaries without pressuring you to do something you're uncomfortable with.

When you understand and practice mutual respect and kindness, you can apply these principles in real-life situations. Below, you'll find a case study about two individuals who treated each other with kindness and respect. You will also find a kindness and respect challenge that you and your friends can participate in to further cultivate these essential qualities in your relationships.

Lily and Sam

Lily and Sam were childhood friends who lived in the same neighborhood. They played together every day and shared everything. However, as they entered high school, they started to drift apart due to their different interests and groups of friends.

During this time, Sam's parents divorced, and she struggled to cope with the changes in her life. She felt lonely and isolated. Lily noticed the change and decided to reach out.

Lily made a point of sitting with Sam at lunch, listening to her concerns, and offering support. She also invited her to join her group of friends. Her friends welcomed Sam with open arms.

Sam appreciated Lily's gesture and started to feel less alone. Over time, their friendship was rekindled, and Sam learned the importance of being there for someone when they needed it the most. As they moved through high school, they remained close friends, always valuing their shared history and the kindness they had shown to each other.

Answer the following questions about Lily and Sam's friendship.

1. How did Lily demonstrate kindness and respect towards Sam?

_____

_____

_____

2. Why was Lily's support so crucial for Sam during her parents' divorce?

_____

_____

_____

3. How did Lily's actions impact their friendship and Sam's well-being?

_____

_____

_____

4. In what ways can you show kindness and respect to friends who may be going through a tough time, even if you've drifted apart?

_____

_____

_____

Activity: Kindness and Respect Challenge

This activity aims to help you improve your friendships by intentionally practicing kindness and showing respect towards your friends. You might be surprised by the positive impact it can have!

Decide on a Time Frame
Choose a specific period for your challenge, such as two weeks or a month. The grid provided has space for 14 days, but you can adjust it according to your chosen time frame.

Perform Acts of Kindness
Each day, carry out at least one act of kindness towards a friend. It could be something small, like helping them with a task or offering a compliment, or something bigger, like supporting them through a challenging time.

Display Respect
In addition to your act of kindness, make a conscious effort to display respect in your interactions with friends each day. This could include listening actively, acknowledging their feelings, or respecting their boundaries.

Record Your Actions
Use the grid template provided to track your acts of kindness and displays of respect. In the "Act of Kindness" and "Display of Respect" columns, jot down your specific actions for each day.

Reflect on Your Experiences
In the "Observations and Notes" column, write down any notable experiences, reactions from your friends, or personal reflections related to your actions. Consider how these actions may have influenced your friendships.

Evaluate Your Challenge
At the end of your chosen time frame, review your grid and reflect on the overall impact of your actions on your friendships and your personal growth. Did you notice any positive changes in your relationships? What did you learn about the importance of kindness and respect?

Remember, this challenge is an opportunity for self-reflection and growth in your friendships. Be genuine in your actions and enjoy positively impacting your relationships through kindness and respect.

CHALLENGE LOG

	ACT OF KINDNESS	DISPLAY OF RESPECT	OBSERVATIONS & NOTES
DAY ___			
DAY ___			
DAY ___			
DAY ___			
DAY ___			
DAY ___			
DAY ___			

 **Key Takeaways**

Kindness and respect are essential ingredients in any successful friendship. These qualities not only help resolve conflicts and improve communication, but also strengthen the bond between friends. You can cultivate kindness and respect in your friendships by expressing thanks to your friends, helping them, and openly communicating with them. Choosing kindness and respect can transform your relationships and create the foundations of fulfilling, lifelong friendships.

CONCLUSION

Congratulations on finishing this book! You've embarked on a fantastic journey into the world of friendships, and now you're armed with all the knowledge you need to be the best friend you can be. Real friendships are built on respect, trust, empathy, and kindness. Each chapter has given you the tools to navigate friendships in your teenage years and beyond, whether they're in person or online.

You now know how to approach new people, manage different personalities within your group of friends, and overcome challenges like jealousy and peer pressure. You've even learned how to cope with the loss of a friend and how to handle the changes that come with growing up.

This is just the beginning! Your challenge now is to put all this knowledge into action in your own life. As you do, you'll become a better friend, attract better friends, and keep the good friends you already have. So go out there, embrace the lessons you've learned, and build those strong, positive, happy friendships.

You've got this!

A TWEEN GIRL'S GUIDE TO FEELINGS & EMOTIONS

Mastering Self-Love and Building Self-Esteem

The Essential Emotional Wellness Handbook for Young Girls

Abby Swift

INTRODUCTION

"When dealing with people, remember you are not dealing with creatures of logic, but with creatures of emotion."
— **Dale Carnegie**

Being a tween is anything but simple. With all the emotional rollercoasters, physical changes, and growth happening during puberty, it's a time full of challenges. One of the most crucial skills you can develop during this time is mastering your emotions. However, despite its importance, emotional development often doesn't get enough attention.

That's where "A Tween Girl's Guide to Feelings & Emotions" comes in. This book aims to help you understand your emotions better and boost your emotional intelligence. These skills are key to making your teen years smoother, helping you tackle the tough emotions and situations you might face.

Tweens and teens have a lot on their plates, from school and family to social lives and activities. With so much going on, learning about emotions might not seem like a priority. However, experts in education and psychology stress that social-emotional skills are incredibly important — sometimes even more so than academic skills. Emotionally intelligent kids tend to do better in school, have better relationships, and are more empathetic.[1]

If you haven't focused much on developing these skills yet, don't worry — it's never too late to start. "A Tween Girl's Guide to Feelings & Emotions" is designed to be your roadmap through this complex world of feelings. It's packed with discussions, exercises, and activities that not only help you understand your emotions, but also provide you with the tools you need to grow emotionally.

One key component of emotional development is opening yourself up to discussion. Discussions with family, peers, and people you trust, as well as having honest conversations with yourself, are essential for emotional growth. A big part of emotional development also involves learning how to navigate difficult conversations and uncomfortable situations in a healthy way.

"A Tween Girl's Guide to Feelings & Emotions" is an interactive book. Throughout the book, you'll find exercises, activities, and reflections to use and interact with. When you see the worksheet symbol, it's time to do the corresponding worksheets. Simply scan the QR code below to access these worksheets. Try to complete these activities, as they will help you develop a deeper understanding of yourself and your emotions, as well as teach you the tools needed to process your emotions and interact with others.

Top Tip

Take your time with this book and enjoy the process of learning more about yourself and your emotional intelligence. The skills you learn from this guide will serve you your entire life and can be applied repeatedly in numerous situations. It can feel uncomfortable to sit with your emotions and frightening to reflect on strong feelings, but only by doing so can you really develop a relationship with your emotions and learn how to process and control them healthily.

Scan this QR code to receive the free accompanying worksheets, which correspond to the activities in the book.

UNLOCKING EMOTIONAL INTELLIGENCE

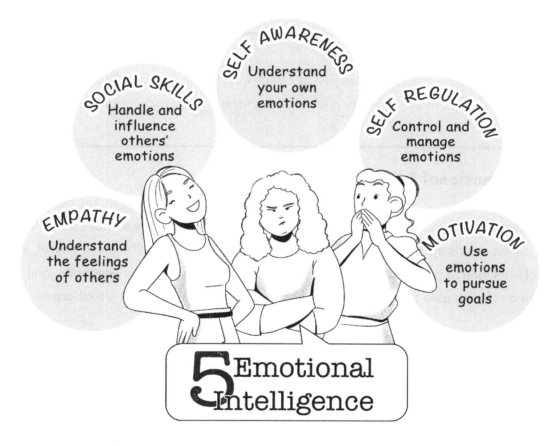

SELF AWARENESS
Understand your own emotions

SOCIAL SKILLS
Handle and influence others' emotions

SELF REGULATION
Control and manage emotions

EMPATHY
Understand the feelings of others

MOTIVATION
Use emotions to pursue goals

5 Emotional Intelligence

Have you ever wondered why one day something makes you extremely mad or frustrated, but another day the same thing doesn't seem to bother you? Your reactions to events and situations aren't random; they're controlled by your emotional intelligence, or EI for short. Think of your EI as a compass guiding you through your day. Like a captain sailing a boat, you are the leader of your life.

Like a compass, your emotions provide positive and negative signals telling you how to feel and which way to go. However, if you misread your emotional compass, you may steer yourself into a storm!

As captain, it is essential to understand your emotions and develop a strong EI so you can read your compass successfully and navigate each day. If your compass is broken and you don't know how to read it, you'll struggle to keep your boat on course!

 DID YOU KNOW?

Your emotional intelligence directly relates to your ability to handle stress, manage life changes, and develop and maintain healthy relationships with others.

What Is Emotional Intelligence?

You possess many types of intelligence. You may be good at math, excel at sports, be musically talented, or have strong writing skills. These are all examples of different types of intelligence. Emotional intelligence is your ability to interact with others, handle your emotions, and respond to them. It means being able to respond appropriately to others in different situations.

For example, imagine you're working on a group project at school and there's a disagreement. Strong EI allows you to recognize your frustration without letting it take over, communicate your thoughts calmly, and listen to your classmates' ideas.

Now, imagine a different scenario. You find out about a party that everyone seems to be invited to — except you. EI helps you manage disappointment, embarrassment, sadness, and anger.

Developing emotional intelligence also means learning how to respond correctly to challenging situations. For instance, if you fail a test after studying hard, emotional intelligence helps you understand that yelling at the teacher isn't the right approach, even if you believe the test was unfairly difficult. Instead, it guides you to process your feelings and then calmly discuss the test with your teacher.

EI plays a crucial role in many aspects of life, including school, friendships, family, and social interactions. Without well-developed EI, you might struggle to react appropriately in social and emotional situations. While some people may naturally have a high level of emotional intelligence, others need to work to develop it. However, everyone can improve their EI by learning and practicing specific skills. Remember, like any skill, some days it will be easier to apply your EI than others, as it can be affected by your overall well-being and environment.

Your emotional intelligence works like a gas tank — some days, it is full, and others, it needs fuel and maintenance.

Have you ever felt "hangry?" Hangry means angry because you're hungry. It is a perfect example of your tank needing fuel! If you're hungry, your blood sugar is low, making you cranky, irritable, and more likely to handle situations poorly.

The opposite happens when your tank is full. If you've slept well, scored an A on a test, or made the soccer team, your emotional tank is full and you can handle stressful situations better. Self-care is another way to keep your emotional tank full. Hanging out with friends, enjoying your favorite hobbies, and spending time with loved ones are all great ways to keep your EI topped up.

Emotional Intelligence consists of five key components:

- **Empathy:** This allows you to understand why a friend is upset over something that didn't directly affect you.

- **Social Skills:** These are crucial for interacting appropriately with others, such as not shouting in class or cutting off your friends mid-conversation.

- **Self-Awareness:** This helps you recognize your own feelings and reactions, such as why you might bounce your knee when you are anxious or feel queasy before a big event.

- **Self-Regulation:** This is about managing intense emotions, ensuring you don't lash out physically or burst into tears under stress.

- **Motivation:** This fuels your ambition to achieve goals, such as making the sports team or landing the solo in the spring concert.

Understanding how all five components work together and building upon your strengths is how you develop strong emotional intelligence. Now that you know the basics of EI and its importance, let's dive into each of the five components, starting with empathy.

"When awareness is brought to an emotion, power is brought to your life."
— Tara Meyer Robson

Empathy

Empathy is the ability to understand and share the feelings of others. Empathy is a critical human skill because it allows you to show compassion to others. By employing empathy, you can temporarily set your needs and wants aside and look at a situation from someone else's point of view. For example, imagine you and your best friend tried out for the school play. You are cast in the lead, and your friend receives a small part. You feel excited, but your friend may be sad or disappointed. Empathy allows you to set aside your emotions temporarily and see things from your friend's point of view.

Social Skills

Social skills are your ability to interact with other people. Social skills include [2]:

- Listening skills
- Conversation skills
- Manners

- Self-control
- Cooperation
- Assertion

A solid grasp of what's appropriate and when and how to interact with others is essential to developing EI. Your EI helps you function at school and in social situations. For example, you understand that being responsible means arriving to class on time or offering support to someone who's being teased.

Self-Awareness

Self-awareness is perceiving who you are as a person. It is about truly understanding yourself as an individual, including your personality, actions, values, beliefs, emotions, and thoughts.[3]

You have public and private self-awareness. Your public self-awareness controls how you behave in most social situations.

Public self-awareness is how you behave at:

· School
· Church
· Social situations
· Playing sports or performing

Private self-awareness is something only you experience. Examples of private self-awareness include:

· Looking in the mirror
· Feeling nervous before singing a solo
· Remembering you forgot to study for a test
· Feeling butterflies in your stomach when you see your crush

Take a moment to think about the different emotions you've felt this week and what caused them. Did you feel excitement because your favorite team won? Or perhaps you felt disappointed when your parents said you couldn't attend a party this weekend? Reflecting on these emotions is self-awareness.

Self-Regulation

Self-regulation is the mind's ability to control thoughts, functions, mental states, and inner processes. It means controlling our feelings and thoughts even when we don't want to!

Toddlers have tantrums because they lack self-regulation skills. Teens and tweens like you have much better self-regulation skills than little kids. You know not to throw your dinner on the floor if you don't like it, and you won't cry over getting the blue cup instead of the green one.

Self-regulation is key to reacting appropriately, especially in tense situations. It helps us avoid responses that we might regret later.

MOTIVATION

Motivation comprises three things:

- **Activation:** The decision to start taking action or initiate a behavior.

- **Persistence:** The continued effort to achieve a goal and overcome obstacles.

- **Intensity:** The concentration and focus that goes into pursuing a goal.

Motivation is *why* you choose to do something. There are two types of motivation: intrinsic and extrinsic.

- **Intrinsic motivation** is personal motivation from within yourself — for example, reading a book for enjoyment or going for a walk to relax.

- **Extrinsic motivation** comes from an outside source. You usually receive an award of money, praise, awards, or social recognition. Examples of extrinsic motivation are studying for a test to get a good grade or doing chores to earn your allowance.

MOTIVATION

Motivation comprises three things:

- **Activation:** The decision to start taking action or initiate a behavior.

- **Persistence:** The continued effort to achieve a goal and overcome obstacles.

- **Intensity:** The concentration and focus that goes into pursuing a goal.

Motivation is *why* you choose to do something. There are two types of motivation: intrinsic and extrinsic.

- **Intrinsic motivation** is personal motivation from within yourself — for example, reading a book for enjoyment or going for a walk to relax.

- **Extrinsic motivation** comes from an outside source. You usually receive an award of money, praise, awards, or social recognition. Examples of extrinsic motivation are studying for a test to get a good grade or doing chores to earn your allowance.

The Importance of Emotional Intelligence

EI is an essential skill to learn. Like all skills, some people are better at it than others.

Do you know anyone on the autism spectrum or who has ADHD? People with autism or ADHD tend to have lower levels of EI or emotional quotient (EQ).[4] This means they don't always know how to respond in social situations. For example, they may say inappropriate things, fail to make eye contact, or interrupt and talk out of turn.

However, having a lower EQ doesn't equate to lower intelligence. Many neurodivergent individuals with challenges in EI shine in other areas, like math, science, music, or art.

Famous Neurodivergent People[5,6]

- Albert Einstein (scientist)

- Emma Watson (actor)

- Nikola Tesla (inventor/scientist)

- Bobby Fischer (chess master)

- Bill Gates (business owner/inventor)

- Andy Warhol (artist)

- Justin Timberlake (musician)

- Pablo Picasso (artist)

- Simone Biles (gymnast)

- Emily Dickinson (poet)

The great news is that even if you struggle with EI, there are ways you can improve it! Like developing any skill, improving your EI takes time. Much like learning to play a musical instrument, you won't perform a flawless solo right away. It takes time, effort, and hard work.

EI is uniquely human. As far as we know, animals do not possess it. It is one of the earliest skills humans begin developing, alongside language. It is such a crucial skill that preschool and kindergarten teachers say that a child learning social-emotional skills is more important than mastering the basics like the alphabet or counting.

Workplaces are also starting to recognize the importance of emotional competence. While you're still young, there's no better time to develop the EI skills that future employers are looking for in young hires.

TWEEN GIRLS AND EMOTIONAL DEVELOPMENT

During your tween years, both your body and mind undergo significant changes. You might find yourself riding a rollercoaster of emotions, feeling one way one moment and completely different the next. This whirlwind of feelings is perfectly normal, even though it can sometimes be frustrating. Remember, it's all part of growing up.

As a tween, your mind and body are still developing. This journey of change will continue over the next few years. In fact, science tells us that our brains continue to develop into our 20s![7] Even at 18, when you're considered an adult, your brain is still in its adolescent stage of growth.

For girls, physical changes tend to occur earlier than for boys (though the emotional changes you experience may be quite similar). It's natural to have lots of questions about these changes, and you might notice their impact on your self-esteem or confidence levels. It's crucial to understand that all these shifts are normal, driven by the hormones active in your body during this time.

As you enter puberty, your body gets flooded with hormones, which triggers the many changes your body undergoes.

This is important to understand, because much of what you're experiencing is part of a gradual process influenced by factors beyond your control. Remember, mastering your emotions doesn't happen overnight. Many adults are still working on their emotional skills. The good news is that, as a tween or teen, you're already ahead of where you were as a younger child when it comes to managing your emotions.

To navigate your ever-changing emotions, consider practices like meditation, yoga, deep breathing exercises, and journaling. Physical activities such as walking or dancing, spending quality time with friends, and engaging in your favorite hobbies or activities can also be incredibly beneficial.

Sometimes, just recognizing that your emotions are influenced by your body's changes and hormonal shifts can help you pause, reflect, and regain your calm.

Teen Emotional Skills

- Empathy: Understanding the feelings of others.

- Recognizing and naming different emotions: Identifying your and others' feelings and emotions.

- Impulse control: Being able to pause, think, and control your reactions.

- Maintaining friendships: Building strong friendship bonds.

- Understanding right from wrong: Developing a clear understanding of what is and is not acceptable.

- Patience: Developing the ability to wait, including coping with the frustration of delays.

- Problem-solving: Resolving issues thoughtfully.

As your hormones fluctuate and change, you may also begin experiencing some less pleasant emotions and changes [8]:

- Mood swings

- Concern about your appearance or clothes

- Short temper with siblings and parents

- Lack of confidence in physical appearance or abilities

- Sadness or even depression

- Peer pressure

- Confusion and uncertainty

Emotional Intelligence Basics [9]

- Everyone has feelings: We all have emotions and a built-in level of EI.

- Improves relationships: Developing your EI improves your relationships with others.

- Builds confidence: Strong social-emotional skills give you self-confidence.

- Social skills can be learned.

- Social rules vary: What's acceptable changes based on the situation.

- Being shy is fine: It's okay to be shy, but you can't avoid all social situations.

- Builds communication skills: Strong social-emotional skills equal strong communication skills.

- Helps you in everything: Your social-emotional health affects your school performance, mood, and physical health.

Discovering Your Strengths

Before you start working on understanding and managing your emotions, it's really important to figure out what you're good at. Think about the things you enjoy and excel in. Are you a fantastic singer, or can you play the piano beautifully? Maybe you're a whiz in subjects like science or history, or perhaps you have a talent for painting or helping others with patience and kindness. Recognizing these strengths does more than just make you feel good about yourself — it lays a solid foundation. When you know what you're good at and feel confident about it, you're in a much better position to tackle the challenge of improving how you handle your feelings and emotions.

 ## Discovering Your Strengths Worksheet

Take a moment to write down your strengths. These could be skills like playing soccer or writing, or traits that make up your personality, such as being funny, helpful, or compassionate. List them all out, whatever they may be.

Next, make a separate list of everything you like about yourself. Focus on your abilities, strengths, and achievements, rather than how you look. Some items might overlap with your strengths, and some might be different — and that's perfectly fine.

Once you have both lists, take a good look at them and identify anything that might relate to your EI. Traits like patience, kindness, politeness, problem-solving skills, effective communication, making friends easily, and the ability to learn new skills all contribute to EI.

Now that you have a better idea of your strengths, you can use them to enhance your emotional intelligence. Likewise, you'll better understand your weaknesses, and can start turning them into strengths, boosting your EI.

Fostering Personal Growth

To grow and learn, we often have to step outside our comfort zone and do something uncomfortable or even a little scary. Our comfort zone is like a safety net — it's the place we feel most secure.

Perhaps you're used to playing goalkeeper, and your soccer coach moves you to play midfield for one game. Suddenly, you're in a new, unfamiliar position, unsure of what's expected of you.

Or maybe you're scared of snakes, but you visit the zoo and attend a demonstration where you can pet a snake. Do you step outside your comfort zone or hide at the back of the room? Often, it's much easier to try things that make us uncomfortable in a safe and secure environment.

Trying new things or stepping outside your comfort zone might feel uncomfortable. It is often hardest when you're worried you'll fail, be embarrassed, or get hurt.

You might fear embarrassing yourself, not being good at something, or failing. There are so many worries!

You'll only know if you try. Success, learning, and growth come from taking that leap. Think of something you're good at, like a sport, drawing, or cooking. Now, try to remember what it was like the first, second, or even fifth time you tried it. You probably weren't an instant expert! The reason you weren't good is that it was a new skill. But with practice and hard work, what was new and challenging became easier, more enjoyable, and something you're now good at.

Learning EI is the same. Only now, with the strengths you've already identified, you have a foundation to build upon to expand your EI.

DEVELOPING EMOTIONAL INTELLIGENCE

Using your strengths, you can begin to enhance your EI.

Controlling Emotions

One of the first steps is learning to name and control your emotions. You can do this by expressing your feelings. If you enjoy writing, use a journal to track your emotions. If you'd rather talk, chat with someone you trust about your feelings. And if you're an artist, you can paint, draw, or dance out your emotions! The more you express your feelings, the better you'll understand them and be able to control them.

Developing Empathy

Another crucial step is looking at situations from other people's point of view. This is called empathy, and it allows you to step back from a situation and see it differently. [10]

For example, if you're mad at your little brother for barging into your room without knocking, think about why he came in. Does he want to play with you? Is he excited to show you something? This is the perfect opportunity to practice controlling your emotions and using empathy.

Building Your Social Skills

Building your social skills means working on your interactions with others. A great way to enhance your social skills is to interact with other people more. Find people you can compliment or help — even strangers!

10 Tips for Great Conversations

1 LISTEN ATTENTIVELY
Pay attention without interrupting.

2 ASK OPEN-ENDED QUESTIONS
Encourage meaningful discussions.

3 SHARE EXPERIENCES
Connect by sharing stories.

4 BE EMPATHETIC
Show understanding and support.

5 RESPECT DIFFERENCES
Be open-minded and respectful.

6 STAY POSITIVE
Focus on uplifting topics.

7 PRACTICE ACTIVE LISTENING
Engage and show you value their input.

8 STAY CURIOUS
Ask questions and learn from others.

9 MIND YOUR BODY LANGUAGE
Maintain good posture and eye contact.

10 END POSITIVELY
End with thanks & leave the door open for future talks.

Engaging in conversations is another way to build your social skills. Find people with shared interests to talk to, or start a conversation with someone while waiting in line at the store (or with your favorite teacher before class begins).

Practice Active Listening

Active listening helps you develop empathy and conversation skills. Show you are listening by repeating details back to the person who is speaking. Maintain eye contact and face the person while they speak to you. Do your best not to interrupt or turn the conversation about yourself.

Ways to Build Emotional Intelligence

· Think about things from different points of view.

· Talk to people more.

· Try new things.

· Express your emotions.

- Engage in mindfulness (yoga, exercise, meditation).

- Focus on and use your strengths.

- Practice being assertive (when appropriate), saying "No" to things you don't want to do.

- Learn your body's non-verbal cues (for example, do you roll your eyes, cross your arms, or sigh when frustrated?).

- Accept your emotions (there are no bad emotions!).

REMEMBER!

Your EI is under construction. It grows, changes, and improves as you develop and age. The more you practice your social-emotional skills, the quicker and easier they'll develop.

EXPLORING YOUR EMOTIONS

"Our emotions need to be as educated as our intellect.
It is important to know how to feel, how to respond,
and how to let life in so that it can touch you."
— Jim Rohn, Motivational Speaker

Emotions are a natural state of being. As a human, you are constantly feeling and experiencing emotions. You might be bored in class or excited about your upcoming game. You may be nervous about a first date or happy it is Friday afternoon.

Human philosophers, psychologists, and scientists have been trying to define and explain human emotions since the time of the ancient Greek philosopher Aristotle (4th century B.C.E.). According to Aristotle, humans experience 14 different base emotions[11]:

- ☆ FEAR
- ☆ ENMITY
- ☆ ENVY
- ☆ CONFIDENCE
- ☆ SHAME
- ☆ INDIGNATION
- ☆ ANGER
- ☆ SHAMELESSNESS
- ☆ EMULATION
- ☆ FRIENDSHIP
- ☆ PITY
- ☆ CONTEMPT
- ☆ CALM
- ☆ KINDNESS

In 1872, naturalist and biologist Charles Darwin theorized that humans only experienced five emotions[12]: fear, anger, sadness, happiness, and love. However, 130 years later, Robert Plutchick believed humans experienced more than 90 different emotions![13]

The currently accepted theory, put forth by psychologist Paul Eckman, narrows the list to seven base emotions[14], including happiness, sadness, fear, and anger. Eckman's theory suggests that these seven emotions are the foundation from which all other emotion variations derive.

The table on the right lists the six most common basic human emotions. Fill in the chart with as many versions of the same emotion as possible.

Happiness	Sadness	Fear	Anger	Disgust	Surprise
Confidence Love		Anxiety	Frustration Hurt		

If you're a fan of Disney-Pixar movies, you might recognize these basic emotions from "Inside Out." The film explores tween Riley's mind as she navigates the challenges of moving to a new city and making new friends. She experiences anger toward her parents for the move, sadness for missing her friends and ice hockey, and fear of attending a new school and living in an unfamiliar place, among other feelings. The film provides a glimpse into the emotional rollercoaster a tween can experience.

It's entirely possible to feel all of these emotions in one day. You may even feel them in a matter of hours or even minutes, depending on the situation you're experiencing.

Tweens and teens often have trouble identifying and connecting emotions to their thoughts and experiences. However, as Jim Rohn's quote earlier in the chapter points out, understanding your emotions is key. He says, "It is important to know how to feel, how to respond, and how to let life in so that it can touch you." Mastering your feelings allows you to fully experience all that life has to offer!

Identifying Emotions

It's usually clear when you're experiencing happiness, sadness, or anger, and the sensations of surprise or disgust are familiar, too. Chances are, you can recall many instances when you've felt each of the seven fundamental emotions: happiness, sadness, fear, anger, disgust, surprise, and love.

But you have probably also experienced situations where you weren't exactly sure what you felt, and the emotion was incorrectly labeled as something else. Labeling our emotions can be tricky, especially in highly charged emotional moments.

Are you familiar with the Harry Potter series by J. K. Rowling? The fifth book, "Harry Potter and the Order of the Phoenix", is often referred to as being full of teenage angst and emotion. The main characters are now 14 and 15 years old. On top of trying to stop an evil wizard from returning to power, they're dealing with puberty, social situations, school, and family pressures. When you read the books, you can see the whirlwind of emotions. Each feeling piles on top of another, making it impossible to separate, understand, and identify them individually.

Humans are capable of feeling a range of emotions, but emotions are like colors that blend into each other. Sometimes, fear might also feel like worry. Likewise, happiness might feel like peace or confidence. When basic emotions don't fully explain how we're feeling, an emotion wheel can help.

Using an Emotion Wheel

An emotion wheel is like a map that shows many different feelings. It helps us find the exact word that matches our emotions. If you're feeling something but can't quite describe it, the emotion wheel can help you better understand yourself. It's a handy tool for exploring all the feelings that bubble up inside us, making it easier to see and name each one.

Trying to figure out and understand your emotions, just like in the Harry Potter books, is often challenging! So, how do you identify confusing and unfamiliar emotions? With patience, practice, and getting to know yourself better!

Getting to Know Yourself

To better understand your emotions, you must get to know yourself better. How does your brain work? What situations do you handle easily, and which do you find stressful?

Take a few minutes to take the Emotion Quiz to discover which base emotion you connect with the most.

Getting to Know Yourself Worksheet

After taking the quiz, were you surprised by the results, or did it sound just like you? Remember, these quizzes are mostly for insight, and are not an official diagnosis or indicator of any medical or mental health condition. Nonetheless, answering the questions honestly gives you a good idea of how you respond emotionally to situations.

Connecting Emotions and Thoughts

Part of getting to know yourself is connecting your thoughts with the emotions you are experiencing. Our thoughts and emotions are internal, but they influence our external actions and behaviors. For example, you might feel angry because your sister borrowed your favorite sweatshirt without asking, so you go into her room and yell at her. Or, you might be frustrated while studying for your science test, so you slam the book shut and throw it on the floor.

When you understand your emotions, you can better control your actions and make them situationally appropriate. This means you'll be able to behave appropriately for the place you're at and the people you're with.

There is nothing wrong with crying, being angry, showing nerves, etc., but you may not wish to cry in front of your peers for failing a test, and you know that punching a wall is inappropriate.

A lot of times, strong emotions cause us to respond without thinking. If you're able to understand your emotions and their connection to specific behaviors, you'll learn how to slow your brain down and think before responding.[15]

Ready for another quiz? Try the worksheet to discover your emotional type.

 **Emotional Type Worksheet**

Knowing your emotional type gives you insight into how you respond to various situations. Once you understand your emotional type, you'll see how you mentally and physically react to emotional situations. The way your body physically responds is called body language. Our bodies can tell us and others a lot about what we are thinking and feeling!

Body Language and Sensations

Our bodies and faces can tell an entire story without us saying a single word! You probably engage in various actions or faces when experiencing emotions without realizing it.

Using the chart below, think of a time you felt each base emotion, then write down sensations in your body, actions you took, or any other thoughts related to the situation.

For example, when you are nervous, maybe you bounce your knee. Or, when you're excited, maybe you talk loudly and quickly.

When I Feel..	I...
Happy	
Sad	
Angry	
Scared	
Disgusted	
Surprised	
Love	

Journaling is another excellent way to connect your thoughts to your emotions. At the end of the day, spend five minutes journaling about an emotional experience you had that day.

You can write about a good or bad experience. Sometimes, we think big emotions are only negative, but they can also be joyous and exciting. For example, getting the lead in the school musical, scoring the winning goal, or being asked out by your crush are all reasons you might feel big emotions!

The Science of Emotions

Scientists have narrowed down the emotional range to what they call the Four Irreducible Emotions: happiness, sadness, anger, and fear.[16] These are the emotions we feel in our most basic, animal-like form.

Research says these are the four emotions we are all born with, and your cultural and social experiences influence the range of these four emotions you feel.

A 2020 research study showed that humans have 16 universal facial expressions [17]:

- Amusement
- Anger
- Awe
- Concentration
- Confusion
- Contempt
- Contentment
- Desire

- Disappointment
- Doubt
- Elation
- Interest
- Pain
- Sadness
- Surprise
- Triumph

Pause and think about how you are sitting right now. Are your shoulders scrunched up or your teeth clenched? Have you rolled your eyes reading any of this? Perhaps you're fidgeting with a toy. These are all body language expressions you might not even know you're doing!

CONTAGIOUS EMOTIONS

Science also tells us that emotions can spread from person to person. This is typically a subconscious action, meaning that you are unaware it is happening. [18]

Imagine being at a big game when your team scores. The wave of excitement that sweeps through everyone cheering is emotional contagion. Or, perhaps your teacher announces a test on Friday. Your best friend tells you they're nervous about this test after class. Suddenly, you find yourself feeling anxious, too!

Research indicates that people tend to feel happier when their friends are happy. [19] So, if you're feeling down, talking to a cheerful friend might help improve your mood. But remember, your emotions can also spread to others, so aim to share positive feelings!

Emotional Output Self-Reflection

- What emotions do I give off, and how does that affect others?

- Do I let others affect my emotions? Do I even know it is happening?

- Are my friends positively or negatively affecting my emotions? Are these the people I really want to surround myself with?

- What changes could I make about how I express my emotions?

Are you interested to know how easily emotional contagion affects you? Take the quiz! [20]

 **Emotional Contagion Worksheet**

Emotional Reflections

"You can't manage what you can't measure."

Regular emotional reflection is the best way to learn more about what you feel, how you feel it, and when you feel it. There are numerous ways to pause and reflect on your emotions. What works best for you will depend on your likes, interests, and dislikes.

- Journaling: Journaling is a private way to record your emotions and thoughts. It is also a very healthy way to express strong feelings.

- Emotional Tracking: Emotion or mood tracking helps you learn your triggers, control your emotions, and develop strategies to overcome strong emotions and negative or impulsive behaviors.

 **Emotional Tracker**

- Meditation/Mindfulness: Regular meditation and mindfulness activities help you connect with your feelings and inner thoughts. They are also a great way to calm down and recenter yourself when experiencing strong negative emotions. Check out YouTube for meditations made especially for kids and teens!

- Listening to or Playing Music: Music is an emotional experience. Find music that mirrors your mood or the mood you want to feel. If you play an instrument, sing, or dance, do one of those activities to connect with your emotions and feelings.

REMEMBER!

You must understand and identify your emotions to control and react to them appropriately. Take time to get to know yourself better. Learn your natural emotional responses and reflect on your nonverbal expressions, such as body language and facial expressions. Reflecting on your emotions each day is the best way to learn about them.

EXPRESSING YOUR FEELINGS

"Control what you can control. I can control my emotions, my attitude, and my effort every day."
— Michael Trubisky, Athlete

The quote above is from Michael Trubisky, an NFL quarterback who played for the Chicago Bears and Pittsburgh Steelers. Sports are often highly emotional for those playing and watching. Tempers often flare, and so does excitement. Playing sports at a high level teaches players to control strong emotions and express them healthily.

Yelling at a referee or screaming in a coach's face are inappropriate ways for athletes to show frustration and may result in them getting benched and taking an early shower. Instead, they can choose to accept the decision, even if they don't like it, vent to a teammate, and then use that disappointment to get back out there and try again. These are all healthy ways to express emotion.

An angry athlete is an example of expressing feelings positively and negatively. Now, it's your turn! Think of a time recently when you felt a strong emotion.

Maybe you argued with one of your parents about not being allowed to go to a party, or you lost a battle in Fortnite with only you and one other player remaining. These are emotionally charged situations that often result in big expressions of emotion. Big, however, doesn't necessarily mean bad. Big emotions are OK as long as they are appropriate to the situation.

You can express big emotions positively or negatively, but the emotion itself isn't good or bad. There are no bad emotions, because all feelings are valid, even when they feel uncomfortable.

Think again about the recent situation where you felt strong emotions. How did you handle your emotions? Did you behave appropriately, or is there something you could have changed about your emotional expression? Did you slam a door when you could have taken a deep breath instead? Did you say something unkind instead of asking for space with your thoughts?

In this chapter, we will explore what emotional expression is and looks like, explore tips for controlling your emotions, and discuss healthy ways to express big emotions.

What Is Emotional Expression?

Emotional expression is how we verbally and non-verbally communicate our feelings to others. Most of us know when we feel angry, sad, or happy. But do you know what your body and face look like when you feel those emotions? Are you aware of any habits or things you commonly do when you feel specific emotions?

In the previous chapter, you practiced connecting your emotions to body sensations and body language. You also learned about yourself and how different emotions feel in your body.

Those feelings, sensations, and actions are all part of your emotional expressions. Most of the time, you are probably in control of your emotional expressions — but no one is *always* in control. Even adults lose their tempers, cry, and shout in excitement.

Some people like being alone when angry, while others yell or throw things. When you're nervous, maybe you bite your fingernails or snap at anyone who talks to you.

While some emotional expressions, like frowning or smiling, are common, everyone experiences and expresses emotions differently. What you see is not always the truth behind what someone is feeling.

We usually think of crying as a sad emotion, but many people also cry when happy. Some people may frown or scowl when thinking or are confused, while others smile, laugh, or joke when nervous.

Learning the many layers of emotional expression will help you better express yourself and represent your true feelings.

I felt angry because... (Describe the situation)	I felt sad because...	I felt overwhelmed because...
How I expressed it: (Eg. Did you shout, argue etc?)	How I expressed it:	How I expressed it:
Instead, I could have... (Explain how you could have reacted)	Instead, I could have...	Instead, I could have...

Use the chart above to think of three different times you felt a big emotion and didn't handle it as well as you could have. Describe what you did, your emotional expression, and a possible alternative solution. We listed angry, sad, and overwhelmed, but if you have an example of another big emotion, use that instead!

The exercise you just did allowed you to examine your current emotional expression tactics and techniques. Most of the time, you probably handle your emotions in healthy ways. For example, you don't yell at your mom when she asks you to clean your room or kick your little sister when she annoys you.

But, as a tween or teen, your emotions and ability to understand and express them are still developing. Just like developing any other skill, the more you practice, the better you'll become! Let's examine some healthy ways to express emotions and tips to keep yourself in control, even during the most emotional experiences!

Healthy Ways to Express Emotions

Expressing your emotions is super important. If you keep them all bottled up, they'll stagnate inside you. No matter how hard you try to keep them hidden, they'll burst out eventually — and often not in good ways. Keeping all those feelings inside can make you more stressed, bring down your mood, and even hurt your physical and mental health.

Imagine you're like a volcano that's ready to erupt. All that pressure just keeps building and building until it explodes. This explosion usually comes out as anger, even if you're feeling scared, embarrassed, sad, or jealous. When you let it all out like that, how you show your feelings doesn't match up with what you're truly feeling inside — and that's not a healthy way to deal with emotions. You might end up saying things you didn't mean, unfairly taking out your frustration on someone else, or acting in ways you regret later.

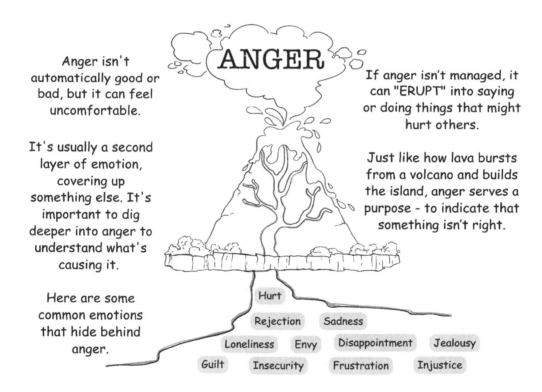

Anger isn't automatically good or bad, but it can feel uncomfortable.

It's usually a second layer of emotion, covering up something else. It's important to dig deeper into anger to understand what's causing it.

Here are some common emotions that hide behind anger.

ANGER

If anger isn't managed, it can "ERUPT" into saying or doing things that might hurt others.

Just like how lava bursts from a volcano and builds the island, anger serves a purpose - to indicate that something isn't right.

Hurt
Rejection   Sadness
Loneliness   Envy   Disappointment   Jealousy
Guilt   Insecurity   Frustration   Injustice

When emotions get bottled up, it's often the tough ones like anger that build up pressure. But it's key to remember that there's nothing wrong with feeling anger or any other emotion. Emotions aren't good or bad — they're just part of being human. Anger, for example, is a normal and healthy emotion.

The real issue is how you choose to express that anger. If you don't figure out a positive way to show how you're feeling, you might express your emotions in an unhealthy manner.

Why We Experience Emotions Differently

Why do we all feel things so differently? It's because we're all unique — not just in how we see the world, but also in how we respond to it. A big part of how you handle your emotions comes from what you've seen growing up. If a parent or someone close to you gets angry and shouts or slams doors, you might do the same. But if you've seen someone stay cool and collected in tough times, you're more likely to pick up those calm vibes.

Your own body plays a role, too. For instance, people with ADHD might find themselves getting super mad really fast. Meanwhile, someone dealing with depression might not show much emotion at all. And if you're someone who gets anxious, stress can feel extra heavy. [21]

Here's the good news: Learning to express your feelings in a healthy way is a skill — and, like any skill, you can get better at it. But it'll take some effort and patience. You don't have to try every method out there — just pick a few that seem like they might work for you and give them a shot. After a while, take a moment to reflect on times you felt really emotional and see if you handled things better. If not, no worries — just try something else. The key is to keep at it and not give up.

Activities to Improve Your Emotional Expression

- **Practice Gratitude:** People who are grateful experience less stress and more happiness. Gratitude reduces uncomfortable emotions like stress and anger and improves mental health. [22] Using a gratitude journal to write down a few things you're grateful for each day is an excellent way to express healthy emotions. If you're struggling with gratitude, try adding the phrase "I get to do this" to activities. For example, if you don't want to clean your room, say, "I have a safe home and a room of my own, and I get to do this!" This is called re-framing. Re-framing a situation helps you find the positive in a situation, and will remind you how lucky you are that you have a bedroom to make messy and have to clean!

- **Enjoy the Moment:** Try to really enjoy what you're doing in the moment. Many of us, especially teens and tweens, get swept up in capturing everything on our phones, like snapping selfies or videos. How about putting your phone aside and just soaking up the moment, without worrying about sharing it or posting online? Spending too much time on social media can actually make you feel worse about yourself, mess with your sleep, and even cut down on how much you move around, all of which can affect your mood and emotional well-being. [23]

- **Get Active:** Being physically active helps lower stress and increases your energy, leading to a better mood. When you're feeling good, it's much easier to express your emotions in a healthy way!

- **Spend Time Outdoors:** Spending time outdoors has been scientifically proven to improve your mental and physical health. [24] Whether gardening or engaging in other outdoor activities, being outside can lift your spirits and help you manage stress better. Even indoor gardening is excellent for your mental health and can teach you to be more empathetic by taking care of plants. [25]

- **Practice Mindfulness:** Mindfulness can help you calm your mind and deal with strong feelings by giving you a moment to pause between feeling and reacting. Taking time to quietly think about what you're feeling lets you understand and respond to your emotions in a healthy way. You can find mindfulness exercises and meditations suited to different feelings on YouTube or meditation apps.

- **Get Creative**: Activities like listening to music, playing an instrument, dancing, drawing, and coloring can lower stress and help you process your emotions. Use your feelings as inspiration to create something unique, whether writing a story, painting a picture, or choreographing a dance. Turning your emotions into art is a positive way to express and understand them.

TECHNIQUES FOR STAYING IN CONTROL DURING EMOTIONAL EXPRESSION

Everyone faces times when emotions run high and it's challenging to keep your cool. Maybe you've felt your temper flare up or been overwhelmed by frustration. Fortunately, there are strategies you can use to better manage your emotions during these intense moments:

- **Practice Empathy**: Empathy is the ability to look at a situation from another person's point of view. For example, imagine your best friend is upset because someone they like turned them down, and they come to you for comfort. Being empathetic means putting yourself in their shoes and feeling their disappointment.

- **Be an Active Listener**: The better you are at listening to others, the better your emotional expression will become. Don't rush the person talking so you can have a turn. Instead, listen to what they are saying and try to understand what they are telling or asking you.

- **Be Forgiving**: Choosing to forgive others is a sign of maturity and helps you let go of heavy emotions. Forgiveness doesn't mean you're okay with being hurt or wronged—it means you're choosing to move past those hard feelings in order to communicate and express yourself more effectively.

Practicing Healthy Expression

So far in this chapter, we've examined emotional expression, tips to improve your emotional expression abilities, and techniques for staying calm when experiencing big emotions. Now, we will examine some active steps you can take to practice healthy expression.

Just like you can't hit a home run in a game if you've never swung a bat before, you won't be able to express yourself effectively in emotional moments if you haven't practiced the skills.

- **Try an Emotional Checklist**: An emotional checklist asks you a series of questions to help you process big feelings. By answering the questions truthfully, you will gain an understanding of what's going on and find ways to express emotions in a healthy way.

 **Emotional Checklist**

- **Write or Draw About Your Emotions:** If you're experiencing powerful emotions, write about them or draw a picture. For example, imagine writing to the person who upset you, or draw a picture of your feelings. These activities provide clarity and help you practice expressing your feelings.

- **Talk to the Mirror:** Have practice conversations in the mirror. It may seem silly or weird, but talking it out to the mirror is an outlet to practice emotional expression. When you say something out loud, you might realize how hurtful it could sound, or that it doesn't adequately communicate your feelings. Pretend the person you need to talk to is right there in the mirror and say what you need to say!

- **Practice Empathy with Characters**: When you're reading a book or watching a movie and you hit an emotional scene, take a moment to pause. Think about what the characters are feeling. Write down your thoughts on each character's emotions, motivations, and whether their actions align with their intentions. Did they achieve what they wanted? Why or why not?[26]

- **Role Play with a Friend or Family Member**: If there's a tough conversation coming up that you know will stir up strong emotions, try practicing it with a friend, family member, or even a school counselor whom you trust. Whether it's talking about ending a relationship or expressing a change in interests, like not wanting to play the piano anymore after years of lessons, rehearsing what you'll say can be really beneficial.

The Power of Words

Words are powerful tools. While many animals communicate using sounds and signals, humans are the only species that has developed language. It is easy to take the gift of language for granted and forget its power.

You've probably heard the saying, "Sticks and stones may break my bones, but words will never hurt me." While it sounds reassuring, it's not always true. Words can be deeply hurtful, especially during intense emotional moments, and their effects can last a long time.

However, this doesn't mean you should keep your feelings to yourself. The key is choosing your words thoughtfully and with care. Expressing our emotions offensively or inappropriately can harm our relationships with others. For instance, if you feel overwhelmed about an audition and snap at your best friend to "shut up and go away," you will likely hurt their feelings.

Instead, if you say, "Hey, I'm really nervous and I need some space. Can we chat later?" a real friend will get where you're coming from and give you the space you need.

Choosing the right words — words that are safe and respectful — helps us feel closer to the people we care about. Knowing the best words to use and the right time to use them is crucial for keeping our relationships strong and healthy.

STEPS TO CHOOSE WORDS AND EXPRESSIONS

1. **Take a Moment:** Before you say anything, pause and identify what you're feeling.

2. **Calm Down First:** Anger can make you defensive. If your feelings fall along the anger spectrum (mad, frustrated, annoyed, irritated, etc.), calm down before you start talking.

   ☞ Try a word other than "anger" for the feeling that remains, such as disappointed, sad, or scared. Using these types of words can decrease your defensiveness.

3. **Use "I Feel..." Statements:** Start sentences with "I feel..." to discuss your feelings without blaming anyone. For example, "I felt disappointed when you didn't show up as planned."

4. **Explain Why:** Provide more details about why you felt a certain way. "I felt disappointed because it made me feel like you didn't value my time or friendship."

Following these steps gives you space to think and choose words that clearly express how you feel, without causing blame or hurt. This approach can prevent arguments and helps ensure your message is understood.

Slowing things down can also help you manage difficult emotions by allowing you time to reflect and understand what you are feeling in the moment.

REMEMBER!

Sharing how you feel is good for you, and there's no such thing as a "bad" emotion. Some feelings are just bigger, stronger, or more uneasy than others. Learning how to stay calm, picking the right words, and getting better at showing your emotions will help you express yourself in a healthy way.

MANAGING DIFFICULT EMOTIONS

Sometimes, when we feel strong emotions, it's because we feel a situation is unfair, we're embarrassed, we're in pain (physically or emotionally), or we aren't feeling our best (like when we're tired, sick, or hungry). During these times, diving into our emotional toolbox and pulling out the necessary skills to keep our emotions in check is crucial.

In *Chapter 3: Expressing Your Feelings*, we explored ways to share how you're feeling and techniques for staying calm while doing so. This chapter will expand upon that theme and focus on managing difficult emotions.

Being open about your emotions is important, but it's just one piece of the puzzle. Knowing how to manage those emotions is equally important, especially when you can't talk about them right away — like during a nerve-wracking test or a high-stakes sports game.

Below, we'll introduce several strategies for effectively managing intense emotions when they arise. These techniques are tools for your emotional toolkit, ready to be used whenever you need them most!

Strategies for Difficult Emotions: Handling Stress, Anger, and Sadness

Dealing with emotions like stress, anger, and sadness is tough. It's something even adults find challenging. The first thing to keep in mind is that there are no "bad" emotions. Some emotions might make us feel uncomfortable, but that doesn't mean they're wrong to have.

Thinking of emotions as good or bad can make us feel like we're not supposed to experience certain ones. The truth is, all emotions are valid. The key is learning how to understand and navigate these feelings.

- **Accept What You Can't Change**: Learning to accept situations and other people is a big step in emotional maturity. For example, if you have to take a surprise quiz or don't make the sports team, focus on what you can control. This could mean staying on top of your schoolwork to be ready for quizzes or practicing more for the next tryouts.

- **Breathing Exercises:** When you feel stressed or overwhelmed, try controlled breathing to help your brain return to a calm place. Close your eyes, slowly breathe in through your nose for five counts, and then out through your mouth for five counts. Place your hands on your belly to feel the breath entering and leaving your body.

- **Take a Break from the Situation:** Taking a break from the discussion, task, or activity provides time to pause and reflect. Saying something like, "Let's pause this discussion and come back to it later," gives everyone time to cool down. The more frustrated and emotional you become during an argument or activity, the less able you are to express yourself healthily.

- **Use an Emotional Checklist:** As we explored in *Chapter 3*, an emotional checklist can help you understand and identify your feelings. Sometimes, what seems like anger is disappointment or frustration. Understanding your true feelings is the first step in managing them effectively.

- **Use an Emotion Wheel:** If you're unsure what you might be feeling, use an emotion wheel to pinpoint your emotions.

Coping Techniques: Methods for Managing Fear, Anxiety, and Jealousy

Fear, anxiety, and jealousy can often disguise themselves as anger. This is because they're closely related emotions, and anger is a fundamental emotion we all know well. The ways to deal with sadness, anger, and stress can also help with anxiety, fear, and jealousy.

Breathing exercises, for example, are great tools for nearly any tough emotion. Deep breathing can calm your nerves and reduce fear and anxiety.

Understanding Jealousy and Envy
Jealousy is a tricky emotion, and shouldn't be confused with envy.

JEALOUSY vs ENVY

Jealousy is when you're worried someone will take what's yours.

Envy is when you wish you had what someone else does.

EXAMPLES

- Feeling upset because your best friend is spending more time with someone else.
- Worrying your sibling is getting more attention from your parents.
- Being afraid your pet dog likes your brother/sister more.
- Concerned a classmate might get the lead role in the play that you wanted.

EXAMPLES

- Wanting the same smartphone your friend just got.
- Wishing you could score as well as your classmate on a math test.
- Wanting your neighbor's new bike.
- Hoping to get as many likes and followers on social media as your friend.
- Wanting the same cool backpack your teammate has.

- **Jealousy** is when you are afraid someone will take what you already have. For example, if you're worried about losing a solo in the spring concert to another student because you're sick, that's jealousy.

- **Envy** is when you want something that someone else has. When you see someone with the brand-new Nike sneakers you want and an uncomfortable feeling creeps in, that feeling is envy.

Tips to manage envy or jealousy:

- **It's Okay:** Remember that jealousy, in small doses, is a normal, healthy reaction.

- **Mindfulness:** Use mindfulness to work through your feelings.

- **Practice Gratitude:** Focus on what you have. Maybe you don't have the latest Nike shoes, but you got a lovely new dress last weekend.

- **Practice Positive Self-Talk:** Lift yourself up! Remind yourself of all your skills, talents, and great qualities.

- **Share Your Feelings:** Talk to someone about how you feel.

Dealing with Jealousy in Relationships

Feeling jealous, especially when it comes to relationships, might be something new for you as a tween or teen. You may be starting to find others attractive, or even beginning to date. It's important to know that jealousy can strain a relationship and affect how you feel about yourself.

Jealousy is a natural reaction that often comes from feeling threatened, like if someone is a bit too friendly with the person you're dating. Even if there's no real danger, it can still feel like a big deal to you.

If you've begun dating and are experiencing jealousy, here are some tips to help you manage your feelings before they grow out of control:

- It's okay to admit you are feeling jealous.

- Accept that, when left unchecked, jealousy can harm your relationship.

- Decide to work on your behavior and reactions.

- Trust your partner. Never spy on them.

- Discuss the roots of your jealous feelings.

- Understand that you cannot control someone else, but you can control how you respond to situations.

- Speak to a counselor, trusted adult, or therapist.

Understanding and Processing Grief

Grief is a very uncomfortable and difficult emotion to manage, especially for young people. If you're fortunate, you might not have faced much grief yet — but if you have, you probably found it hard to understand and deal with those feelings.

We feel grief when we lose something. It could be because of the death of a pet, the end of a relationship, or moving away from a place you love. Grief changes over time and differs with each loss. You might feel overwhelming grief when a pet dies, but only a small amount of grief if you lose something like your favorite necklace.

Despite these differences, there are ways to manage grief, no matter the situation. Here's a look at how to navigate through the grieving process:

- **Talk to Someone:** Find someone to talk to. It can be a friend, parent, teacher, counselor, or religious leader.

- **Express Your Feelings:** Try journaling or expressing your grief through art or music.

- **Allow Yourself to Grieve:** Remember that grief is normal. It is OK to feel grief.

- **Don't Bottle It Up:** If you've lost a loved one, find ways to keep their memory alive. Listen to their favorite music, keep pictures of them around, and talk about them.

- **Take a Break from Social Media:** Avoid discussing your grief on social media platforms. Expressions of grief on social media can be twisted and altered by rumors or people who don't know what you're feeling, which may make the grieving process harder.

- **Write a Goodbye Letter:** Writing a letter to the person or thing you are grieving can be a powerful way to process your feelings.

 Goodbye Letter Worksheet

- **Use a Stages of Grief Worksheet to Help You Process Your Emotions:** The stages of grief can happen in any order, and you can bounce around between them many times, but acceptance always comes last.

- Stages of Grief:
  - ☞ Denial: Not accepting that it has happened.
  - ☞ Anger: Being angry at the person, God, someone else, or even yourself that it has happened.
  - ☞ Bargaining: You want to create an alternate situation where it didn't happen.
  - ☞ Depression: Feeling sad and hopeless about it.
  - ☞ Acceptance: Learning to be OK that it happened.

Breathing Exercises and Mindfulness Techniques

We've discussed breathing exercises and mindfulness several times already in this book, and that's because they're handy tools for calming down and reflecting on one's emotions.

Here are some excellent breathing exercises and mindfulness techniques for managing tough emotions anywhere, anytime!

Breathing Exercises

- **8–4–7 Breathing**: The 8–4–7 exercise is very common and can be done anywhere. Breathe in through your nose for eight counts, hold your breath for four, and exhale through your mouth for seven. Slowing down your breathing sends a message to your brain to relax.

- **Cupcake Breaths**: Imagine you have a cake or cupcake with a candle in front of you. Try to blow out the candle slowly. This makes you breathe out gently and helps you calm down.

- **Blowing Bubbles:** You may feel like a little kid, but blowing bubbles from a bubble wand is a great way to practice breathing. The act of blowing bubbles forces the breath to come out slowly, which can decrease anxiety and stress.

Mindfulness Techniques

Mindfulness is the simple practice of bringing a gentle, accepting attitude to the present moment.

- **Engage Your Five Senses:** This simple exercise can distract you from complex emotions and help you focus on the present.

  - ☞ Right now, I see...
  - ☞ Right now, I hear...
  - ☞ Right now, I am touching...
  - ☞ Right now, I smell...
  - ☞ Right now, I feel...

- **Mindful Listening:** Sit quietly with your eyes closed and listen to everything around you for a few minutes.

- **Perform a Body Scan:** Starting at your head or your toes, slowly scan your entire body, notice where you're holding tension, and try to release it.

- **Listen to a Meditation:** Apps like Calm and Headspace have meditations for kids and teens that target specific emotions. You can also find meditations on YouTube.

- **Do Yoga:** Yoga releases tension and stress from your body and mind.

- **Focus on a Mindful Word:**

  - ☞ Think of a word that creates calm images, like waves, sunlight, or peace.
  - ☞ Think about the word, saying it silently as you breathe in and out. Stay focused on the word.
  - ☞ If/when your mind wanders, gently bring it back to your word.
  - ☞ Continue for one to five minutes.

Personal Coping Strategies Toolkit for Emotional Regulation

Chapters three and four were full of ideas, tips, and strategies for regulating emotions and processing big or complex emotions. Not every method will work for everyone, so building a personal toolkit with strategies that work for you is important.

1. **Experiment with Different Strategies:** Try various tips to see which fits you best.

2. **Track What Works (and What Doesn't):** Keep a list of strategies you've tried, noting which helped and which didn't make much difference.

3. **Identify Your Emotional Triggers:** Pay attention to the situations that often require you to use emotional regulation tools. It could be before an exam, during sports events, at social gatherings, or when you're speaking in public.

4. **Find a Creative Outlet:** Choose a creative activity, like writing, drawing, playing music, or dancing to express your feelings. Remember, you don't have to share your creations with anyone unless you want to.

5. **Talk to Trusted People:** Build a support network of people you can open up to, such as teachers, friends, family members, or mentors.

6. **Prioritize Self-Care and Hobbies:** Allocate time for activities that bring you joy and relaxation. Engaging in hobbies and self-care practices is crucial for emotional well-being.

7. **Incorporate Relaxation Techniques:** Make sure your toolkit includes relaxation methods, like yoga, meditation, or breathing exercises. Find what helps you unwind and make it a regular part of your routine.

REMEMBER! Difficult emotions are not fun, but they need to be handled and processed to prevent resentment, anger, and other uncomfortable emotions from building up and bubbling over. To manage difficult emotions, it is important to find ways to express yourself and distract your mind when needed. Find people you can talk to, hobbies you enjoy, and breathing or mindfulness techniques to help you relax and calm down.

BUILDING RESILIENCE AND SELF-ESTEEM

Resilience and self-esteem are two essential pieces of the puzzle that make you who you are! There are a lot of parts to your personality, but your self-esteem is one of the most crucial pieces. It is the center of who you are and how you feel about yourself. It's your overall sense of value or worth, and a measurement of how much you like, appreciate, and value yourself. [27]

Your self-esteem can change based on different factors, like how you're feeling physically, where you are, what you're doing, and who you're with. For instance, you might feel super confident and valued on the soccer field because you're a great player, and your self-esteem is likely high in that setting.

But if science isn't your strong suit, you might feel less confident in the chemistry lab, especially if it takes you longer to grasp new concepts, or if you have to ask for help more often than your classmates.

It is important to understand that not being a chemistry whiz doesn't make you any less valuable as a person — it just means the lab isn't where your strengths lie. Remember, your value doesn't decrease because of your challenges in certain areas.

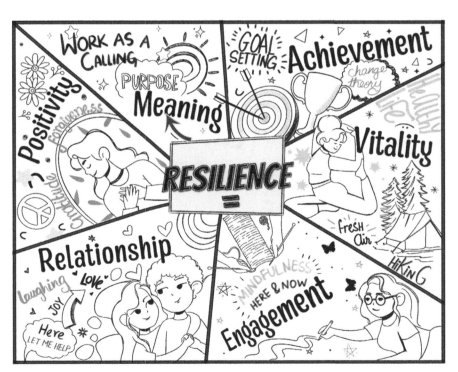

This is where resilience comes into play. According to the American Psychological Association, resilience is "the process and outcome of successfully adapting to difficult or challenging life experiences, especially through mental, emotional, and behavioral flexibility and adjustment to external and internal demands." [28]

Put simply, resilience is the ability to keep trying and going, even when things are tough. It is the ability to push your body and mind further and say, "It's OK that I am not the best at chemistry; I will still do my best and give it my all."

When you hit a tough spot, try asking yourself a few questions:

· Why is this getting to me?

· What can I do differently?

· Who can I ask for help?

· What small goals can I set for myself?

· How can I use what I'm good at to help me through?

Everybody has resilience, but if you don't practice it, it will become like a muscle that is never exercised: weak and ineffective. To strengthen your resilience, you need to use it repeatedly when facing challenges that threaten to knock your self-esteem.

So, how do you boost your self-esteem? Can you just say, "I've got this?" and move forward? In some cases, yes — but sometimes you might need to use a few more strategies.

Boosting Self-Esteem and the Importance of Resilience

Humans are emotional creatures that respond to people and situations. We're also affected by physical conditions like hunger levels, the amount of sleep we get, and even the weather. Because of this, our self-esteem and resilience can change from day to day.

For example, imagine it's the day of your gymnastics meet. If you slept well, enjoyed a nutritious breakfast, and received encouraging words from your best friend, you will likely feel confident.

But, if you were too anxious to sleep, woke up late, rushed your breakfast, and had a disagreement with your mom, your self-esteem might take a hit.

However, your gymnastic skills haven't changed. You've practiced just as much, and your body knows what to do. This is when resilience needs to kick in and crank up your self-esteem, allowing you to feel confident and perform your best, no matter the circumstances.

Why Building Your Resilience Matters: [29, 30]

· Resilience helps you rebound from setbacks or challenges, such as failing a test, missing the winning shot, or going through a breakup.

· Resilience helps you process and overcome challenges.

· Resilience can help you tap into your strengths, reach out to your support systems, and work through problems.

· Resilience helps you move forward, even when things don't work out as planned. It's the inner strength to carry on, even if you forget your lines in a play.

· Resilience allows you to learn and grow from failure and be less fearful of future challenges.

Tips to Boost Your Self-Esteem

· **Focus on Your Strengths:** Reminding yourself what you're good at can boost your confidence.

· **Get Physical:** Physical activity improves our mood and energy levels, which can improve your self-esteem.

- **Meditation and Mindfulness:** Meditation and mindfulness activities help you calm and center your feelings, making sense of why you feel a particular way. Being calm can help you feel more confident and self-assured.

- **Avoid Negative Influences:** If you have friends or even adults in your life who are negative influences, try to avoid them as much as possible. Avoid people who tease you, put you down, and make you feel small or unimportant. Surround yourself with people who support you!

- **Find a Hobby You Love:** Engaging in a beloved hobby or activity will make you feel good about yourself. Not only are you doing something you enjoy and are probably skilled at, you're also spending time with people who enjoy the same thing!

DEVELOPING RESILIENCE: HOW TO BUILD RESILIENCE TO FACE EMOTIONAL LIFE CHALLENGES

Now that you understand why resilience is important, let's discuss how to develop the skill.

Resilience builds over time, like muscles getting stronger the more you use them. Just as certain actions can build your resilience, others might wear it down. Tanya Kowalenko, an educator and writer, likens resilience to a bank account. The more positive actions or "deposits" you make into this account, the greater your resilience becomes.[31]

How do you fill up your resilience account and keep it topped up? Here are a few tips.

Tips for Building Resilience

- **Practice Gratitude:** Remembering what you're grateful for will make you feel stronger and more positive.

- **Volunteer:** Helping others gives you perspective on other people's lives (empathy) and makes you feel good.

- **Consider How You've Overcome Challenges in the Past**: What has worked before, and can you apply it to a new situation? For example, did breathing exercises calm you down before taking a big test? Maybe they'll also work before the homecoming dance.

- **Do Something Nice for Someone Else**: Similar to volunteering, helping others makes us feel good about ourselves and our abilities.

- **Practice Mindfulness**: Mindfulness keeps popping up because it is an excellent tool for connecting with your inner thoughts and feelings.

- **Reframe Negative Thoughts**: Instead of saying, "There's no way I am going to finish this assignment on time," say, "I am going to do the best I can with the time available, and then I will talk to the teacher tomorrow if needed."

- **Have Fun**: Having fun boosts your energy, improves your mood, and makes you feel good in general, making you more resilient.

- **Spend Time with People You Care About**: Spending time with people who make you feel good about yourself is a guaranteed way to fill up your resilience account.

- **Get out into Nature**: Go for a walk, bike ride, or sit outside with a book.

Learning from Failures and Overcoming Emotional Challenges

Learning from failures and overcoming emotional hurdles are essential reasons why building resilience is so important. Facing failure is hard — it can leave you feeling embarrassed, disappointed, sad, or even angry, especially when you've invested a lot of effort. However, failure and disappointment are part of life, and everyone experiences them at some point.

Here are five incredible examples of people who failed numerous times before finding success: [32]

1. **Walt Disney** had his share of failures before creating his animation studio. Did you know he was fired from an early newspaper writing job for lacking creativity?

2. **J.K. Rowling** submitted "Harry Potter and the Sorcerer's Stone" to 12 publishers, all of which rejected her book. They said no one would want to read a story about a boy at a magical boarding school. They were wrong, of course!

3. **Bill Gates** dropped out of college and faced numerous failures before creating Microsoft, the largest computer company in the world.

4. **Michael Jordan** didn't make it onto his high school basketball team, and missed many crucial shots as a young player, but he became one of the greatest basketball players of all time.

5. **Abraham Lincoln** lost countless elections and suffered several personal tragedies, but he persevered and is well-known as one of the most influential American presidents.

Imagine how different the world would be if any of these five people gave up after their first, second, or third failures! Instead, each took what they learned from their failures, adapted, made changes, and tried again. That is resilience in action.

Think of something you've recently struggled with. Did you try once and give up? Maybe you tried two or three times before you quit. Why did you decide to quit? Was it because it was too hard, or because you lost interest?

If something doesn't interest you, there might not be a reason to keep trying. But if it is something you enjoy or are determined to accomplish, keep going.

1. **Talk to someone knowledgeable in the area**. What insight can they provide?

2. **Do some research**. Read about it, watch how-to videos, or listen to interviews with people who have accomplished what you're trying to do.

3. **Decide why it is important to you**. Perhaps it is a matter of passing the next test so you don't fail the class, or maybe it's your dream to sing on a stage like "American Idol." Your motivations play a big role in how resilient you are in a situation.

What Does Failure Teach You? [33]

· **Resilience:** The ability to keep trying.

· **Humility:** The understanding that you can't be perfect or the best at everything, and that to fail is human.

· **Flexibility:** Learning how to grow, change, and try something different.

· **Creativity:** Learning to think outside the box, create new ideas, and find new ways of doing something.

· **Motivation:** The desire to keep trying. If everything were easy, we'd lose the motivation to try new things.

By learning from your failures and developing resilience, you are already on your way to boosting your confidence and improving your self-esteem. But there are other positive steps you can take to improve your self-perception.

REMEMBER!

Managing difficult emotions can feel uncomfortable, especially big feelings like jealousy, anger, or grief, but these uncomfortable emotions aren't necessarily bad. They need to be treated with care and support so you learn how to process them and move forward. Use your mistakes as learning opportunities to build resilience and self-esteem. Your strengths make you unique, and you can utilize them to process difficult emotions.

Techniques for Improving Self-Perception and Confidence

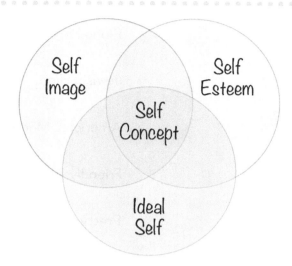

Much of this chapter has covered self-esteem, but remember, self-esteem is just one part of your broader self-concept, or how you see yourself. Your self-concept is your overall view of yourself, answering the question "Who am I?" [34] It includes your self-image, ideal self, and self-esteem. Your self-concept might include aspects like:

- Gender: Female

- Age: 13

- Height: Tall

- Hair Color: Brown

- Roles: Big sister, daughter

- Hobbies: Piano player

- Religion: Jewish

- Nationality: American

- Personality: Friendly

- Appearance: Pretty

Your self-esteem reflects how much you value each of these traits and abilities. You might feel just okay about being female and wish for a slight boost in how you see this aspect of yourself. Yet, you might really cherish being a big sister, and feel proud and confident in this role!

For the same list, your self-esteem values may look like this:

- Female: Moderate
- Age 13: Low
- Tall: Low
- Brown Hair: Moderate
- Big Sister: High
- Daughter: High

- Piano Player: Moderate
- Jewish: High
- American: Moderate
- Friendly: High
- Pretty: High

Self-concept can also be viewed as a circular system, with one factor constantly affecting the others.

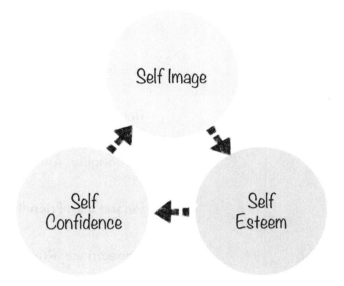

Because self-esteem and self-concept are linked, there are ways to boost one by strengthening the other:

- **Positive Self-Talk and Affirmations:** Positive self-talk can greatly boost your self-image. Tell yourself that you can score the goal, do the audition, or ace the test!

- **Practice Makes ~~Perfect~~ Improvement:** Remember, there is no such thing as perfect — but the more you practice a skill, the better you'll become. If you want to shine at the recital, practice your playing. If you want to become a better pitcher, get out there with a ball and pitch!

- **Listen to Others:** Other people will sometimes view us differently than we view ourselves. When it is people we trust, listening to their opinions and insights can help us. For example, your best friend may tell you that how you spoke to another classmate sounded mean and disrespectful. Maybe that wasn't your intention, but taking a moment to consider the interaction might help you get to know yourself better.

- **Journal and Reflect:** Using a journal to jot down your thoughts while they are fresh is helpful for understanding your motivations and feelings at a specific moment. A journal is something you can reference time and again when you need insight into your self-concept.

- **Recognize and Celebrate Your Strengths:** Everybody's good at something. Pat yourself on the back for everything you *can* do!

How to Recognize Your Strengths

To celebrate your strengths, you must first recognize them. Use the following activities to identify and appreciate your personal strengths and achievements:

1. **"I am…":** Using a piece of paper and a pencil or pen, write as many positive "I am" statements as possible. For example, "I am a girl," "I am honest," "I am a good student," etc.

2. **Flip It:** Using 3x5 index cards, write out several recent mistakes, disappointments, or failures you've made or had. Now flip them over one at a time and turn them into positives. For example, one might read, "I didn't get the part I wanted in the musical." On side two, you could write, "I got a callback for the lead, and I was cast in the musical."

3. **Visualize Success:** Close your eyes and take a few minutes to imagine a situation where you've accomplished a goal. Use your five senses to describe what that feels, looks, sounds, tastes, and smells like. How did you accomplish this goal? What strengths did you utilize?

4. **Find Your Strengths**: Using the words in the boxes below, circle the ones that best reflect your strengths.

Wisdom	Artistic Ability	Curiosity	Leadership
Empathy	Honesty	Open Mindedness	Persistence
Enthusiasm	Kindness	Love	Social Awareness
Fairness	Bravery	Cooperation	Forgiveness
Modesty	Common Sense	Self-Control	Patience
Gratitude	Love of Learning	Humor	Spirituality
Ambition	Creativity	Confidence	Intelligence
Athleticism	Discipline	Assertiveness	Logic
Optimism	Independence	Flexibility	Adventurousness

NAVIGATING RELATIONSHIPS

"Communication is the lifeline of any relationship."
— Elizabeth Bourgeret

Understanding Emotional Dynamics

Emotional dynamics are all about how we react and interact with different people in our lives, and they play a big part in how we communicate. How you feel and act can change based on who you're with, where you are, and your mood before everything starts. But, no matter the situation, it's always possible to communicate in a kind and effective way. Let's look into some scenarios to see how emotional dynamics play out in real-life situations.

Scenario #1: A Stressful Morning

Imagine that you and your mom had a disagreement last night about your need to be more responsible. Today, you overslept because you forgot to set your alarm. Now, your mom is rushing you so she won't be late for work.

· The emotional dynamic between you and your mom is pretty tense. You're upset because you didn't live up to your promise to be more responsible, and she's frustrated about possibly being late. Mornings are usually hectic, but today feels extra stressful. Maybe you're a bit snappy or don't want to talk.

Scenario #2: A Day of Wins

Now picture a totally different day in which you aced your history test, your best friend lent you her favorite shirt, you got the first chair in the orchestra, and you scored in your soccer game. Plus, after school you're hanging out with your best friend at Starbucks.

· Your mood is way better. In fact, you're over the moon! Everything's going your way, and you're feeling excited and proud. You're all smiles, sharing your happiness with your best friend.

In both scenarios, the emotional dynamic was affected by who you were with, what happened, and how you felt about what was happening.

Now, take a look at a third scenario and decide what you think the emotional dynamic is.

Scenario #3: Anxious Excitement

Tonight, you're going out with friends, including your crush, who doesn't know you like them. You've decided tonight's the night you'll tell them, but you're in a bind: You can't find the jeans you wanted to wear, and your backup outfit doesn't match the shirt you picked out. To top it off, your best friend isn't replying to your texts for fashion advice.

Describe the emotional dynamic in the scene above:

Emotional dynamics will change from day to day, and sometimes from hour to hour. Thanks to puberty, as a tween or teen, you're going through a lot of changes. Hormones are reshuffling everything, including your feelings, changes in your body, your thoughts, and even how you interact with others. [35]

At this point, it's crucial to learn how to deal with the emotional ups and downs in different situations, whether with friends, family, acquaintances, or professional relationships.

Your relationships can be imagined as a set of circles around you.

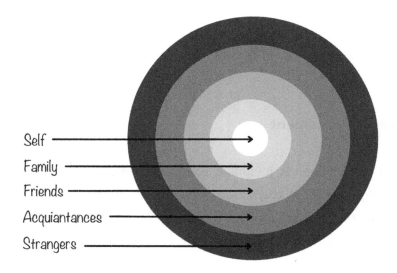

Self
Family
Friends
Acquiantances
Strangers

In the middle is you. The next ring is your immediate or closest family members. The next one out is for close friends and relatives. Further out are the rest of your friends — maybe your teammates or church youth group members. Beyond that are acquaints or people you are not close to emotionally, like your teachers, the barista you see daily, co-workers at your part-time job, and your school bus driver.

The way you feel and interact changes based on how close you are to someone and how you're feeling in the moment. Often, the most complex feelings come out when you are around the people you're closest to because that's where you feel safest being your true self.

Let's dive into the different levels of emotional dynamics and explore some tips for handling them effectively.

FRIENDSHIPS

*"Always love your friends from your heart not
from your mood or need."*

How many close friends do you have? How many of those friends would you trust with your biggest secrets? Navigating friendships as a tween or teen can feel like walking a tightrope. You want to be seen as cool, smart, and likable, all while trying to figure out where you fit in. When things don't go as planned, like embarrassing yourself or feeling left out, it can really shake your confidence. You might even try changing who you are just to feel accepted.

Remember, your true friends appreciate you for who you are. They will want to be friends with the true you. If you find yourself acting differently, dressing a certain way, or pretending to like things just to fit in, those people might not be your genuine friends.

Peer pressure is a big part of being a tween or teen. You might feel pushed to act in certain ways or make choices based on what your friends think is cool. But it's okay to stand up for what you believe is right, even if it means going against the crowd.

For example, imagine a scenario where a friend wants you to skip class, but you know it's a bad idea. You want to seem "cool," but you also don't want to disappoint your parents or miss out on learning. Or, maybe a new friend invites you to a party, but you've already committed to helping with a youth group event. Choosing between disappointing a friend and missing out on something fun can be tough.

How do you deal with these challenging situations? How do you stay true to yourself and keep your friendships and values intact? Sometimes, you might be able to find a balance; other times, you might need to think hard about what those friendships mean to you. Staying true to yourself is key, even when it's not the easiest decision.

Questions to Ask Yourself

· Think about the emotional dynamic of the friendship. Is this friendship a healthy choice? Do you feel good about yourself when you are with this friend? Is this friend there for you when you need them? Do you value this friendship?

· What are the possible outcomes of saying yes or no to a friend's request? What is the best and worst that could happen? How do you feel about those options?

· If a friend says or asks something of you that makes you feel uncomfortable or that you know is wrong, what would disagreeing with them look like? Would it ruin the friendship, or would they consider your opinion? If your disagreement ruins the friendship, it probably isn't a true friendship.

Additional Ideas to Consider [36,37]

· Value honesty in your friendships. If you cannot be honest with your friends or they are not honest with you, that is a red flag.

· If you're struggling with a friend's opinion or suggestion, evaluate who they are. List their good qualities. Was this incident outside their normal behavior? Sometimes, people don't realize they said something offensive if they haven't been exposed to it before.

> ☞ Talk to them about why their opinion upset you using "I feel" statements. For example, "I felt sad when you said (blank), it was an unpleasant comment, and it hurt me," or "I felt disappointed when you used the term (blank). It's offensive, and that's not cool."

· Think of people you admire and want to emulate. Maybe your mom is a great friend and role model. Maybe there's a celebrity or professional athlete you look up to. What traits about them make them good people? You should seek those traits in your friendships and for yourself.

· Be the friend you want others to be to you.

- Ultimately, you can't change anyone who doesn't want to be changed. If a friend is exhibiting behaviors you don't like and you've discussed your feelings with them, it might be time to cut ties with them.

- Establish boundaries within your friendships and stick to them. For example, if a friend stands you up at Starbucks twice, you might decide not to make advance plans with them anymore. Or, if someone returns a borrowed shirt with a stain on it, you might tell them you won't share clothes with them again unless they can return items in good condition.

- Be able to forgive. Not every mistake needs to end a friendship. If a friend messes up, you can set a new boundary, but also forgive them. This gives them a chance to prove they're sorry, allowing both of you to move on together.

Family

Many of these tips also apply to family relationships. You'll find that some family members, like your parents and siblings, are very close to you, while others, like aunts, uncles, cousins, and grandparents, might not be as close.

The big difference with family is that you don't get to choose them like you do your friends. However, you do have some say in how and when you interact with them, even though it might be limited. Family relationships can be complex, and it's up to you to figure out who you feel closest to and who might be more on the outskirts of your inner circle.

Tips on Talking to Your Parents

Tweens and teens often find talking to their parents challenging. There is a belief that your parents won't understand or listen to you. There is also the thought that parents don't know what it is like to be a kid today. In many ways, that is true.

Your parents likely grew up without smartphones, iPads, laptops, social media, or even Netflix! The way they hung out with friends and interacted with the world was very different. They might have had a family computer, and perhaps a laptop towards the end of college, but personal devices like smartphones likely weren't a part of their lives until much later.

Your parents couldn't share photos, thoughts, and memes via social media like we can today, and their actions weren't recorded and saved forever in a digital data bank.

It makes sense that your parents might not fully grasp the ins and outs of social media safety, usage, and protecting you online, which is ultimately what they want to do.

So, try your best to remember how different their teen years were when attempting to talk to them. Try some of these tips for effective communication:

- **Use "I feel" statements**. We've mentioned these a lot because they are a very effective form of communication that removes blame from the conversation. For example, "When you tell me I have to do my homework as soon as I get home, I feel overwhelmed and frustrated because I haven't had any time to relax or recover from the school day."

- **Be honest with your paren**ts. Trust must be earned! Lying to your parents about who you're with, what you're doing, and where you are will not help build your relationship.

- **Talk to your parents as often as you can**[38], even if it's just about simple stuff, like the weather, something you did at school, or a YouTube video you watched. The more you talk to your parents, the easier it will be.

- **Share your interests with them**. Your parents want to know what you like, but they may need to learn how to talk to you about it. Offer to teach them about Fortnite, fashion, or your favorite rapper.

- **For sensitive discussions, plan what you want to say to your parents ahead of time**. You can even practice it in front of a mirror.

- **Pick the right moment**. Starting a conversation about why you don't want to play violin anymore isn't ideal when your mom is busy getting your little brother ready for school.

Whether navigating friendships, family relationships, or more casual relationships, the keys to effective communication are using "I feel" statements, being calm and courteous, and being honest with yourself and the person you are speaking with.

However, despite our best efforts, conflicts can sometimes occur. When they do, there are some unique strategies you can use to calm things down and find a resolution.

Conflict Resolution Techniques

Whether you're disagreeing with your best friend over which dress to pick for the prom or having a heated discussion with your dad about getting a nose piercing, there are effective methods to calm tensions and resolve conflicts.

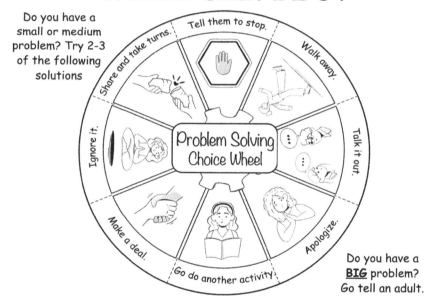

WHAT CAN I DO?

Do you have a small or medium problem? Try 2-3 of the following solutions

Share and take turns.
Tell them to stop.
Walk away.
Talk it out.
Ignore it.
Problem Solving Choice Wheel
Make a deal.
Go do another activity
Apologize.

Do you have a **BIG** problem? Go tell an adult.

- **Take Turns:** Taking turns or sharing is a simple solution, especially with siblings or classmates. Suppose you're arguing every morning with your sister over who gets to use the bathroom, and when. Make a schedule and take turns. Each person has to agree to the schedule and then stick to it. It may not be ideal, but it is fair!

- **Tell the Person to Stop:** If someone is doing something inappropriate, hurtful, or that makes you uncomfortable, tell them to stop. You don't owe them an explanation. However, you can always use "I feel" statements to discuss why you told them to stop.

- **Talk About It:** Talking is a great way to solve conflicts. Find a safe space and allow each person to speak without interruption. Be sure to use "I feel" statements. When listening, don't think about what you want to say next. Truly listen to what the person is telling you.

- **Do Something Else:** If the conflict is minor and not worth arguing over, simply do something else. If you're fired up and angry and need space before you talk, doing something else is a great way to distract your mind and calm down before a discussion.

- **Apologize:** If you made a mistake, own it and apologize. Be sincere in your apology. Simply saying "I'm sorry" usually won't cut it, especially since it is overused.

- **Ignore It:** Is what happened simply not worth the time and effort to discuss? If so, then just ignore it. Maybe your brother accidentally grabbed your towel from the dryer, or your friend forgot the book she said you could borrow. These types of minor infractions don't need a big discussion, even if they're irritating.

- **Look at the Situation from Their Point of View:** In a conflict, it is easy to forget that the other person has opinions, feelings, and ideas, too. Try to look at the conflict from their side and use empathy to understand.

DEVELOPING EMPATHY

Empathy is a useful tool for navigating relationships and solving conflicts, and that's why it comes up so often. It is the ability to see a situation from another person's point of view, giving you a glimpse into their feelings and motivations. This understanding can guide how you react and what you do next.

Feeling empathy might be tough sometimes, like if your sibling breaks a prized possession of yours. But even a small amount of empathy can ease tension and help you handle the situation better.

Tips to Develop Empathy

· Build safe and secure relationships with your parents (or another trusted adult if your parents aren't an option). Research shows that teenagers with secure relationships with at least one adult are more empathetic to their peers and friends.

· Read about history and the struggles of different people throughout time. The more you know about the world you live in and how people got where they are, the more empathy you'll develop.

· Look at every situation from all possible points of view. The more expansive your understanding of a subject, the more empathy you will have for the other people involved. [39]

· Study art and photography. Art is a wonderful way to develop empathy, because you can look at a piece and try to imagine what the artist was feeling or what the picture represents. It is a good way to practice your empathy skills. [40]

Empathy Exercises

Want to practice and develop your empathy further? Try these empathy exercises:

· What's going on in this picture?

☞ Take a look at the photo above. Try to imagine the story behind it.

☞ What might the person be thinking or feeling? What do you think led up to the moment before the photo was taken?

· What does the following quote mean? How is it related to empathy?:

"If you look into someone's face long enough,
eventually you're going to feel that you're looking at yourself."
— Paul Aster

· Fill out this empathy table.

EMPATHY

Empathy means seeing things from someone else's perspective rather than your own. Empathy helps you get along with others. It also helps you to build stronger relationships.

How can you practice empathy:

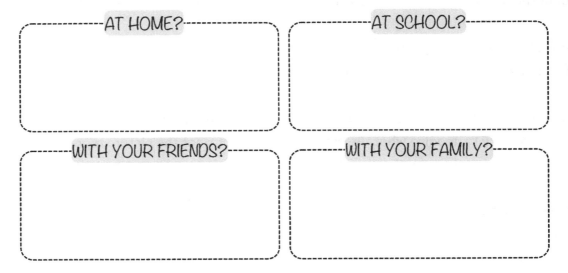

AT HOME?

AT SCHOOL?

WITH YOUR FRIENDS?

WITH YOUR FAMILY?

REMEMBER!

Empathy is a powerful relationship tool. It helps you see a situation from another person's point of view, providing fresh insight you may have missed, which is useful when interacting with other people. When empathy alone isn't enough to navigate a relationship, there are conflict resolution techniques you can try to build stronger communication between you and your friends and family.

THE DIGITAL WORLD AND EMOTIONS

Before starting this chapter, consider all the different ways you interact on social media. Do you have X (Twitter), Snapchat, or Discord? Do you watch videos on YouTube and TikTok? What about Instagram, Facebook, or Twitch?

The apps and sites mentioned are only some of the options teens use regularly. There are many more you might have tried or know about. According to data gathered in 2022, over half of U.S. teens use at least one social media platform, and 97% of teens use the Internet every day! [41]

YouTube, TikTok, Instagram, and Snapchat were the most visited sites among teens. Does that match your online activity? If so, are you aware of how to stay safe on these platforms? Do you know about the potential risks to your mental health and the impact of too much social media use or gaming on your brain?

Researchers across various fields, including science, psychology, and education, have been closely studying the effects of social media and digital technology on teens, especially focusing on mental health aspects. Their findings reveal a significant connection between social media use in teens and increased rates of depression and anxiety. [42]

Given these findings, it's essential for you as a tween or teen to understand the impact that the digital world can have on your emotional well-being. It's equally important to know how to navigate the online space safely, ensuring you protect both your physical and mental health while using the Internet.

How the Digital World Affects and Influences Emotions

Digital technology is still relatively new. The Internet has only been around since 1969, and didn't become common in homes until the mid-1990s [43] — around the time your parents might have been your age. Social media is even more recent, but has rapidly become a significant part of our lives.

The Internet and digital technology have evolved quickly over the last 30+ years, but research into their effects on us is still in its early stages. However, findings so far are worrying, especially the links between social media usage and increased rates of depression and anxiety among teenagers.

Computers, smartphones, and digital technology are now a part of our everyday lives, making them hard to avoid completely. However, becoming aware of their potential risks is the first step towards effectively managing and reducing screen time.

Social Media

Social media began in 1997, but didn't truly catch on until the launch of MySpace in 2004. This means social media has only been a part of our lives for about 20 years, making it a relatively young phenomenon.

Facebook, an early social media giant, started in 2004 as a platform for Harvard students, later expanding to other colleges and certain companies before opening to the general public in 2006. Today, it boasts over 3 billion registered users, with more than 2 billion active every day. [44]

Facebook usage among tweens and teens has declined, but you may use or have heard of WhatsApp or Instagram, which the company also owns. Platforms like Snapchat, launched in 2011, and TikTok (2018) have surged in popularity, particularly among tweens and teens. [45]

A Pew Research Center study highlighted the fact that a significant portion of teens are almost constantly on social media, with YouTube, TikTok, Instagram, and Snapchat the most popular. [46]

Think back to the question at the beginning of this chapter: How many different social media apps do you use? Are there any others not mentioned here that you use frequently?

Over half of the teens in the same study said it would be hard to give up social media. Is that number too high or too low? How would you feel if you had to give up social media for an hour, a day, or even a week?

DID YOU KNOW?

According to a recent study, girls use social media more than boys — an average of 3.4 hours per day, compared to 2.1 hours per day for boys. [47] Girls also said it would be harder to give up than boys. [48]

The older the teens, the greater their dependence on social media. That's likely due to the addictive nature of social media.

Did you know that checking your favorite app and getting likes and comments triggers a dopamine release in your brain — the same chemical that makes us feel good? Every time you get a dopamine hit, your interest in using that app goes up, which means you keep going back for more.

Unfortunately, spending a lot of time on social media can lead to some negative situations: [49]

- Low self-esteem: Seeing everyone else's "perfect" lives online can incorrectly make you feel like yours isn't as good.

- Loneliness: Although social media connects people, it can also create feelings of isolation and loneliness.

- Poor school performance: Using screens too much can make it hard to focus on homework or studying, leading to poor grades.

- Depression and anxiety: Spending too much time on social media can make some people withdraw socially and feel down.

- Lack of empathy: Social media can make it harder to feel or express empathy face-to-face.

- FOMO (fear of missing out): Worrying about missing out can lead to even more social media usage. [50]

- Trouble sleeping: Using social media or screens right before bedtime can negatively affect sleep.

- Less exercise and physical activity: Time spent on screens tends not to be active, which may affect your overall health.

- Fewer real-world connections: While online friendships can be great, they don't quite meet the need for real-life connections with people close to you (friends, family, teammates, etc.).

Constantly comparing ourselves to others online can lower our self-esteem, change how we see ourselves, and make us worry about how we look to others.

INFLUENCERS

Influencers are a big part of why we might feel left out (FOMO) or compare our lives to others on social media.

Influencers only show the very best moments of their lives. They take lots of shots to get it right, use special lighting, and often have brands giving them free stuff to show off. Remember, what many influencers show isn't real life.

Nonetheless, watching their perfect-looking lives on YouTube or Instagram can make you feel not good enough and hurt your self-esteem.

Sometimes, you might know the people you're talking to online, but other times (like when you're looking at influencers' posts), you don't know them at all. Talking to someone online without seeing their face is called faceless communication.

While talking to people without seeing them is common, it's not always clear, and can make you feel upset or misunderstood.

FACELESS COMMUNICATION

Most social media and digital communication is faceless, meaning you can't see the person you're interacting with. If you text with your friends you know and see regularly, you may not worry too much about this. However, if you interact with people you don't know on social media platforms, there is no guarantee that the person you're speaking with is who they say they are.

Pictures and profiles are constantly being faked, and with the increase of AI technology, it is even easier to fake photos.

The safest way to interact online is to ONLY accept friend requests from people you know.

If you do not know the person at the other end of the chat, never provide them your real name, age, address, photo, where you live or go to school, or any information they can use to identify who and where you are.

Never click on any links sent to you or open any attachments.

If a person's comments ever make you feel uncomfortable or are inappropriate, block the person and tell a trusted adult.

It's important to remember that faceless communication, even from people you know, can also negatively impact your emotional well-being.

CYBERBULLYING

Cyberbullying (bullying that happens over texting and social media) is a trend on social media, and one that parents and teachers often have trouble detecting.

What exactly is cyberbullying? According to stopbullying.gov, "Cyberbullying includes sending, posting, or sharing negative, harmful, false, or mean content about someone else. It can include sharing personal or private information about someone else, causing embarrassment or humiliation." [51]

If you're experiencing cyberbullying, it's really important to get help. Talk to an adult you trust about it as soon as you can.

Try not to reply or fight back. Instead, block the person causing you trouble and consider taking a break from social media and your phone. Before you delete any hurtful messages, make sure to take screenshots. This way, you'll have proof of what happened.

Also, report the person bullying you to the website or app where it's happening. The site's administrators might be able to stop the bully from using the platform.

DOWNSIDES OF FACELESS COMMUNICATION

Faceless communication, like texting or chatting online, misses out on a lot of important cues we get from talking in person. When we're face-to-face, we can see someone's expressions, hear the tone of their voice, and notice their body language. Without these, it's easy to get confused or misunderstand each other.

Here are some problems that can come from communicating without seeing or hearing each other:

- **Arguments from Misunderstandings**.

- **Slow Response Time**: Sometimes, you need a quick answer, like knowing if you have a ride to soccer practice. Waiting for a text reply can be frustrating.

- **Saying Mean Things:** People might say things online they'd never say in person, especially if they're anonymous. They might feel more comfortable being mean or inappropriate without seeing the other person's reaction. It feels "safer" to hide behind a screen.

- **Feeling Disconnected:** It's tough to connect with someone emotionally if you can't see or hear them.

If you're finding it hard to connect with people because you're not seeing them in person, or if spending a lot of time online is making you feel down, there are ways to deal with these feelings and improve your emotional well-being.

Navigating Emotional Challenges Online

Dealing with the emotional ups and downs of online life can be tough. Here are some strategies to help you handle these challenges:

- **Take a Break:** Stepping away from social media can be really good for you. One study found that by simply reducing online time by 15 minutes per day for three months, people slept better, felt more positive, and got sick less often. [52]

- **Talk to Someone Real:** Find someone you trust to talk to in person, like a family member, teacher, or friend.

- **Don't React Immediately:** It's easy to react immediately when you see something upsetting online, but it's often better to wait. When you're emotional, you might not make the best choices.

- **Get Active:** Spending a lot of time on your phone or computer can mean you're not moving around much. Exercise can make you feel happier and healthier — plus, getting some sunshine is great, too!

- **Set Boundaries**: It's important to have rules for yourself about how you use social media:

  ☞ Think about how long you should be online each day.
  ☞ Decide who you will interact with online.
  ☞ Have a plan for what to do if someone makes you feel bad or says something that's not okay.
  ☞ Choose which websites or apps are good for you to visit.

Making these choices can help you feel better and keep your online life healthy.

CREATE A DIGITAL WELL-BEING PLAN

Creating a Digital Well-Being Plan is a smart way to manage how social media and digital interactions impact your mental and physical health. Here's how you can start:

Understand Your Usage

Think about and answer these questions:

· What role does social media play in your life? Is it crucial to you? If so, why?

· Are there any apps, websites, or games you feel you can't live without?

· Do you think you're spending too much time online? Explain your reasons.

 **Digital Wellbeing Worksheet**

Track Your Usage

Log your digital activities for a week:

· Note down how long you spend on each site or app. For example, if you play a game from 5:15 PM to 7:15 PM, that's two hours. If you're on Facebook from 3 PM to 3:30 PM, write down 30 minutes.

· Try to be as accurate as possible to understand your habits better.

Use tools to help:

· iPhone users can check their app usage in "Screen Time" under settings.

· Android users have "Digital Well-Being" in their settings to track app usage. You can also set limits for apps you use too much.

Reflect on Your Feelings

- Regularly note how you feel before and after using social media. Does your mood change? Do you feel happier, more stressed, or the same?

Adopt Good Habits

- Keep devices out of your bedroom at night and turn off electronics 30–45 minutes before bedtime. Use this time for non-screen activities.

- Try setting your screen to grayscale to reduce the rewarding feeling you get from colorful screens.

Setting Limits

- Consider setting a usage limit if you find you're using an app more than you'd like. Your phone can help by blocking access to the app once you've hit your daily limit.

By following these steps, you'll be well on your way to creating a balanced digital life that supports your emotional well-being and keeps you safe online.

REMEMBER!

Using digital devices, particularly for social media, can impact your emotional well-being. But that doesn't mean you have to give them up completely. Take a realistic look at how and if social media and digital engagement affect you, and make a Digital Well-Being plan to stay healthy and connected with the world around you.

GROWING TOGETHER — FAMILY ACTIVITIES

"Families are the compass that guides us. They are the inspiration to reach great heights and our comfort when we occasionally falter."
— Brad Henry

Our families are essential to our well-being and development. Every person on this planet has a family. Some are luckier than others and have families that love, support, and guide them. We hope that you are one of those people.

This chapter might be challenging to read if your family is not a place of comfort and support. But know that you can create your own group of people who care about you and support you by reaching out to other trusted adults, friends, and people within your community.

The Family's Role in Supporting Emotional Development

Parents are a child's first teachers. They taught you how to socialize, speak, and interact with others. They were crucial in your early emotional development, and they still have an important role to play in this regard. Did you know that, for young children, a mother's voice plays an essential role in their health and development, impacting their stress levels, social bonding, feeding skills, and speech processing? [53]

As you get older, your instinct might be to turn away from your parents when faced with an emotional challenge. A recent study showed that teens are biologically designed to tune out their mother's voices in favor of their peers. [54] Scientists believe these changes in brain development allow teens to develop healthy social skills among their friendship groups. But, even if you are biologically designed to tune out your parents, they are still an excellent source of guidance to help you develop emotionally.

Your parents and immediate family should be a place of comfort and safety. Your family is your base for exploring feelings and relationships. Families help guide you as you navigate experiences in different settings, including school, social settings, or your first job.

Your family teaches you about values, culture, social norms and behaviors, responsibility, and independence. For example, you may have learned from your family that stealing is wrong, showing respect to older people is expected, or that you should take your shoes off when you enter a house.

You may have family rituals and customs centered around specific holidays, roles, and religious ceremonies. You might have learned to respect hard work and care for those less fortunate than you.

These learned skills and scenarios have developed who you are and shaped your social-emotional development — but your family's job isn't done yet!

As a tween, your family is a valuable resource for shaping how you interact with and perceive the world.

Activities to Foster Family Bonding and Emotional Engagement

Ever since birth or adoption, you have been building an emotional bond with your family. As a baby, your bond started with feedings, diaper changes, playtime, and your parents talking and interacting with you.

That bond has continued to grow and deepen throughout your life as your family has become a source of comfort, safety, and trust. As a tween, you might start questioning your role in the world and within your family, and struggle to figure out where you belong. This is normal, and you're not alone in asking these questions.

Research has shown that children develop vital social skills and higher self-esteem when families enjoy activities together. Daily activities, specially planned activities, and games are great ways to foster the bond between you and your family.

Daily Activities That Foster Emotional Development

There are a number of everyday activities you can adopt to develop your emotional development and create deeper bonds with your family, including:

- **Carpooling:** Asking your parents to help you carpool with friends to school, sports events, church, etc., teaches you about responsibility, problem-solving, and teamwork. You are sharing the responsibility of arriving on time with your peers, and teamwork is required to ensure everyone arrives on time.

- **Family Meals:** Eating meals as a family is a powerful bonding opportunity. Family meals provide a sense of security and belonging. While it's not always possible every day, try to find a few nights per week to sit and eat together.

- **Scheduling Time Together**: Make time with your family for a scheduled event. Ask your parents to go to the mall or the movies together. Go to a sports event or visit a museum in the city. Your parents might not realize that you, as a tween, want to spend time with them! Make an effort and ask *them* to hang out.

- **Choosing Family over Friends:** As a tween, the urge to hang with your friends is strong, but sometimes family needs to come first. Choosing special family events, rather than your friends, boosts your empathy, responsibility, and emotional management.

- **Earning an Allowance:** If your parents don't provide an allowance, discuss the possibility of earning one in exchange for work and chores around the house. Working for your allowance teaches you financial responsibility and the importance of self-discipline and hard work.

- **Volunteering Together**: Volunteering as a family is an excellent way to bond and build empathy. The more we give and help others, the more grateful we feel about our lives. Sharing these emotional experiences with your family can strengthen your bond. [55]

-

GAMES AND ACTIVITIES TO FOSTER FAMILY BONDING

In addition to daily or routine activities, you can play games and activities as a family specifically designed to strengthen the family unit. These include:

- **Family Game Night:** Game nights are a fun way for your family to bond. Family members can take turns choosing the game, or you can play games on a rotation. Playing games with your family provides a shared experience and a sense of unity and bonding. Plus, it gives the winner bragging rights for the week!

- **Team Sports:** If your family is active, turn family game night into team sports. You could play two-on-two basketball in your backyard, go bowling, or play minigolf. Remember, it's not so much about winning but about spending time together.

- **Role-Playing Games:** Role-playing is a great way to practice new behaviors and skills. For example, if one family member struggles with expressing their emotions, a role-playing game might help. This could include games like charades, where you practice acting out emotions or switch roles with your parents and pretend to be the adult.

- **Emotions Ball:** This activity is perfect for kids who struggle with or are uncomfortable expressing their feelings through words. You'll need a permanent marker and a beach ball. On each colored section of the ball, write down different emotions, such as anger, happiness, anxiety, etc. Sit in a circle with your family and pass the ball around. Whoever catches the ball should share a personal experience or moment when they felt the emotion written on the section facing them on the ball. [56]

- **Family Meetings:** Family meetings can be an excellent time to check in and openly discuss concerns or future plans. For instance, a family meeting might be the perfect time to discuss changes to your family chore rotation, or more exciting things like vacations, holiday plans, or a family outing. [57]

- **Miracle Question:** This exercise encourages family members to imagine a future where their problems are miraculously solved. Each family member describes what their life would be like if, overnight, any issues they might have disappeared. This exercise helps family members share problems, goals, and desires. It creates opportunities to openly discuss the steps needed to move closer to that ideal future. [58]

Discussion Guide to Enhance Emotional Discussions Between Parents and Tweens

Talking with your parents about big emotional issues and concerns might be challenging for you right now. It might feel awkward, uncomfortable, or even embarrassing, especially if you don't typically talk to your parents about sensitive or personal topics. You might not realize it, but your parents aren't always 100% sure what to say to you, either! They may feel uncomfortable, embarrassed, or awkward!

The more you talk to your parents, even about the simple and easy stuff, the easier it will be to open up about the big stuff. If you're struggling with talking to your parents and need tips to start conversations, here are some discussion guide ideas and questions to enhance emotional discussions.

You could turn these questions into a game or activity by writing prompts on slips of paper and choosing one at random to answer.

Personal Questions:

1. What is something you like about yourself?
2. What is one of your earliest memories?
3. What's one of your favorite memories?
4. What are things you're working on improving? How are you doing that?
5. What do you like to do for fun?
6. When do you feel happiest?
7. What helps you feel better when you're upset or stressed?
8. When have you felt angry recently?
9. When are some times you've felt worried recently?
10. What do you do to cope with your feelings?
11. What is something you're looking forward to?

12. What are you most proud of this past year?
13. What's the best compliment you've ever had?
14. What does your perfect day look like?
15. If you could be famous, would you? What would you want to be famous for?

Family & Friends

1. What are our family values?
2. What are our most important family traditions?
3. What do you like most about me/your other parent/siblings?
4. What would you change about me?
5. What do you think I like most about you?
6. What do you think I would change about you?
7. What is something you wish I would do more often?
8. Do you feel comfortable talking to me about anything?
9. Is there anything you wish our family would do together more often?
10. Do you think the discipline in our family is fair? What would you change?
11. Who are your closest friends now?
12. What do you enjoy doing with your friends?
13. Have your friendships changed in the past year? How? Why?
14. What do you look for in a friend?
15. How do you know if someone is not your friend?

Current Events/Culture

1. What are your favorite shows? Why?
2. What is an event that you heard about recently that concerns you? Why?
3. What social media platforms do you use? What do you like about that platform?
4. What are some positive things you've experienced about social media?
5. If you could travel anywhere in the world, where would you go?
6. What is your biggest goal in life?
7. What do you hope your life will be like 10 years from now?
8. If you had $100,000 to spend, how would you spend it?
9. Would you ever get a tattoo? Why or why not? What would it be?
10. What are the things that my generation doesn't understand about your generation?

REMEMBER! Your family should be a source of support and comfort. If they're not a safe place, you can find other adults you trust, like teachers, coaches, or other relatives, who you can use as a source of stability. Talking to your parents isn't always easy, but they're probably unsure how to talk to you, too. If you struggle to talk to your parents, use a conversation starter or find a common interest you can share with them. The more you talk to your parents and work on developing your bond, the easier communication will become and the stronger your bond will be.

YOUR EMOTIONS, YOUR CREATIVITY

"Every artist dips his brush in his own soul, and paints his own nature into his pictures."
—Henry Ward Beecher

Art and creativity are closely tied to emotions.

When actors play different characters, they portray the characters' feelings to make us believe them. When songwriters write songs, they tell stories or express their feelings through words. When artists paint a peaceful beach or a bustling city, they put their feelings and experiences onto the canvas.

Creativity is a great way to express your emotions. For instance, you may listen to different songs when happy, sad, anxious, or angry.

Writers create poems about all sorts of feelings, including love, hatred, and jealousy. Artists have captured scenes of love, destruction, serenity, and wonder. Dancers use their bodies to express passion, joy, and sadness.

Do you have a preferred way to express yourself creatively? Do you sing, draw, write, knit, or play a musical instrument? Or do you find engaging with creativity a healthy way to process emotions? Perhaps you like to listen to music, watch movies, or visit art museums.

There is no wrong way to express yourself creatively, as long as it is healthy and not harmful or offensive to others.

Take a few moments to draw or color how you're feeling right now in the frame below. It can be scribbles and swirls, stick figures, or a detailed picture.

How did drawing your emotions feel? Did you enjoy it? Were you surprised by any of the emotions? If you liked this activity, you can do it whenever you feel the need to express your emotions creatively. All you need is blank paper and something to color or draw with!

Even if you don't consider yourself a creative or artsy person, there is probably some form of art you connect with. It's just a matter of finding it.

In addition to being a healthy way to express your emotions, creativity has many other benefits for your body, brain, and well-being.

The Benefits of Creative Emotional Expression

> ☆
>
> *"Creativity is intelligence having fun"*
>
> *-Albert Einstein*

There are many great quotes about creativity, but the one above by Albert Einstein is simple yet true. To be creative, you must also have intelligence.

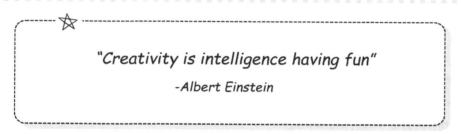

DID YOU KNOW?

Animals also exhibit creativity and problem-solving skills. Their creative behaviors often lead to survival advantages, demonstrating creativity's importance beyond just art and culture.

Creativity isn't just about making art — it also helps us solve problems, handle complex emotions, and find comfort or purpose. It also offers a method of self-discovery, self-expression, and emotional release, combating uncomfortable emotions and helping us reframe our thoughts. [59]

Through creativity, we get to know ourselves better, express our feelings, and sometimes shift our moods by simply doing something different.

When you're creative, you step out of your daily routine. It makes your brain focus on something new, which can be a refreshing break from whatever is bothering you.

Creativity also breaks you free from your routine and forces your brain to think and focus on something other than your emotions. Sometimes, this break is enough to lighten your mood and help you refocus. [60]

All forms of creative expression are beneficial, but different types of creativity may offer different kinds of relief.

Music

Creative expression through music includes everything from playing an instrument or singing to dancing or listening to music. These different types of emotional expression benefit your body and brain in many different ways, including:

- **Making You Feel Good:** Physical activities like dancing release dopamine and serotonin. These feel-good hormones lift your mood and foster happiness. [61]

- **Helping Reduce Stress:** Dancing helps reduce stress levels.

- **Social Bonding:** Singing in a choir or group or making music with others creates positive feelings toward those people by producing oxytocin, which helps with social bonding. [62]

- **Building Trust:** Listening to music also releases oxytocin and builds our ability to trust others.

Writing

Writing takes many forms. It can be storytelling, poetry, song lyrics, letters, or journaling. Writing is a healthy way to express emotions in a safe and private space. Nothing you write ever has to be shared with anyone else, but it can provide a great outlet to process uncomfortable emotions or difficult events. In short, writing is great. Its benefits include:

- **Stimulating the Brain:** Writing stimulates the mind, improving cognitive function and enhancing mental abilities. [63]

- **Developing Creativity and Imagination:** Storytelling involves imagination and creativity, and provides an outlet for expressing emotions in make-believe settings.

- **Thought Processing:** Writing about your emotions forces you to slow down and organize your thoughts. Through the writing process, you will learn how to recognize and regulate your emotions better. [64]

Art

Have you ever looked at a painting and been drawn into the picture or setting? Art is naturally emotive. This means that you automatically feel something when you look at a piece of artwork. Of course, you might not always like what you see, but it will usually trigger an emotion. You might find it calming or upsetting. It might make you happy or sad. When you interact with art, you often imagine another person's feelings and point of view, and when you create art of your own, it can be an avenue to release your own feelings. Art's benefits also include:

- **Helps Develop Empathy:** Interacting with art, especially from other cultures, develops empathy. [65]

- **Helps Relieve Stress:** Drawing and painting relieve stress. [66]

- **Boosts Brain Functioning:** Painting and drawing strengthen the brain, increasing cognitive function. [67]

- **Increases Memory:** Engaging in art increases memory. [68]

- **Builds Patience:** Creating art teaches you patience, and that mistakes and re-starts are OK. Without making mistakes, you'll never figure out what works best and why! [69]

OTHER CREATIVE EXPRESSIONS

Beyond your typical forms of creative expression, like music, dancing, art, and writing, there are other ways to express your emotions creatively and improve your overall emotional mindset and coping skills. These include:

- **Puzzles** improve cognitive function and stimulate the brain. Whether you like traditional jigsaw puzzles, LEGO kits, crosswords, or sudoku, they all positively affect your brain.

- **Cooking** gives you a space to be creative and provides a sense of accomplishment. It teaches patience and can improve your relationship with food. Cooking also gives you an opportunity to care for and connect with others. [70]

- **Gardening** teaches you how to care for other living things. Plus, being outside and interacting with nature has been proven to improve your mood.

- **Knitting, crocheting, and sewing** are all relaxing, and another way to express yourself creatively. Consider making items to donate to those in need, as helping others also helps improve your mood.

- **Playing board games** teaches many life skills, including communicating with others, problem-solving, and developing self-confidence. [71]

Where to Start: Creative Projects to Explore Emotional Experiences

Starting a new project or learning new skills might feel scary. You might worry you won't be good at it, or that you will embarrass yourself. However, your form of creativity is neither good nor bad, because every person sees things differently. How you view the world is very different from how anyone else sees the world, so all you have to do is start! Pick one of the projects below that interests you, and give it a try. Then, come back and try another one.

Journal about your experiences and the emotions you explore through the process as another way of monitoring how your emotions ebb and flow.

DANCE

There are many different ways to dance, including tap, salsa, ballet, hip-hop, modern, and Irish step dance. If you're not interested in taking formal dance classes, look for dance tutorials online.

YouTube has almost every dance style you can imagine for viewing and learning. You can practice in the privacy of your room, and no one will judge you because no one can see.

If you're not interested in formal dance, anytime you feel a big, uncomfortable emotion, put on some music and just move. Don't worry about how you're moving — simply let it all out!

ADULT COLORING BOOKS

If you think coloring books are only for little kids, then you're wrong! There is an entire market for adult coloring books. Adult coloring books are more intricate and detailed than your standard Mickey Mouse or Peppa Pig books. Using adult coloring books has been proven to be relaxing, improve brain function, reduce anxiety and stress, and improve your sleep.[72]

Because adult coloring pages have much more detail than a children's coloring book, they take longer to complete a page. This gives you a project to focus on and provides a sense of accomplishment and completion when you are done, much like finishing a big puzzle.

MURALS AND MOSAICS

Murals and mosaics are two styles of artwork that require creativity and patience. A mural is a large painting that usually goes on the side of a building. You often find them in cities or large towns. Mosaics combine tiny pieces of stone, gems, glass, etc., to create a picture.

Both of these types of projects require planning and strategy. You have to plan what you want, how you will create it, and what materials you will use, and use time management to complete it.

Through the process of planning the project, you'll explore many emotions. You can use the project to work through any uncomfortable or challenging emotions or experiences you are going through.

Don't worry if you don't have a wall available. You can also paint a mural on a large piece of wood or a series of canvases.

WRITE A STORY

Writing a story is an incredibly beneficial way to express your emotions creatively. Like your art or your dance, no one has to see it or read it if you don't want them to, but it still provides an outlet to pour all your feelings onto paper.

DID YOU KNOW? Many famous writers and poets dealt with depression, anxiety, and other mental illnesses.[73,74] They found writing to be highly therapeutic:

- Ernest Hemingway
- Sylvia Play
- Virginia Woolf
- Charles Dickens

- F. Scott Fitzgerald
- Emily Dickenson
- Edgar Allen Poe

Activity: Emotional Art Project to Visually Express Feelings

If you need a way to express your feelings visually but don't know what to do or don't have the time for a big project like the ones already listed, try one of these emotional art activities.

 Creative Project Worksheets x3

- Wordplay Association Worksheet

- Art Sequence Worksheet

- Words to Live by Collage Worksheet

REMEMBER! Emotions and creativity are linked and can inspire each other. Use your creativity to channel uncomfortable or big emotions you're struggling to process or need more time to sit with. But remember, creativity isn't only for feelings we think of as negative. We can also express positivity and joy! Use dance, music, art, writing, or whatever creative outlet speaks to you the most, and try your hand at expressing your emotions creatively.

LOOKING AHEAD — BUILDING YOUR EMOTIONAL FUTURE

"Emotional self-awareness is the building block of the next fundamental emotional intelligence: being able to shake off a bad mood."
— Daniel Goleman

As American psychologist Daniel Goleman said, emotional self-awareness is the building block of emotional intelligence. To grow emotionally, you have to be aware of your emotions and know how to manage them. Put simply, it is important to be able to shake off a bad mood.

It sounds simple, but controlling your emotions, especially as a tween or teen, can be complicated. Fortunately, it's not impossible. Creating an emotional growth plan, developing a strategy, and working toward short- and long-term goals are building blocks you can put in place to secure a healthy emotional future.

You may not be worried about your emotional health or future emotional well-being right now. You might have more important things to worry about, like your science test, making the softball team, and who is going to the homecoming dance with whom. Those are all valid and realistic concerns and thoughts for someone your age.

But what happens if you fail the science test, you make the softball team but your best friend doesn't, and the person you hoped would ask you to the homecoming dance is going with someone else? Do you have the tools to handle those situations and emotions?

The more you practice emotional growth and strategies, the easier it will become. Then, when you are older and have other adult-sized situations and emotions, you'll be prepared to handle whatever comes your way.

Preparing for Your Emotional Future

What does preparing for your emotional future even look like? It starts with a five-step process[75], some of which you've already done by reading this book and completing the exercises.

1. Assess Your Emotional Intelligence Level
2. Set Realistic and Meaningful Goals

3. Daily Practice of Emotional Intelligence Skills
4. Learn and Grow from Your Mistakes
5. Celebrate Your Successes and Progress

Let's examine each of the five steps in more detail.

Assess Your Emotional Intelligence Level

If you want to grow emotionally, you need somewhere to grow from — a baseline. Throughout this book, there are exercises and activities designed to help you assess and work on your emotional intelligence. *Chapter Two: Exploring Your Emotions* has quite a few. If you haven't done those exercises yet, or it's been a while and you'd like to revisit them, take time before reading further.

If you need more help evaluating your current emotional intelligence level, here are a few more activities you can try.

Emotional Scale [76]

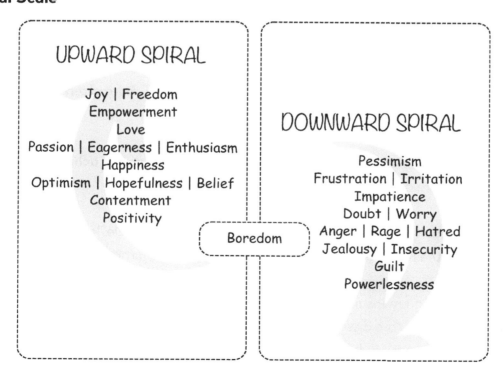

UPWARD SPIRAL

Joy | Freedom
Empowerment
Love
Passion | Eagerness | Enthusiasm
Happiness
Optimism | Hopefulness | Belief
Contentment
Positivity

DOWNWARD SPIRAL

Pessimism
Frustration | Irritation
Impatience
Doubt | Worry
Anger | Rage | Hatred
Jealousy | Insecurity
Guilt
Powerlessness

Boredom

Evaluate your current emotional state on the scale. What actions can you take to move yourself to where you'd like to be to keep the scale balanced? The Emotional Scale is handy in the mornings, when your emotions are fresh and not influenced by the day's activities. Use it each morning to establish a baseline of your emotional well-being.

Why not try the emotional intelligence activity to explore further?

 **Emotional Intelligence Worksheet**

Now that you've better understood your emotional intelligence, you are ready for step two: planning for your emotional future and setting realistic goals.

Set Realistic and Meaningful Goals

What do you want to accomplish emotionally? Think short-term and long-term, and make a list. For right now, make the list as long as you want. Don't worry about how far-fetched or unrealistic a goal might seem; write everything down.

Once you've created your list, decide which are the most important. Pick two or three. Maybe your goals include developing better study habits, learning to say "No" more often when you don't want to do something, and being less annoyed at your sibling.

When choosing goals, use the acronym **SMART: specific, measurable, achievable, relevant, and time-bound.** Let's take developing better study habits as an example.

· **Specific:** Developing better study habits means creating a schedule, lessening distractions, and finding a spot in the house or outside the home (like the local library) where you regularly study.

· **Measurable:** You can measure this goal by tracking how many days you follow your schedule, noticing how often you are distracted and what those distractions are, and keeping track of how frequently you use your study spot and if it is useful. You can also measure if your study habits have improved by how much homework you are completing and the grades you are receiving.

- **Achievable**: Developing better study habits is an achievable goal.

- **Relevant:** Better study habits are a relatable goal because they will improve your school performance and help you develop time management and problem-solving skills, which you will need throughout your life.

- **Time-bound**: You have one week to develop your plan, and then you will follow it until your history final three weeks later and reassess your goal.

This example shows you how to use the acronym SMART to decide if your goal is right for you. You can apply SMART to any short- or long-term goal.

You won't achieve every goal you set because that would be impossible. When failure happens — and it will — you'll be prepared to handle that failure and disappointment because you've been regularly practicing your emotional intelligence skills.

Daily Practice of Emotional Intelligence Skills
Practice makes improvement.

In theory, the more you practice something, the better you become. Skills like ballet, piano, soccer, and cooking improve with practice. Everyone has a point at which they will peak with a skill, no matter how much work they put into it — and that's okay, because once you reach your peak, practice equals maintenance. Practice is how you keep the skills you worked hard to achieve at the level they should be.

Use a journal to record what's working and not working for you. Then, assess why specific techniques or skills aren't improving. For example, are you practicing meditation daily, but not feeling more relaxed? Maybe you need to lengthen the time you meditate, find a new spot, or sit or lie in a different, more comfortable way.

Use a mirror or record yourself when practicing skills that require speaking and body language. This way, you can watch yourself and make adjustments.

Breathing exercises, reframing negative thoughts, and grounding exercises can be done almost anywhere. Breathing in and out while counting from one to five in your head is helpful for calming nerves. You can reframe any negative thoughts, and an excellent grounding technique if you're feeling anxious or overwhelmed is to name one thing you can see, hear, feel, smell, taste, and touch.

For example: "I can see the trees outside the classroom." "I hear the clock ticking." "I feel the fleece of my sweatshirt." "I smell the cleaning solution used in the classroom." "I taste the gum I am chewing."

Learn and Grow from Your Mistakes

Learn to look at mistakes and failures as opportunities for growth and change. Failure is a part of life. It might feel disappointing, but you can still use it as an opportunity to learn and grow.

If your initial goal of being less annoyed at your sibling isn't working, think about what you could do differently. Could you talk to them about what bothers you? Think about the other options you can try, and then try again.

If your failures and disappointments are big, like not getting the lead you dreamed of in the school play or failing your driving test, take the time to grieve, reframe the situation, and try again. You can't go back in time and get the lead in this school play, but are there other places to audition? What about a local community theater? What other opportunities exist for performing? If there are none and you simply have to wait until the next school play, use the experience to practice emotional regulation.

Celebrate Your Successes and Progress

Your successes deserve celebration. If your goal was to use your new study habits to get an A on your history test, and you did just that, then celebrate! You can decide what a worthy reward is. You could give yourself the night off from homework, buy your favorite Starbucks drink, or go to the bookstore and pick out a new book.

Another way to celebrate your success is to tell people what you've achieved and be proud of your progress. If you've been working on calming your nerves or being more socially outgoing, share your results with others and talk about how you achieved your goals. Maybe you'll inspire someone else to focus on a new goal themselves!

Navigating Change

Change is inevitable. It happens to everyone. We experience small changes every day. You may have wanted vanilla creamer in your iced coffee, but someone used the last bit of it, so now you have to use plain. Perhaps you planned to wear your purple dress today but realized it's in the wash and had to choose something else. These are small changes we deal with every day.

But what about big changes? How do you handle major life changes, like moving to a new city, breaking up with your boyfriend, or switching schools?

These types of significant life changes can bring up some uncomfortable and confusing feelings.

The good news is that some of the very strategies you've already learned about for processing and handling emotions can also guide you through these major life changes.

Strategies for Managing Emotions During Significant Life Transitions

Strategies for managing your emotions during major life events are also known as coping skills. Life changes can bring about stress, anxiety, fear, and physical ailments.[77] Knowing what strategies are available and which work best before you need them can help you cope with a significant life change.

Journaling

Journaling is a fantastic hobby and skill for any emotional situation. It is private, expressive, and creative. You can write and say whatever is needed to help you process your feelings. Journaling also provides a reliable tool for looking back later if you need help understanding what you felt at the time.

Try a New Hobby

Refocus your energy by learning a new skill or hobby, or getting involved with an older hobby that's been dormant. Having another place to focus your thoughts and energy releases tension and can provide joy and contentment.

Taking up a new hobby is also the perfect way to meet new people. If your life change involves moving or switching schools, it can help you get to know people with common interests who may turn into friends!

Sleep

Getting enough good-quality sleep is vital for your emotional well-being.[78] Maintain a consistent sleep schedule and try to keep your sleep on track, even on the weekends. Most teenagers don't get enough sleep, which is another crucial reason to take sleep seriously.

Tweens and teens need at least 8–10 hours of sleep per night.[79] How much are you getting?

Lack of sleep impairs cognitive functioning, which affects memory, problem-solving skills, emotional regulation, and critical thinking.

Engage in Self-Care

Self-care is discussed a lot among parents, especially moms, but you need self-care, too! Life can be stressful for tweens and teens. Between school, friends, sports, music, church, and whatever else you have going on, there's a lot to stress you out.

Plus, in our world, most of us have 24/7 access to news and social media, which is not always good for our minds and self-care practice.

Self-care means engaging in anything that makes you feel happy and relaxed, and that relieves stress and anxiety[80]. That could include getting a haircut or your nails done, going for a bike ride or a jog, or binge-watching your favorite movie with a tub of Ben & Jerry's ice cream.

The only wrong way to do self-care is not to do it at all. Just like engaging in a hobby, self-care redirects your thoughts elsewhere and gives you time and space away from the emotions you are working to process.

Therapy

Therapy is a valuable tool for anyone at any age. You don't have to have a diagnosed mental health condition to see a therapist. If you're struggling with a significant life change, ask the school counselor for help.

If your parents would be open to the suggestion, ask them if they can help you find a therapist to talk to. Many therapists offer telehealth visits now, so it's possible to get care from the privacy of your bedroom.

Mindfulness

Like journaling, mindfulness is a versatile skill that can help you in most significant emotional situations. Mindfulness might mean doing a breathing exercise, closing your eyes and listening to music, walking in nature, or meditating. Meditation helps you be aware of the moment and reduces stress and anxiety.[81]

Mindfulness can be practiced in different ways, so explore options and see what feels right for you.

Activity: My Emotional Growth Plan for Setting and Achieving Emotional Growth Objectives

An emotional growth plan, also known as a personal development plan or individual development plan, is a plan used to develop your personal growth, self-awareness, and self-improvement. [82]

To successfully grow emotionally, you have to be committed to making changes. It's not enough to simply say you want to grow and change — you have to mean it!

Key Notes:

· Commit to change. Make the commitment to yourself to grow and change emotionally.

· Avoid judging yourself. Being non-judgemental is key to accepting change and working through your emotions.

· Be honest and open. Trust yourself and the process.

· Avoid blame. Try not to blame yourself or others for your emotions. Situations and people can affect and change your emotions and growth, but it is important to avoid blaming others for your feelings and any obstacles you encounter.

Five Steps to Creating an Emotional Growth Plan

· Choose the area of development. What are the basic skills that you want to work on? Is it anger management, stress, or anxiety?

· Develop objectives and goals. What specifically do you want to do? For example, "I want to reduce my anxiety in social situations" or "I want to improve my response to situations that anger me."

· Choose the techniques or behaviors you will use. They might include breathing exercises, journaling, and art. You might also choose to exercise, meditate, and sleep more.

- What specific actions will you take to make these changes happen? For example, you could set a timer each day to ensure you get out for a walk on time, or go to the paper store to purchase a new journal and pen.

- Pick a review or completion date. How soon do you want to achieve this goal? Make sure it is realistic. Most changes need three to four weeks to cement new patterns.

REMEMBER!

You control your future and develop your future self. Other people will influence and affect you, but only you can commit to taking control of your emotions and responses to the world around you. Journaling, new hobbies, self-care, and therapy are all ways you can manage your emotions and work on your emotional growth.

CONCLUSION

Emotional development and expression are some of the most critical life skills you will ever develop. Without emotional skills, you cannot interact with the world and people around you in a healthy and successful way. Emotional skills support every aspect of your life. They foster social skills, cognitive development, and academic ability, and boost self-esteem and independence.

But even as you develop your emotional skills, remember there is always room for more growth. Emotional development is an ongoing skill that you can foster your whole life. *"A Tween Girl's Guide to Feelings & Emotions"* is a source you can return to again and again because emotional growth never stops.

The more you explore your emotions, the more you grow. When you face a new or uncomfortable emotional situation, you can turn to this guide for tips and tools.

As you grow and develop, your emotions and emotional capability will, too. If you find a tool no longer works the same way, return to the guide and try something new. Or, if you're experiencing an emotion you've never felt before or don't understand, revisit the emotions wheel to name it.

There are many ways to explore and process your emotions. The best part is that many of the tools you learned in this book apply to multiple situations! For example, if you love journaling, you can use it to understand, process, and express an emotion.

Your emotions are ever-changing, and are some of the incredibly unique things that make you who you are. No one else feels or experiences the world as you do, and that fact alone should remind you how important and valid your emotions are. No emotion you feel is ever wrong, even if it feels uncomfortable.

Every emotion you've ever felt or will feel is valid, unique, and entirely yours. No one else will feel exactly what you are feeling, which is why learning to understand your emotions is so vital. Your goal in life should be to learn, change, and continually grow from each new emotional experience.

Each skill you learn from this book will serve you elsewhere in your life. As you build upon your emotional intelligence, you will learn to love yourself, accept your failures, and celebrate your successes, becoming more independent and continually increasing your emotional well-being. Emotional growth is a never-ending journey that can accompany you no matter where your life takes you.

"Emotions are what make us human. Make us real. The word 'emotion' stands for energy in motion. Be truthful about your emotions, and use your mind and emotions in your favor, not against yourself."
— Robert T. Kiyosaki [83]

Good luck on the wonderful journey ahead.

THANKS

FOR READING MY

BOOK!

I appreciate you picking this guide to help your tween girl understand and navigate the exciting yet sometimes puzzling journey of puberty.

I would be so grateful if you could take a moment to leave an honest review or a star rating on Amazon.
(A star rating is just a couple of clicks away.)

By leaving a review, you'll help other parents discover this valuable resource for their own children. Thank you!

To leave a review & help spread the word

REFERENCES

BOOK 1. A TWEEN GIRL'S GUIDE TO PUBERTY

1. *Body image.* (n.d.). National Eating Disorders Collaboration. https://nedc.com.au/eating-disorders/eating-disorders-explained/body-image/

2. Breehl, L., & Caban, O. (2023). *Physiology, puberty.* StatPearls Publishing.

3. Byzak, A. (2018, August 20). *5 ways the sun impacts your mental and physical health.* Tri-City Medical Center. https://www.tricitymed.org/2018/08/5-ways-the-sun-impacts-your-mental-and-physical-health

4. *Cellulite.* (2021, October 28). Cleveland Clinic. https://my.clevelandclinic.org/health/diseases/17694-cellulite

5. Cherry, K. (2022, November 7). *What is self-esteem?* Verywell Mind. https://www.verywellmind.com/what-is-self-esteem-2795868

6. *Everything you wanted to know about puberty.* (n.d.). Nemours Teens Health. https://kidshealth.org/en/teens/puberty.html

7. *55+ Strong Women Quotes to Inspire You* (2019, April 2). Shutterfly. https://www.shutterfly.com/ideas/strong-women-quotes/

8. Greep, M. (2022, February 2). *How the 'perfect body' has changed throughout the decades.* Mail Online. https://www.dailymail.co.uk/femail/article-10467643/How-perfect-body-changed-decades.html

9. *Growth spurts & baby growth spurts.* (2021, November 19). Cleveland Clinic. https://my.clevelandclinic.org/health/diseases/22070-growth-spurts

10. *Heavy menstrual bleeding.* (2022, August 17). Centers for Disease Control and Prevention. https://www.cdc.gov/ncbddd/blooddisorders/women/menorrhagia.html

11. Holland, K. (2019, December 5). *What causes extreme mood shifts in women.* Healthline. https://www.healthline.com/health/mood-swings-in-women

12. Jitesh, A., Chaabna, K., Doraiswamy, S., & Cheema, S. (2021, May 18). *Importance of sleep for teenagers.* Weill Cornell Medicine — Qatar. https://qatar-weill.cornell.edu/institute-for-population-health/community/stay-safe-stay-healthy/issue/importance-of-sleep-for-teenagers

13. Mandal, A. (2022, December 6). *What are hormones?* News Medical. https://www.news-medical.net/health/What-are-Hormones.aspx

14. Makvana, H. (2023, June 1). *10 important conflict resolution skills for teenagers.* Mom Junction. https://www.momjunction.com/articles/important-conflict-resolution-skills-for-teenagers_00106119/

15. McCallum, K. (2021, September 24). *Menstrual cramps: 5 tips for getting relief from period pain.* Houston Methodist. https://www.houstonmethodist.org/blog/articles/2021/sep/menstrual-cramps-5-tips-for-getting-relief-from-period-pain/

16. *Menstrual cycle.* (2022, June 9). Better Health Channel. https://www.betterhealth.vic.gov.au/health/conditionsandtreatments/menstrual-cycle

17. *Puberty.* (n.d.). Planned Parenthood. https://www.plannedparenthood.org/learn/teens/puberty

18. Sheehan, J. (2010, February 17). *Mood swings: PMS and your emotional health.* Everyday Health. https://www.everydayhealth.com/pms/mood-swings

19. Tallman Smith, S. (2017, November 14). *How to manage mood swings naturally.* Everyday Health. https://www.everydayhealth.com/emotional-health/how-manage-mood-swings-naturally

20. *10 tips for improving your self-esteem.* (n.d.). Reachout. https://au.reachout.com/articles/10-tips-for-improving-your-self-esteem

21. *The first bra guide: how and when to buy your daughter a bra.* (2019, May 17). Lingerie Outlet Store. https://lingerieoutletstore.co.uk/magazine/the-first-bra-guide-how-and-when-to-buy-your-daughter-a-bra/

22. Watson, S. (2019, March 8). *How to deal with premenstrual mood swings.* Healthline. https://www.healthline.com/health/pms-mood-swings

***

BOOK 2. A TWEEN GIRL'S GUIDE TO FRIENDSHIPS

1. Cherry, K. (2023, March 11). *The Big Five Personality Traits*. Verywell Mind. https://www. verywellmind.com/the-big-five-personality-dimensions-2795422

2. Degges-White, S. (2017, November 1). *Confronting Conflict With Friends*. Psychology Today. https://www.psychologytoday.com/za/blog/lifetime-connections/201711/ confronting-conflict-friends

3. Dowshen, S. (2015). *Everything You Wanted to Know About Puberty (for Teens)*. Kidshealth.org. https://kidshealth.org/en/teens/puberty.html

4. *Dr. Seuss Quotes About Being Different*. (n.d.). A-Z Quotes. Retrieved June 30, 2023, from https://www.azquotes.com/author/13348-Dr_Seuss/tag/being-different

5. *Healthy Relationships in Adolescence*. (2022). Office of Population Affairs. https://opa.hhs.gov/ adolescent-health/healthy-relationships-adolescence

6. *How to be respectful and respected*. (n.d.). Kids Helpline. https://kidshelpline.com.au/teens/issues/ all-about-respect

7. Miguel, M. (2018, May 7). *Define Friend: A Good Understanding of the Friend Definition*. Betterhelp. https://www.betterhelp.com/advice/friendship/ define-friend-a-good-understanding-of-the-friend-definition/

8. Nurick, Jennifer. (2021, November 8). *Healthy vs. Unhealthy Friendships*. https://jennynurick.com/ healthy-vs-unhealthy-friendships/

9. *Our Definition of Bullying*. (n.d.). Anti-Bullying Alliance. https://anti-bullyingalliance.org.uk/ tools-information/all-about-bullying/understanding-bullying/definition

10. *Personality Test*. (n.d.). Attitude. https://www.attitude.org.nz/personality-test

11. *7 Body-Language Hacks to Try When Meeting New People*. (2017, August 7). Entrepreneur. https:// www.entrepreneur.com/leadership/7-body-language-hacks-to-try-when-meeting-new-people

12. *What Is Kindness?* (n.d.). Kindness Is Everything. https://www.kindnessiseverything.com/faqs/ what-is-kindness/

***

BOOK 3. A TWEEN GIRL'S GUIDE TO FEELINGS & EMOTIONS

1. Teaching Emotional Intelligence in Early Childhood | NAEYC

2. What Are Social Skills? (Definition, Examples & Importance) (socialself.com)

3. Self-Awareness: Development, Types, and How to Improve (verywellmind.com)

4. How does EQ impact neurodivergent professionals? (welcometothejungle.com)

5. Successful People with Neurodivergent Disabilities — Student News (manchester.ac.uk)

6. Neurodiversity: The Definitive Guide | Ongig Blog

7. At What Age Is The Brain Fully Developed? — MentalHealthDaily

8. Young Teens (12–14 years old) | CDC

9. What Are Social Skills? (Definition, Examples & Importance) (socialself.com)

10. Emotional Intelligence (for Teens) — Nemours KidsHealth

11. How Many Human Emotions Are There? (verywellmind.com)

12. Basic Emotions: A Reconstruction — William A. Mason, John P. Capitanio, 2012 (sagepub.com)

13. The Nature of Emotions: Human emotions have deep evolutionary roots, a fact that may explain their complexity and provide tools for clinical practice on JSTOR

14. How Many Emotions Can You Feel? | Psychology Today

15. Relationship between thoughts, emotions and behaviours — Complete guide — Visit MHP

16. How Many Human Emotions Are There? (verywellmind.com)

17. Reading Facial Expressions: 7 Expressions, Interpret Them (verywellmind.com)

18. Emotions are contagious: Learn what science and research has to say about it — MSU Extension

19. SOCIAL NETWORKS AND HAPPINESS | Edge.org

20. The Emotional Contagion Scale | Psychology Today

21. The Biology of Emotions | Brain & Behavior Research Foundation (bbrfoundation.org)

22. Reprogram Your Brain for Happiness (psu.edu)

23. 5 Ways Social Media Affects Kids' Mental Health (And How Parents Can Help!) — FamilyEducation

24. The wellness benefits of the great outdoors | US Forest Service (usda.gov)

25. Gardening is beneficial for health: A meta-analysis — ScienceDirect

26. Fostering-Empathy-Reflectively.pdf (b-cdn.net)

27. What Is Self-Esteem? A Psychologist Explains (positivepsychology.com)

28. Resilience (apa.org)

29. What Is Resilience? Your Guide to Facing Life's Challenges, Adversities, and Crises (everyday-health.com)

30. Resilience: Build skills to endure hardship — Mayo Clinic

31. Building Resilience — CMHA Haliburton, Kawartha, Pine Ridge (cmhahkpr.ca)

32. 55 Famous Failures Who Became Successful People (developgoodhabits.com)

33. Why Learning from Failure Is Your Key to Success (betterup.com)

34. What Is Self-Esteem? A Psychologist Explains (positivepsychology.com)

35. Understanding Emotion in Adolescents: A Review of Emotional Frequency, Intensity, Instability, and Clarity — Natasha H. Bailen, Lauren M. Green, Renee J. Thompson, 2019 (sagepub.com)

36. 7 ways to help your teen strengthen their friendships — ReachOut Parents

37. 10 Tips To Help Your Teen Navigate Friendships (grownandflown.com)

38. Talking to Your Parents or Other Adults (for Teens) | Nemours KidsHealth

39. Help your teenager develop empathy — ReachOut Parents

40. 5 Strategies for Teaching Empathy to Teens — Connections Academy

41. Nearly half of US teens use the social media 'almost constantly' | World Economic Forum (weforum.org)

42. Social media harms teens' mental health, mounting evidence shows. What now? (sciencenews.org)

43. History of the Internet: Origin and Timeline — Tech Quintal

44. Facebook User & Growth Statistics to Know in 2024 (backlinko.com)

45. The History of Facebook and How It Was Invented (thoughtco.com)

46. Teens, Social Media and Technology 2022 | Pew Research Center

47. Social media harms teens' mental health, mounting evidence shows. What now? (sciencenews.org)

48. Teens, Social Media and Technology 2022 | Pew Research Center

49. Social Media Addiction: What It Is and What to Do About It (healthline.com)

50. 5 Ways Social Media Affects Kids' Mental Health (and How Parents Can Help!) — FamilyEducation

51. What Is Cyberbullying | StopBullying.gov

52. Social Media Use and Poor Health | Psychology Today

53. How a mother's voice shapes her baby's developing brain | Britannica

54. New Study Reveals the Reason Teens Seem to Tune Out Their Mom's Voice : ScienceAlert

55. How to Strengthen Family Bonds (verywellfamily.com)

56. 10 Family Therapy Activities for Building Relationships (healingcollectivetherapy.com)

57. How to Strengthen Family Bonds (verywellfamily.com)

58. 10 Family Therapy Activities For Building Relationships (healingcollectivetherapy.com)

59. What Is Creativity? Top 5 Mental Health Benefits (mind.help)

60. How Creativity Positively Impacts Your Health (verywellmind.com)

61. Working out boosts brain health (apa.org)

62. How Creativity Positively Impacts Your Health (verywellmind.com)

63. What Is Creativity? Top 5 Mental Health Benefits (mind.help)

64. Writing about emotions may ease stress and trauma — Harvard Health

65. Children and Art: Creativity, Empathy, and Cultural Awareness (kneebouncers.com)

66. How Creativity Positively Impacts Your Health (verywellmind.com)

67. What Is Creativity? Top 5 Mental Health Benefits (mind.help)

68. How Creativity Positively Impacts Your Health (verywellmind.com)

69. Why being creative is good for you (bbc.com)

70. 7 Ways Cooking Can Boost Your Mental Health (livekindly.com)

71. How Creativity Positively Impacts Your Health (verywellmind.com)

72. Interested in Coloring? 7 Benefits of Coloring for Adults (webmd.com)

73. 7 Famous Writers Who Lived with Mental Illness — H2H (halfway2hannah.com)

74. The 10 Most Famous Writers Who Suffered With Mental Illnesses — whatNerd

75. What do you do if your emotional intelligence is lacking when it comes to preparing for the future? (linkedin.com)

76. Assessing Emotional Intelligence: 19 Valuable Scales & PDFs (positivepsychology.com)

77. Life Transitions: 8 Effective Ways to Cope (copepsychology.com)

78. 8 Ways to Cope With Life Transitions | Psychology Today

79. Sleep for Teenagers | Sleep Foundation

80. 8 Ways to Cope With Life Transitions | Psychology Today

81. 8 Ways to Cope With Life Transitions | Psychology Today

82. How to Create a Personal Development Plan: 3 Examples (positivepsychology.com)

83. Robert T. Kiyosaki Quote: "Emotions are what make us human. Make us real. The word 'emotion' stands for energy in motion. Be truthful about your em..." (quotefancy.com)

Made in the USA
Las Vegas, NV
07 November 2024

11302364R00184